One agent is already missing, and now the U.S. government's most confidential secret is in danger of falling into a power-hungry dictator's hands.

The top-secret agents of ARIES are the world's only hope.

Agent Ethan Williams: Haunted by childhood memories of his parents' deaths, this millionaire playboy is deadly serious about protecting those close to him. And these days that means his alluring new partner, Kelly Taylor—a woman he can't keep close enough....

Agent Kelly Taylor: She may look innocent, but this young linguist is no stranger to danger—or desire. She's always wanted to be an operative, and she's finally gotten her chance. But posing undercover as Ethan's lover has awakened another longing....

Samuel Hatch: A lifetime in the CIA has shown him secrets the rest of the world would never imagine. And as director of the top-secret ARIES agency, it's up to him to make sure those secrets stay safe. His agents are the best of the best, and he's not going to lose one now....

Dr. Alex Morrow: Hatch's most covert operative is missing somewhere in war-torn Europe. Morrow's last message mentioned mythical jewels with devastating powers, but the transmission was unclear. If ARIES can't locate the good doctor soon, the world may pay the price....

Dear Reader,

This month we have something really special on tap for you. *The Cinderella Mission*, by Catherine Mann, is the first of three FAMILY SECRETS titles, all of them prequels to our upcoming anthology *Broken Silence* and then a twelve book stand-alone FAMILY SECRETS continuity. These books are cutting edge, combining dark doings, mysterious experiments and overwhelming passion into a mix you won't be able to resist. Next month, the story continues with Linda Castillo's *The Phoenix Encounter*.

Of course, this being Intimate Moments, the excitement doesn't stop there. Award winner Justine Davis offers up another of her REDSTONE, INCORPORATED tales, *One of These Nights*. A scientist who's as handsome as he is brilliant finds himself glad to welcome his sexy bodyguard—and looking forward to exploring just what her job description means. *Wilder Days* (leading to wilder nights?) is the newest from reader favorite Linda Winstead Jones. It will have you turning the pages so fast, you'll lose track of time. Ingrid Weaver begins a new military miniseries, EAGLE SQUADRON, with *Eye of the Beholder*. There will be at least two follow-ups, so keep *your* eyes open so you don't miss them. Evelyn Vaughn, whose miniseries THE CIRCLE was a standout in our former Shadows line, makes her Intimate Moments debut with *Buried Secrets*, a paranormal tale that's as passionate as it is spooky. And Aussie writer Melissa James is back with *Who Do You Trust?* This is a deeply emotional "friends become lovers" reunion romance, one that will captivate you from start to finish.

Enjoy! And come back next month for more of the best and most exciting romance around—right here in Silhouette Intimate Moments.

Leslie J. Wainger
Executive Senior Editor

Please address questions and book requests to:
Silhouette Reader Service
U.S.: 3010 Walden Ave., P.O. Box 1325, Buffalo, NY 14269
Canadian: P.O. Box 609, Fort Erie, Ont. L2A 5X3

The Cinderella Mission
CATHERINE MANN

Silhouette®

INTIMATE MOMENTS™

Published by Silhouette Books

America's Publisher of Contemporary Romance

Special thanks and acknowledgment are given to Catherine Mann for her contribution to the FAMILY SECRETS series.

To Joanne Rock, a fabulous critique partner and an awesome friend. Thank you for the tireless reads, endless support and countless bags of shared Jelly Bellies!

 SILHOUETTE BOOKS

ISBN 0-373-27272-3

THE CINDERELLA MISSION

Copyright © 2003 by Harelquin Books S.A.

Visit Silhouette at www.eHarlequin.com

Printed in U.S.A.

Books by Catherine Mann

CATHERINE MANN

began her career writing romance at twelve and recently uncovered that first effort while cleaning out her grandmother's garage. After working for a small-town newspaper, teaching at the university level and serving as a theater school director, she has returned to her original dream of writing romance. Now an award-winning author, Catherine is especially pleased to add a nomination for the prestigious Maggie to her contest credits. Following her air force aviator husband around the United States with four children and a beagle in tow gives Catherine a wealth of experience from which to draw her plots. Catherine invites you to learn more about her work by visiting her Web site: http://catherinemann.com.

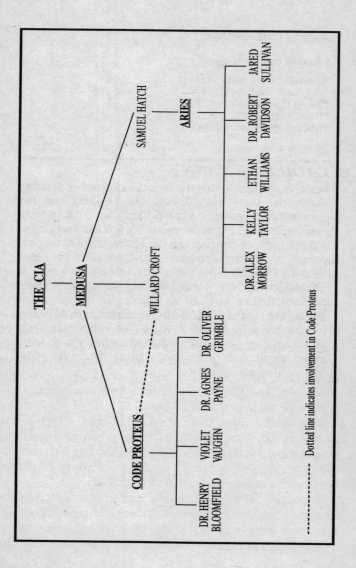

THE CIA

MEDUSA

SAMUEL HATCH

WILLARD CROFT

CODE PROTEUS

ARIES

DR. HENRY
BLOOMFIELD

VIOLET
VAUGHN

DR. AGNES
PAYNE

DR. OLIVER
GRIMBLE

DR. ALEX
MORROW

KELLY
TAYLOR

ETHAN
WILLIAMS

DR. ROBERT
DAVIDSON

JARED
SULLIVAN

--------- Dotted line indicates involvement in Code Proteus

Prologue

Dr. Alex Morrow was dead.

Samuel Hatch feared it all the way to his sixty-year-old, ulcer-riddled gut.

The aging operative bolted back breakfast in his office—two antacids with cold coffee. His job as the Director of ARIES came with countless rewards and endless holes in his stomach. Since Hatch had created the top-secret section of the CIA, ARIES had become his family, his agents the children he and Rita had never been able to conceive.

Now he suspected he'd lost one.

Restrained tension hummed through him, stringing him as taut as the twine he worked to twist around the wilting plant behind his desk. He aimed the sunlamp with meticulous care, grounding himself in the ritual while he plotted how best to utilize his unlimited resources.

One day's silence he could accept, especially given the unstable climate in European Holzberg and neighboring Rebelia. But three days and Alex's tracking device inactive…

Every inch of Hatch's raw stomach burned after ten years

of worrying about his pseudo offspring. Yet their mission was too important to abandon. ARIES operatives embraced assignments no sane CIA agent would touch.

Their country owed these silent knights countless debts that could never be acknowledged.

Hatch anchored the stake on a struggling strawberry plant he'd grafted from home. He mentally sifted through Alex's final transmissions like the soil through his fingers as he looked for the proper texture to bear fruit. Heaven help them all if Alex fell into DeBruzkya's hands. The crazed Rebelian dictator under investigation was a sick bastard.

Heaven help Alex.

His fingers twitched, snapping a limp stem off the plant. He wouldn't let even one of his operatives, especially this one, go down without unleashing the full arsenal at his disposal. Hatch clutched the crumpled leaves in his fist and turned back to the conference area of his office.

And what a mighty arsenal it was, compliments of the government's blank check.

Large flat-screen monitors lined one wall, glowing with everything from CNN to satellite uplink status. Computers hummed from his desk, as well as along the conference table where laptops perched in front of eight seats. Electronic cryptology equipment for encoding and decoding transmissions littered the workspace.

In the midst of it all, he relied on an old-fashioned map of the world with pins marking locations of his operatives. The cover of each agent's private-sector identity offered the freedom to travel anywhere undetected. Already, he'd alerted European operatives to begin searching, but without a narrowed field, there was only so much he could expect.

He needed focus, someone to pull together the minuscule threads of information left behind in a handful of transmissions from Alex. Hatch rubbed the bruised leaves between his fingers like a talisman as he studied the map. Slowly two pins on the board paired in his mind.

The perfect duo for finding answers to the questions left

in those last transmissions. Logical Kelly Taylor would balance well with Ethan Williams, a rogue operative who thought so far outside the box he invented his own rules.

And their personal baggage?

They would either have to work through it or ignore it. He didn't need any fireworks drawing unwarranted—and potentially deadly—attention to this mission.

Hatch reached for one of the seven phones on his desk and punched a three-digit code. One ring later, he carefully placed the mangled leaves on the soil at the base of the struggling strawberry plant. "Taylor, Director Hatch here. I need you to locate Ethan Williams, then meet me in my office with his after-action report from Gastonia."

Her affirmative barely registered. Hatch studied the sole remaining plant from Rita's garden that hadn't been killed by his black thumb. Since Rita's death, that plant and ARIES were all he had left, and by God, they would bear fruit.

Hatch packed the soil around the base of a new sprout and refrained from reaching for the antacids again. Williams and Taylor would find Alex.

Assuming there wasn't—as his roiling gut kept telling him—a Judas in their ranks.

Chapter 1

"**J**udas-freaking-priest!"

ARIES operative Ethan Williams stumbled back a step. His hoarse croak ping-ponged through the cavernous room in a mocking echo. He gasped past the pain exploding in his head.

But he stayed on his feet, damn it.

Ethan swiped his wrist under his bloody nose. Three fast blinks cleared the haze from his vision, if not the dull ache and metallic taste of blood.

Screw pain.

He charged back into the cutthroat battle that reeked of sweat and resolve. He dodged shadows cast by light filtering through the thick plate-glass windows overhead.

Perspiration plastered his T-shirt to his skin. Salt stung the healing nick in his side from a brush with a bullet last week. He ignored it.

The second's hesitation had already cost him his advantage. He needed to stay sharp. After his near miss in Gastonia eight days ago, he feared his edge had dulled. Losing that edge could mean losing his life.

Or worse yet, his job—his only reason for crawling out of bed every morning.

Without it, he might as well step in front of the next bullet. He'd come damned close to doing just that more than once after Celia died, before his recruitment into ARIES had given him the ultimate way to fight back against a world that didn't play fair.

Ethan led with his shoulder in a low blow. His opponent grunted. Adrenaline surged.

ARIES operatives had precious few rules, and Ethan liked that most about his job in the special section of the CIA. Free rein to win in any arena. Essential with life-or-death stakes.

Not that Ethan had much use for his own life. But winning? Yeah, Ethan had a hell of a lot of respect for the thrill of winning.

He pivoted, boxed out, threw in an elbow, looking…for…that…

Rebound!

Basketball tucked to his stomach, he swung around. Ethan on offense now that he had possession, fellow ARIES operative Robert Davidson manned defense in their half-court game.

To some, it might seem a simple hour of pick-up. But even basketball in a CIA training facility in Virginia provided the chance to hone skills, search for potentially lethal weaknesses and overcome them so he could stay in the real game a little longer.

Ethan dribbled, waited, hunting for the opening.

Thump.

Thump.

Thump.

Patience. Don't rush. Find the mojo.

Halogen lights in the gym threw a bluish haze across his opponent. Ethan mentally zoned out the sounds of others shooting hoops on the second court, the bleed-over noise from the connected weight room.

Davidson taunted, "Don't be bringing it to me weak like before, rich boy."

"Gonna go right by you," Ethan promised, ignoring the taunt about his family's obscene bank balance.

This could get ugly. *Oh, yeah.* Excitement pulsed.

Ethan sprinted for the net. Crossover dribble. Nikes squeaked on polished plank. Bolt past. He caught an elbow in the side, his pager digging deep. Ignore it. Keep his hands on the ball, mind on the mission.

Launching into the air, he plowed past for the lay-up. The thrill nudged closer, his elusive edge slipping back into reach.

He jammed it home.

"Weak, my ass." Ethan hung from the rim for an extra three victorious seconds. "I've got a whole lot more of that where it came from."

Davidson landed on his butt, sliding backward. He raised his hands in surrender. "I give. You're one crazy son-of-a-bitch."

No newsflash there.

Ethan dropped to the court and scooped up the ball. A surprise kick of sympathy for Davidson caught him unaware. The guy *had* almost died nearly two years ago. He looked in top form now, but could anyone ever fully recover from the blast of shrapnel he'd taken to the leg?

A ghostly whisper of that stray bullet echoed through Ethan's memory.

He tucked the ball under his arm and extended a hand. "Let's call it quits. Good game, man."

"Thanks." Reaching up, Davidson hooked hands with Ethan. "But it's not over yet."

Davidson yanked.

Ethan lurched forward. The basketball jarred free. He landed with a teeth-jarring thud on the slick wood floor, his pager ramming into his side like a brick. He rolled to his back just in time to see the guy sink a three-pointer.

"Oh, yeah." Davidson punched the air with his fist. "Nothing but net."

Ethan sank back on his elbows. If this had been a real-life operation, that lapse could have cost a life.

Number-one rule, nix the emotions.

He'd pretty much mastered covering the ice block inside himself with a smile. Sure everyone considered him a bud, but he knew the truth. Only with a select few—three to be exact—did he reveal a genuine glimpse of himself. With his boss. With his aunt who'd raised him.

And with Kelly.

Shy Kelly, Hatch's top informations assistant and languages specialist in the operational support unit. Seeing her innocence always reminded Ethan of all the reasons he'd joined the CIA in the first place, back in his idealistic days. Their office friendship had been a real port in the storm for him in his messed-up world.

Until he'd realized she harbored a damned misguided infatuation for him. He'd been with too many women to miss the look that had crossed her face as she'd whispered, *be careful,* just before he'd left for the Gastonia assignment.

Gastonia?

His bullet wound stung.

Ethan swept the rolling ball back into his grasp.

No way was there a correlation between his missing mojo and discovering Kelly's crush. Even considering a link gave too much importance to their friendship when he simply didn't have it in him for anything more.

Ethan leapt to his feet and shook off doubts with a laugh, his most reliable cover for facing the world.

Davidson thumped him on the back. "If style counted for points, my friend, you'd have won hands down."

"Yeah, yeah." Ethan tempered his grousing with a grin. "Go shove your sympathy along with those style points." He smacked the ball out of Davidson's hands.

A humming sound started, low, the buzz of a pager. Ethan and Davidson both slapped their hands on the waistbands.

Ethan glanced down at the LCD screen.

Code Delta. Highest level of urgency. Report to ARIES immediately.

Adrenaline surged double-time.

Davidson's hand fell away. Disappointment shadowed his face. "Just you, rich boy."

"Let 'em know over at the shooting range I won't be making it in this morning. Catch you later," Ethan called, already four steps closer to the door. The drive to the remote ARIES underground compound outside of DC would give him time to get his head together.

Without breaking stride, he swiped his water bottle off the bleachers. Ducking into the locker room, he poured the water over his head and pitched the bottle in the trash. A towel across the face cleared away sweat and blood. A quick hand through his hair slicked back the shaggy length he hadn't bothered to trim since his deep-cover assignment in Gastonia. He snagged his clothes on the way out.

A rogue thought diluted his adrenaline. What the hell would he say to Kelly when he saw her for the first time since his return? God, he hoped he'd read her wrong.

He knew he hadn't.

Ethan took the winding hall at a slow jog, flashing his ID through multiple security checks. With any luck, less than an hour from now he would be back on line for his next mission, away from Kelly Taylor and the feelings in her eyes he didn't know how the hell to handle.

Bitter February wind moaned through the parking garage. Ethan thumbed his remote, disarming the car alarm. He threw his change of clothes over to the passenger side and slid into the embrace of the leather seats in his retooled vintage Jaguar.

Fifteen minutes later, he broke the city limits and opened up the engine. Deserted roads zigzagged in front of him with trees alongside creating a twisting icy tunnel into the Virginia hills.

Steering with his knee, he whipped his T-shirt over his head. He reached to the seat next to him for his black turtleneck. He accommodated for his disdain of ties with great suits.

His car phone chimed over the heater blast.

Ethan yanked the shirt over his head, only blinded for a second before he reached to jab the speakerphone. "Williams, here."

ARIES's number flashed across the screen. He alternated hands on the wheel to slide his arms through the sleeves while waiting for the communications operator to speak the code.

"Confirming your dentist appointment with Dr. Brown."

Ethan rolled out his answer that signified he was alone. "Tuesday at eleven."

"Thank you, sir."

An answer of "I don't have my day planner with me" would have signaled that he could not speak freely because a passenger could overhear.

Modem sounds drifted through the speakerphone in their digital dance to link encrypted lines for secured conversation. Ethan activated cruise control along the empty expanse of rural highway. He kicked off his Nikes and shucked his sweatpants.

The telecommunications squeaks ended. "Confirm we have a secure line. Stand by for your party from Director Hatch's office. Go ahead, ma'am."

Ma'am? Hatch's office?

A burn started in his brain, firing an instinctive awareness that fate had targeted his mojo again. He had a fair guess who the agency *ma'am* from Hatch's office would be. That *ma'am* would be the freaking icing on his bad-luck cake that had started with someone shooting at him as he hurtled through the sky dangling from a streamer parachute.

Foreboding made a drive-by in Ethan's brain with a mere

second's warning before *her* voice flowed through the speakerphone in the last kind of distraction he needed today with a Code Delta in his future.

"Ethan?"

Kelly Taylor's single word swirled through his car and conscience.

"Roger, Kel. I'm here." He kept it light. No way would she discuss anything too deep with the agency monitoring their call. "What do you have for me?"

"Director Hatch requested that I let you know he's waiting in his office when you arrive. Something to do with your Gastonia assignment."

Damned if she didn't have the most incredible voice caressing the airwaves with a richness that could make reading a menu sound like foreplay. And she thought she wanted him when he knew damned well he couldn't have her.

He still remembered the impact of hearing her for the first time two years ago. He'd nearly crawled through the phone line. In five seconds flat, he'd planned seventeen ways to romance her into his bed where he would tangle himself up in that smoky suggestiveness for a solid week.

Then he'd found Kelly Taylor's voice didn't fit the rest of her. At all. Face-to-face, the woman personified innocence and happily-ever-after. He might have wanted those things once, but since Celia, he preferred his women with eyes wide open. Liaisons with innocents were especially taboo. And Ethan suspected they didn't come any more innocent than Kelly Taylor.

So instead of a lover, he'd found a friend, a much more valuable commodity.

"Ethan?" Her voice glided over his name like bourbon swirled on the sides of a glass. "Are you still there?"

"Yeah, Kel." He grabbed his pants off the seat beside him, steadying the wheel as snowflakes dotted his windshield. "Just kinda busy right this second."

"Anything I can help you with?"

Ethan glanced down at his bare legs and boxers. "No, thanks. I've got it under control."

His body tightened.

"I'm always here to give you a hand."

Ethan stifled a groan.

"Are you okay? Should I tell Hatch we'll debrief later?"

Debrief? Ethan resisted the urge to cover himself. He drove one-handed down the lonely stretch of road while sliding into his Brooks Brothers pants. "No thanks."

"If you're sure you're up for the meeting."

He was seconds away from being "up" for a hell of a lot more if he didn't finish this call. He resolved to focus on her words rather than her voice. "I'm only five minutes out. Once I upload my after-action report from the Gastonia assignment—"

"Already done. I had a head start to get on top of things."

An image of her on top of other things nearly sent Ethan into a snow-filled ditch.

Apparently her words posed a hazard after all with each syllable blanketed in her intoxicating tones. The afternoon promised to be long and painful. "Thanks, Kelly."

"My pleasure."

Ethan swerved short of driving up a road sign.

Now that would be a hell of a way to go, pants down and totally turned on by the equivalent of encrypted phone sex.

A voice like that should come with some kind of warning label. *Don't use while others are driving or operating heavy machinery.*

Ethan buckled his belt while driving past the agency radar detector at the designated speed to signify he wasn't under duress. "Need to sign off. Approaching the perimeter."

"See you soon."

The connection died.

Silence echoed in his car. Ethan accelerated around the corner back up to eighty, steering one-handed while exchanging his diver's watch for a Cartier timepiece.

His senses cleared and a mental image of Kelly overlaid the sensual torture of her voice. Large chocolate eyes invited a person to climb right into her soul.

Those vulnerable eyes, too full of some misguided infatuation, offered all the reminder he needed to leave her the hell alone. He knew firsthand how a broken heart crippled a person and wouldn't deal the same blow to anyone else.

Especially not to Kelly.

Besides, he had enough on his agenda with a Code Delta—make or break for a man testing his ability to stay at the top of his game.

Ethan squashed doubts and slowed over the grate in the road that held the covert camera to check the Jaguar's undercarriage for explosives. He would simply keep his mind on the mission. He'd identified his weakness, right? No softening, none of that sensitivity garbage.

Nix the emotions. Just as on the basketball court, he needed to keep his head clear and his emotions locked up tight. He would plant his eyes firmly on her sweet, wholesome face at all times as a reminder that the voice was a red herring.

The rush of an impending job simmered. Every life saved brought the thrill of cheating death, a beast that had already taken too much when it had snatched Celia, when it took his parents.

Ethan plowed around the last curve, the brick quadrangle of ARIES buildings slipping into sight behind a deceptively decorative fence. He only had to endure the next few hours—one day, max—and he'd be back out in the field, far away from Kelly Taylor's romanticized notions.

Kelly Taylor hated Valentine's Day.

After having spent all twenty-four of hers alone, she dreaded the season when Cupid shoved her social ineptitude in her face like a Boston cream pie. And this one promised to be a whopper.

Perched at the conference table, Kelly clicked away on

one of the laptops beside Hatch while they waited for Ethan Williams to arrive. She'd hoped the Gastonia assignment would keep Ethan occupied through the holiday.

Apparently Cupid had ignored her wishes yet again.

She still couldn't believe she'd given herself away to Ethan with one silly look. After two years of keeping the ridiculous infatuation to herself, she'd let a single moment of weakness betray her.

As if the whole crush wasn't embarrassing enough.

Ethan, with all his playboy ways and bad-boy smiles, was totally *not* the sort of guy she wanted for anything other than friendship. Not that her hormones seemed to care one bit what she wanted.

At least she wouldn't be stuck out there with him and all those Valentine's Day decorations some romantic fool had plastered through the stark ARIES lobby in an incongruous display.

Part of her insisted she bore partial responsibility for her dateless status. Years spent in the classroom conjugating verbs from every European language imaginable left her with minimal real-world experience.

So what if she cared more about her career than clothes? Who could keep up with all the trends anyway? And if her mother waved one more make-up gift pack in her face, Kelly vowed she would scream. She'd tried lipstick once and had paid a price far too high for the wrong kind of attention it brought her way.

Never again would she be the helpless graduate student at the mercy of a stalking professor.

The CIA job offer had seemed like a liberating gift from the gods. She certainly hadn't expected to spend ten hours a day behind a desk in operational support. The closest she'd come to a weapon was her docu-binder.

The speakerphone buzzed on Hatch's desk, announcing Ethan's arrival. Kelly's stomach clenched around her breakfast bagel.

Hatch pushed away from the conference table as Ethan

sauntered through the open door. She allowed herself a weak moment to soak up the image of him.

How strange that a man who'd made it to ARIES headquarters in half the normal time still looked as if he'd strolled the whole way. His charcoal-gray suit over a turtleneck hung from his lean body with a negligent élan.

Jet-black hair gleamed with molten life under the sterile office lights. She always liked his hair right after a deep-cover assignment, the longer length giving him a more reckless air—if that was possible.

Deep-blue eyes glinted with the knowledge of things she dreamed of experiencing, places she knew all about but never visited. Ethan Williams personified every risk she'd ever wanted to take and didn't dare, all wrapped up in one dangerous, six-foot-three, bad-boy package.

"Good morning, sir." Ethan shifted toward her, jammed his hands in his pockets and nodded. "Kelly."

Heat crawled up her face and for once she was glad she always forgot to pull her hair back. She longed to duck under the conference table and die of embarrassment over the awkwardness she'd brought to their friendship. But she wouldn't. She was through backing down from life.

"Welcome home, Ethan. Congratulations on the Gastonia mission," she managed to say.

"A simple in-and-out operation. Nothing to worry about."

Her accidental *be careful* warning loomed between them like a big pink elephant on the plush navy carpet.

Director Hatch motioned for him to sit, taking his own seat at the head of the table with a fresh mug of coffee. "Thank you for coming in so quickly, Ethan. I'm sorry to pull you off R and R."

"No problem, sir."

"You'll be rewarded."

Kelly admired the director; he looked more like an old gumshoe with fashion sense almost as bad as her own. Knowing his rumpled appearance covered a man rumored to have more power than the vice-president and the CIA director combined gave her hope for herself.

Appearances weren't everything, damn it.

Man, she wanted to trade her docu-binder in on a SIG-Sauer 9mm. She yearned to step out from behind her desk and into the world reflected in Ethan's world-wise eyes.

Hatch's piercing green gaze met theirs. "Have you heard of Dr. Alex Morrow?"

Ethan hooked an elbow on the chair next to him. "Some kind of rock doctor, right?"

Kelly shoveled her hair out of her face. Typical Ethan to make a multi-degreed scientist sound like a *Rolling Stone* magazine shrink who'd obtained his Ph.D. over the Internet. "Dr. Morrow is a world-renowned geologist."

Ethan nodded. "Right."

Hatch rolled the mug between his palms. "Dr. Morrow has gone missing from a conference in Holzberg. You may have run across Morrow while you were in Gastonia."

"Never met the guy. But I heard some buzz about Morrow attending a European conference on environmental issues. American civilians make too damned tempting targets for terrorist factions these days."

Hatch's hand clenched around his mug, a small but telling gesture from the man who showed so little. "Morrow is one of ours. One of ARIES."

Kelly's head snapped up. "Morrow?"

"You're surprised?" Hatch tipped back his mug for a sip. Were his hands shaking?

Ethan and Kelly exchanged a quick glance across the table. Who the hell was this Morrow person to warrant such a strong reaction?

Ethan straightened in his seat. "Of course not. I'm a prime example of how the CIA and ARIES both recruit from the civilian sector. I'm sure I've crossed paths with more than one ARIES agent without knowing it."

His cover focused on his wealthy background, giving him

blanket acceptance to travel anywhere as one of the idle rich. Sometimes he donned a deeper cover, as he had in Gastonia. Other times, he simply played his role of rich playboy to gain access into the upper echelons of the corrupt wealthy. Once in place, ARIES operatives fulfilled the legacy of their mythological namesake who rescued the persecuted Greek twins Phryxius and Helle.

Lucky Ethan busted bad guys while she sat behind her desk decoding encrypted messages in multiple languages. "How long since we last heard from him?"

"Dr. Morrow went silent three days ago." Hatch clicked through a series of keys on the laptop in front of him. "I'm transferring copies of all the transmissions to your data bases. They've already been decoded, but I'm hoping you'll be able to find something more."

Why all the worry about an agent going silent for seventy-two hours?

Hatch shoved up from his chair, his restlessness apparently winning out as he poured more coffee from a corner bar. "Two hours after the last transmission, we lost total contact. The signal on Morrow's tracking device went dead."

Silence echoed, broken only by the drip of the coffee maker and the low hum of fluorescent lights. The covert transmitters were virtually undetectable, and so pricey only operatives in deep cover warranted the expense. Even super space-power countries with access to a constellation of satellites barely stood a chance of detecting the nanosecond microburst of data from the tracking device, activated only when an agent disappeared.

Just three causes came to mind for a surgically embedded transmitter to fail. Satellite interference. Physical removal.

Or complete destruction of the agent.

Kelly's breakfast bagel weighed like lead in her stomach.

Hatch turned to face them. "I'm employing agents throughout Holzberg to search. Now I need to work the stateside angle. Morrow's last transmission points to a shakedown of some sort at an upcoming European summit in DC. Ethan, your social connections make you the obvious operative to slide in place.''

Damn. Kelly mourned the impending loss of that gorgeous hair of his about to be sacrificed for appearances. ''And why am I here, sir?''

Hatch could have easily sent the transmissions along with a memo.

''The summit ends with a gala celebration and jewel display. We're fairly certain from Morrow's intel there will be a hit. With any luck, tracking those responsible for the attempted heist will give us a lead back to Morrow. For safety's sake Ethan's date needs to be one of ARIES.''

He couldn't mean—

''And what better partner than an expert in the regional languages of the dignitaries attending?''

''Partner?'' Ethan's eyes narrowed.

Already Kelly could feel the constraints of her desk loosening their hold, the weight of that SIG-Sauer in her hand. Excitement tingled over her. Only because of her first real field assignment, right? Not because of her partner on that assignment.

''For the next two weeks, you'll be joined at the hip 24/7 right up to the night of the gala.''

Ethan half stood. ''But, sir…''

''You and Taylor will make the perfect couple.''

Chapter 2

Couple?

Ethan dropped back into his chair. "A couple?"

Just as he chose his women with their eyes wide open, he preferred his partners with more experience. Kelly sat across from him, her peaches-and-cream complexion shouting innocence. She studied him with those doe eyes for three seconds before her head fell forward. All that sable hair glided onto the open file in front of her.

Hatch couldn't really expect to throw her into a Code Delta with only her entry-level training. Ethan's instincts screamed a red alert. A missing agent linked to missing jewels? Something didn't add up.

The ARIES director cupped his mug with both hands. "The couple cover is common, but effective. Hopefully you'll be able to avert a heist attempt prior to the gala. If not, I need you both in place. Taylor's facility in European languages will prove invaluable."

Fan-freaking-tastic.

He would get to spend the next two weeks exchanging language-of-love quips with her.

Kelly looked up. "Sounds like a practical application of my specialty."

Her do-me-honey tones wrapped around languages with as much power as they twined through a man's libido.

His libido.

Ethan reminded himself to stare squarely at her innocent face for his reminder that the voice was a red herring.

Except her warm brown eyes deepened to onyx with excitement over the impending assignment, and he couldn't help but wonder if sex would bring the same heat to her eyes. "Sir, with all due respect, I can handle this one alone."

The spark in Kelly's eyes muted to muddy brown. Ethan refused to let her wounded-puppy look sway him. He was just thinking of her safety.

Yeah, right. "I don't need backup. Kelly can perform any language analysis from here without the risk of putting her in the field."

"Maybe, maybe not." The director's restless feet tracked the room, taking him past a line of mementos down one wall that included diplomas from his scientific background. The man had been a grassroots planner in everything from missile programs to genetic testing. "I'm not willing to risk it. Davidson and Juarez will be at your disposal to coordinate anything you need back here at headquarters. Anything."

Finally the director stopped by a four-drawer safe. Reaching toward the back, he pulled out a bottle of vodka. "Do you know what this is?"

Ethan worked to follow the director's train of conversation. "Aside from the obvious? No, sir."

He turned to Kelly. "Taylor?"

She shook her head, staunchly avoiding Ethan.

Hatch held the bottle up to light. "There's an old tradition in the agency and the military. Many leaders keep a bottle similar to this. Whenever an agent or soldier dies, a toast is lifted in honor. The weight of responsibility is as strong as if a family member has been lost.'' He traced his finger along the empty space a quarter way down the bottle as if remembering a face with every shot glass. ''I don't want a drink with Alex Morrow's name attached.''

Ethan watched remorse flicker through his mentor's eyes and surrendered to the inevitable reality of two weeks with Kelly. Aside from being honor-bound to protect his fellow operative like family, he owed Hatch for giving him a reason to live after Celia died.

If Hatch needed a kidney, Ethan would start cutting. ''Consider Morrow found.''

Hatch nodded. He replaced the bottle with cradling care before turning back to face them, all traces of emotion long gone. The director had returned. ''Taylor, this will be your testing ground. Succeed and I'll expedite your request for upgrade to full operational status.''

She sat straighter, her hair sliding back over her shoulders, swinging along her bulky sweater. ''I'm ready for the challenge.''

''Take the afternoon to review the directives uploaded to your computers and let me know if there are any questions.'' Hatch stepped behind his desk in tacit dismissal.

Kelly stood, swiping wrinkles from her ankle-length skirt. ''Thank you for this opportunity, sir. I won't let you down.''

Ethan gave himself a three-second window to avoid bumping into her outside the door and rose slowly.

''Ethan?''

Hatch's voice stalled his steps. Ethan pivoted. ''Sir?''

The director pinned him with a calculated look that made Ethan want to check his back for an ambush.

''I realize you're going above and beyond coming in off R and R. I consider this a personal favor that deserves to be rewarded. I pulled something for you from the CIA archives.'' He nudged a battered-looking file forward. ''The file on your parents' deaths.''

The file's ragged state declared it to be original, copies no doubt scanned and stored. All the same, those dog-eared documents from a time so close to his parents' deaths brought phantom whispers of deep laughter and lilac cologne. Muddled memories quickly followed of the kidnapping attempt gone wrong that had left his parents dead and Ethan alone except for his father's sister. He ached to know every detail his mind hadn't been able to absorb at five years old.

Hatch's words slowly filtered through the memories. Why would a simple kidnapping attempt on a *Fortune* 500 offspring warrant CIA classified status?

"Finish this for me, and it's yours."

To some it might seem cruel for Hatch to hold that file just out of Ethan's reach. But he knew the rules of the office and that included nixing emotions to get the job done. He respected the man's use of all weapons at his disposal, even as he longed to wrestle the file from the director's desk.

Ethan's elusive edge returned with a full burn. "I see now how you rose to your position."

Hatch's hand fell to rest on the edge of a potted plant beside his desk. "Family is everything."

Kelly charged toward her cubicle, tears and anger battling for domination. Anger won by a long shot.

How dare Ethan try to ruin her chance with his poorly disguised—hell, blatant—disdain at the prospect of working with her?

She wanted to kick him right in his overblown ego. Instead, she took out her frustrations on her office furniture. She yanked her chair away from her government-issue metal desk and flopped down. A wall calendar grinned back at her with a dimple-butted angel.

Kelly ripped a Post-it Note off a pad and slapped it over Cupid's face so hard the divider walls shook.

"Problems, sugar?"

Kelly inched her chair back to look at the woman in the

next cubicle. "Not really, Carla. Thanks for asking, though."

No one would suspect the willowy brunette punching away on the keyboard had once been a field operative—until a bullet to the back during dark ops in eastern Europe had left her in a wheelchair. Now she worked with Kelly in the operational support division, developing high-tech toys for the agents she used to stand alongside.

Carla always insisted she enjoyed her new position since operational support had direct contact with field agents, a fact that had soothed Kelly through two years of waiting for her chance. Hundreds of agency workers never knew the identity of a single agent. In fact, many agents never knew other agents.

All the same, Kelly knew that hadn't stopped the yearning in Carla to step into the field any more than it had in her. Suddenly Kelly felt damned small for being angry when she had the very thing Carla wanted. "I'm fine. Nothing to worry about."

"Men can be a real pain."

"Men?"

"I couldn't help but notice Ethan Williams joined your meeting. I assume he's the reason you're out of sorts."

Carla Juarez's pitying look stoked Kelly's temper back to life. This ridiculous crush had gone on long enough.

With impeccable timing, Ethan rounded the corner. Of course, he would choose now to make his appearance.

And walk toward her.

There'd been a day when she'd waited for him to lounge on the corner of her desk. She'd lived for the occasional invitation to join him for a sandwich in the cafeteria where they would discuss his latest overseas jaunt. Not today.

Not anymore.

Ethan cruised to a stop beside her. The spicy mix of aftershave and masculine sweat wafted her way. Her heart pitched. Damn.

"Kelly, I guess we should get together and review before

meeting with Director Hatch later.'' He sat on the corner of
her desk like countless times before.

''Whatever you say.'' She scraped stray paper clips into
her hand and dumped them into the magnetic holder as if
cleaning her desk might somehow restore her chaotic emotions to order. ''You're the hotshot agent. I'm just a desk
jockey.''

Confusion flashed in those sapphire eyes. ''What's that
supposed to mean?''

The docu-binder suddenly looked like a not-so-shabby
weapon after all if she used it to clock him upside his thick
head. She spun her chair to meet him face on—and came a
little too close to his knees for her comfort level. ''Could
you have been any more obvious in there?''

''What do you mean?''

''Quit being dense.'' She inched her chair back. ''You
know exactly what I mean.''

His face blanked. ''Help me out here.''

She forged ahead. ''Can you imagine how embarrassing
it was for me?''

Still he didn't move or speak. No emotion showed at all,
darn his strong, stubborn chin. He was going to make *her*
spell it out.

''That you don't want to work with me.''

He scooped up her Eiffel Tower paperweight, studying it
as if the snowglobe held answers. ''You're a top-notch informations agent, but you're still operational support.
You're a rookie in field craft. If you can't pull your own
load, it puts me in danger.''

That gave her pause. The story of the mythological Aries
teased through her mind, how the ram was sacrificed after
his mission to save the Greek twins. She wouldn't be able
to live with herself if Ethan died or ended up with a bullet
in his back because of her. Old insecurities marched
over her.

Careful, Kelly. You know how easily you break things.
Watch your step, Kelly. Don't trample Mama's flowers.

After a litany of warnings, the dance had left her feet altogether until she found her sedentary refuge in books, the one place she never stumbled.

Cubicle walls threatened to close in on her with a familiar loneliness. Something she refused to let happen again. She wasn't thirteen anymore, and no one would ever steal the dance from her steps again.

Kelly snatched the paperweight from Ethan and slammed it on her desk. Did he even remember he'd bought it for her? Was he laughing inside over her keeping it?

She launched to her feet. ''Director Hatch wouldn't have put me on the assignment if he didn't have faith in my abilities.''

The cubicle closed in on them both now in a totally different way. She tried to inch away from the insistent heat of him radiating toward her belly.

Kelly backed farther until she bumped the wall. A picture on the other side rattled, then thumped. Kelly winced at her clumsiness. She would apologize to Carla later.

Ethan rose from the desk, brows pinched and his eyes filled with concern or sympathy. She didn't know which but couldn't bear either.

She'd had enough of that from Carla and everyone else in the office. No more hiding behind her hair and her fears. Kelly flipped the too-convenient camouflage of her brown mane over one shoulder and met him nose-to-nose.

Well, nose-to-neck actually, given their height difference. ''Can't you at least be honest with me?''

''About what?''

Damn him, always the agent on the job answering a question with a question. She would give him some answers guaranteed to knock him on his fine butt. ''About why you don't want to work with me.''

His jaw flexed with his gritted teeth for a few telling seconds too long.

Fine. She wanted it out there and acknowledged so they

could sweep it away. "It's because of that ridiculous moment before you left for Gastonia."

His head angled toward her, his voice lowering. "Kelly, there's no need to—"

"My work is the most important thing in my life." This assignment offered hope for finding her voice. She refused to give ground, even though the scent and heat of him swirled through her until she could have sworn she'd pirouetted herself dizzy. "There's no great risk in saying you feel the same about your position here. That being the case, there certainly is a need to discuss anything that interferes with job performance."

He glanced down the length of twenty cubicles, then grabbed her elbow. "Okay, you want to talk, we'll talk. But not here."

She jerked free. "Why not here?"

"Geez, Kelly." The force of his whisper caressed over her. "Do you really want to unroll this for everyone to overhear? Even if they're polite enough to slap on their dictaphones, every word spoken in this building is taped."

"So what?" She rubbed her tingling elbow.

"Kel, I'm just thinking of your feelings here." He reached toward her hair, then stopped midair.

That ripped it.

There was only so much pity a woman could be expected to take in one day, even a woman well-versed in submerging her feelings. First Ethan in Hatch's office. Then Carla. Even Cupid in his fuzzy felt heart, mocking her from behind his Post-it Note mask.

She hated the way her body reacted to Ethan almost as much as she hated the new awkwardness between them. She wanted this dead-end infatuation gone so she could move on with her life and her dreams.

Kelly cursed Cupid yet again for threatening to ruin what should be an incredible day. Nothing, especially not Ethan Williams, would stand in her way. She wasn't the studious mouse any longer, afraid to leave her room for fear of causing ripples in her mother's perfect world. She wasn't the shy student afraid to report a pervert professor to the dean. Time to take charge of her future.

Kelly climbed up onto her chair and filled her lungs for a proper roar.

Ethan watched Kelly climb up on the chair and wondered what he'd missed. He liked to think he understood women, but this had him stumped.

Other than the fact he'd somehow managed to piss her off. A lot.

Fiery resolve crackled from Kelly in surprise heat waves that had Ethan taking a second look to verify what he saw. Back straight, she smoothed her skirt, tugged the hem of her sweater—outlining the most perfect pair of breasts Ethan had ever seen.

Well, damn. His mouth dried right up. She definitely had his attention.

"Hey, gang," Kelly projected down the line of cubicles.

He tore his gaze back up to her face where it belonged.

"You all know Ethan Williams, right?"

Heads popped over the cubicle walls, prairie-dog style. Carla Juarez rolled back six inches.

"Is there anyone here who *doesn't* know that I have the hots for him?"

Ethan choked on his tongue.

All eyes zeroed in on him. Silence reigned supreme. Ethan resisted the urge to squirm like a spider pinned to a science-project board.

"No? Nobody?" Kelly turned on her chair, her skirt swirling around her scrunched socks and tennis shoes as she checked for the consensus. "That's what I thought. Can you believe he only just figured it out? Doesn't say much for his operational skills, if you ask me."

He had to stop this train wreck in the making. "Kelly, you don't want to do this."

She peered down at him with eyes full of steely black

resolve. "Since when are you an expert on what I want, Agent Doesn't-Have-a-Clue?" She returned her attention to her captivated audience. "Now, I suspect I'm not the only one who's appreciated his fine bod. I'm just not too sly about checking out a man."

She jumped down from her chair and planted her hands in the small of Ethan's back. Her shove propelled him into the aisle with surprising strength.

Ethan shot a frown over his shoulder. "Kelly—"

"Of course, what's not to drool over? Killer-blue eyes. And all that hair." She whistled long and soft. "Man, I'll be sorry to see it go." Arms crossed over her chest, she circled him in a slow perusal. "Hmmm, let's talk body specifics."

"Let's not."

"He's got nice legs. Runner's legs. And those washboard abs—" She pivoted to the woman in the cubicle beside her. "What do you think, Carla?"

The woman's gaze raked him with bold appreciation before she gave Kelly a wink and a nod. Heat burned over him. Damn it, he absolutely was *not* blushing.

"Time to go." Ethan grabbed Kelly's arm and started hauling her toward the hall, all the while trying to ignore the soft give of womanly flesh beneath his hand.

He may have been dragging her, but her straight back made it clear she was walking tall at her own pace. She called over her shoulder, "What's the verdict on his butt, Carla? Pretty fine, huh?"

The low rumble of laughs swallowed any answer, laughs from everybody including one from Robert Davidson, who lounged just inside the door. Kelly's eyes turned razor-sharp again in a warning Ethan picked up two seconds too late.

She jerked loose and stood her ground. "But of course we all know his butt's great…since he shows it often enough."

Uh-oh. Ethan jammed his hands in his pockets and prepared to weather the storm.

"As a matter of fact, he was showing that awesome ass of his about four minutes ago. You see, the thing is, now that he *finally* figured out I'm attracted to him, he assumes his hot body is so appealing it will render me incapable of working with him. Now silly little ole me thinks I've managed to do my job quite well for two years with him around. Somehow he must have forgotten that."

Kelly advanced to stand toe-to-toe with Ethan. "Just so everyone's clear, you're a good-looking guy. No question. But you know what else? Big deal. Get over yourself."

She flicked her hair over her shoulder in a tidal wave of silk that caught him square in the libido before she whipped around him and out the door.

Her tennis shoes thudded all the way down the corridor.

Davidson applauded. "Well done."

Low chuckles echoed as everyone ducked back into cubicles.

Davidson shoved a hand through his damp hair. "Nice to see a woman have you on the run for a change."

Kelly? Have him on the run? Ethan didn't like the sound of that at all. And he wasn't on the run, damn it, just off his game today. "I was only protecting her feelings."

"And instead you hurt them."

That stung more than it should have. "Looks that way."

His fellow operative nodded toward an open meeting room and gestured for Ethan to follow. "So you're going to be working with her?"

Ethan paused, then closed the door to the windowless room. Davidson would be briefed soon enough anyway— and probably laugh himself sore.

"The couple-cover deal." Ethan paced around the room, restless energy fueling his feet.

Davidson tugged a chair from the conference table and dropped into it. "Tough gig, working with a woman you're attracted to."

Weary eyes said Davidson had already taken that walk.

Stopping beside a Power Point projector, Ethan readjusted

the cord with too much attention. "Who says I'm attracted to her?"

"You're not?"

Ethan blocked the image of her breasts straining against her sweater, the memory of her voice flowing over him in the car while he dressed. "She's a friend. Or at least she was."

"Whatever." Davidson worked a hand along his left thigh where he'd been hit two years ago. "Sure will kill that playboy image of yours to be seen with her."

Defensiveness crept through Ethan. He'd never thought of Davidson as shallow. Couldn't the guy see the patrician cheekbones Kelly almost managed to hide under all that magnificent hair? And she could layer on enough clothes for an ice storm and it wouldn't disguise the curve of those breasts he suspected were as incredibly generous as the woman.

He opened his mouth to set Davidson straight.

Then stopped.

Rumor had it the man was still reeling from some kind of relationship on his near-fatal assignment in Rebelia. The last thing Ethan wanted was for this guy to go seeking some of Kelly's sweet, gentle warmth.

Not that she'd been particularly sweet three minutes ago when discussing his butt with a room full of co-workers.

If she channeled half that fire into watching his back, they'd be fine. He had to admire the spark of her rampage. The office would talk for years over that one.

She sure knew how to make her point. A smile slid over his face.

"Just a friend, huh?" A smirk twitched Davidson's mouth.

Ethan's smile fell away. "Why do you want to know?"

"Back off, rich boy." He raised his hands in surrender. "I had enough of you on the basketball court this morning. I've got a point here if you'll quit thinking with your libido long enough to listen."

"Then spit it out in plain English so us slow folks can understand."

"She's not your usual type. No one outside this office knows you two have even met, so the couple deal is going to stir questions when you need to keep a low profile."

Why the hell hadn't he thought of all that back in Hatch's office when he needed to persuade his boss to ditch this plan of action? Because it never crossed his mind people wouldn't believe he could be attracted to her.

Damn. He was in serious trouble here. "We'll just have to be convincing."

"She's still going to need some polish if you expect to pull this off."

Fine in theory, if it wouldn't bring the fires of hell down on his head. Or worse yet, some kind of wounded-doe look to her eyes.

He'd been around enough women to know that while a man might appreciate individual assets, women had the unerring knack for zeroing in on the least perceived imperfection. Heaven help the man who failed the *how does this dress look?* test.

As much as he wanted to protect Kelly, Ethan knew Davidson had a point. Other less-discerning eyes might not appreciate her allure. "How the hell am I supposed to take care of that without hurting her feelings? The last thing I need is for her to climb on the roof with a bullhorn to discuss my ass again."

"That's your problem, pal, not mine. Good luck." Davidson stood and rolled the chair back under the table. He headed out the door, laughing under his breath. "Washboard abs…"

Not a reassuring farewell salute to a man with a missing mojo.

ARIES could provide Kelly with all the guns and explosives imaginable. But the social world he cruised would chew her alive if he didn't give her a whole different set of "tools" to protect herself.

His world.

Suddenly Ethan knew the one person he could trust to help Kelly without hurting her.

He just wished he could say the same for himself.

Kelly hunched over her desk, ignoring the persistent ache in her back. Her computer screen hummed in the late-night air, her only company the whir of a janitor's vacuum and a lone light from under Hatch's office door.

Nuances of verb tenses swirled through her head, soothing her with the familiar oblivion of work. She was in control here, with her languages and academics. If only she could find the same control away from her books.

She'd made a fool of herself this afternoon, proving full well she didn't deserve this assignment. Not that Director Hatch had listened when she'd tried to bow out later.

Kelly whipped away the grit in her eyes and reached for her mug of herbal tea. She blew into the steamy heat, hints of raspberry steaming from the mug. She stared at the glowing words on the screen from an intercepted missive. The rural Rebelian dialect, a mix of German and Russian, seemed to be discussing some kind of sapphire. A jewel? Or the color itself?

The color of Ethan's eyes.

She screeched those thoughts to a complete halt. Just a crush, she reminded herself.

Her nose itched with the phantom scent of masculine cologne and sweat mingling with her raspberry tea. A shiver tingled through her and her eyes fluttered closed. She inhaled the memory of Ethan.

So real.

Too real.

Her eyes snapped open.

A shadow fell across her desk. She didn't look up.

"So you really like my butt?" Ethan's rumbling voice filled her workspace.

Mortification seared her. She scrolled through the text on her computer screen as if he hadn't even spoken.

He sat on the edge of her desk as he'd done at least a hundred times before. "Well, I like your smile. And I'm mad as hell at myself for having done something to take it away."

Damn, he was good. Already she could feel her anger melting like a bowl of her favorite rocky road ice cream left in the sun.

"You've earned this assignment, Kelly. I had no right to tamper with that."

She studied her still fingers on the keyboard and mumbled, "As if you could."

"Ah, that's right. I need to 'get over myself.'"

His ability to laugh at himself made him all the more appealing and she could almost hate him for that. Sure he showed that fine butt of his on occasion, but once her anger had cooled she knew he'd been trying to protect her feelings—in his own man-dense kind of way.

Sort of sweet, actually. And gorgeous. And smelling so good she wanted to crawl over the desk to bury her face in his jacket.

Ethan hitched his knee farther on her desk and moved closer. "I looked over the data on Morrow's disappearance this afternoon and came to a conclusion."

He might as well have dangled a carrot in front of her. No way could she resist. "And?"

"Hatch was right about us as a team."

She looked up at him. "Really?"

"I'm okay with foreign languages conversationally." Ethan scooped up her paperweight again. "Written translations, however, are not my strong suit. And I sure as hell don't speak as many languages as you do."

She crossed her arms over her chest. "So you need me."

Ethan went still. His eyes fell from her face, lower. He couldn't be looking at her breasts?

He glanced away, replacing the paperweight. "A good

field operative needs to know his or her limitations. Which means you have to accept I have something you need, too.''

"You do?" she asked, her breasts suddenly warm and heavy beneath her crossed arms.

He swallowed, long and slow, before his eyes locked firmly on her face. "Things could turn ugly at that summit ball. You have to be able to defend yourself. I need to know you can defend yourself or I won't be able to concentrate on my end of the operation."

"Okay." Feet planted, she heeled her office chair back for distance from the draw of those sapphire eyes. "I'll log in extra training hours."

"Not good enough. If you're going to be ready in two weeks, it'll take more than a few extra agency courses. I require a personal reassurance my partner can protect herself, and even watch my back, too. I'll only have that if I take part in the training 24/7."

Kelly scrambled to follow the conversational thread with the scent of him filling her tiny cubicle. She needed air. She needed space.

She needed another partner.

Ethan canted forward. "I think we should live together."

Chapter 3

"Live together?"

If Kelly's horror-filled eyes were anything to gauge by, Ethan guessed he was being subjected to a crash course in "getting over himself." His bruised ego would have to move aside. He had to convince her to move in with him so his Aunt Eugenie could orchestrate a makeover in a way that wouldn't hurt Kelly's tender feelings and he would be one step closer to securing the file on his parents.

Ethan reached to stop her chair before she backpedaled into the next cubicle. "Hear me out."

She smacked his hand away. "If this is your idea of revenge for what I said this afternoon, it's not funny."

"Kelly, this afternoon was," he paused, "surprising. It's not exactly something I'd like to repeat. But no harm, no foul."

"Really?" Suspicion stained her eyes.

He'd have to teach her to hide her emotions better. "You were absolutely right. We're both professionals and I should have treated you as such."

"Now you show that by suggesting we live together?"

Ethan opted to ignore her sarcasm. "Hear me out. You're off office duty once you leave today."

"But the computer intelligence—"

"I have secure link-ups at home. That summit ball is only two weeks away. We need every minute between now and then to trade services."

"What services are you offering at your playboy bachelor pad?"

Her meaning sucker-punched him. Apparently he hadn't hidden his attraction as well as he'd thought.

Kelly's jaw tipped with a defensiveness that spoke louder than her words. "I mean, why not take the warm and willing woman up on her offer? After all, she announced it to a whole room of people."

How could she see herself as nothing more than a warm and willing body? Who the hell had abused her trust?

Guilt pinched him. Hard. But damn it, her safety depended on her cover's believability. He had to trust his Aunt Eugenie could pull off her fairy godmother role for him.

Ethan decided not to acknowledge the "warm and willing" comment and rolled out his excuse for getting her out of the office. "We'll exchange language brush-up lessons for self-defense training."

Her arms fell to her lap. "Oh."

"And I don't live in a 'bachelor pad,'" he felt compelled to add. "When I'm in town, I live in the family home with my aunt."

A grin crept over her face. "You live with your aunt?" She laughed.

He was worrying himself cross-eyed over hurting her feelings and *she* was laughing at *him*.

Kelly clapped a hand over her mouth.

Heat inched up the back of his neck for the second time in one day—hell, for the second time in his life—thanks to this woman. "Kelly—"

Her laughter caressed the air with the same husky sensuality of her voice. "The great playboy of the western world lives with his aunt."

Ethan bristled. "It's a big house."

"I'm sure it is."

"I'm gone a lot. She watches over my stuff."

"Makes sense."

Her laughter faded. Silence fell. Kelly fidgeted with the paperweight. The vacuum cleaner silenced and he still hadn't convinced her. He would have to play dirty. But then rules had never been his strong suit. "I thought you wanted to do whatever it took to get out from behind that desk."

Her hand clenched around the paperweight. He'd won. He could see it in the sigh lowering her shoulders.

"Your aunt won't mind a guest for two weeks?" Kelly offered a final token resistance.

Damn it, Kelly had been pushing his buttons left and right while he was trying to be Joe Sensitive. Well, not anymore. He'd maneuver her where he wanted her, damn it, mouthiness and all. He wouldn't let his rogue feelings get in the way of his quest for that file Hatch had on his parents.

"Aunt Eugenie knows I work for the CIA, just not about ARIES. She doesn't ask questions. I've already spoken to her. Do you want to follow me out there?"

"I don't have a car. I take the train in—"

"Good." His mojo was positively humming. "Then I'll pick you up in the morning."

"Well, I don't know—"

"Be ready by seven. I want to get an early start."

Kelly watched the morning sun creep over the Virginia suburban skyline from the comfort of luxurious leather in Ethan's vintage Jaguar.

A really messy Jag.

She nudged the gym bag at her feet with her tennis shoe in a vain attempt to make room for herself amidst the piles of books on tape and empty coffee cups.

Over the hills and through the woods to Aunt Eugenie's

house they drove. Ice-laden trees and street signs sped past her window outside, while blues music swirled from the CD player inside.

Ethan had steamrollered her in the office the night before. Sure his plan sounded logical, but she could have come up with an alternative if he hadn't been hogging all the air. How could a girl think when she could barely breathe? But she'd surrendered rather than risk spending more time alone with him in the intimacy of the darkened office. She'd waited to start her list of alternatives in the solitude of her apartment.

Three hours and two bowls of rocky road ice cream later, she'd decided his plan had merit, even if not for the reasons he thought. Regardless of her rampage in the office, she doubted her ability to work if she couldn't think whenever he walked into the room. What better way to kill her infatuation than to spend more time with him and uncover his faults?

Ethan stopped for a light. A soda can rolled from under the seat.

Perfect. Her plan was already well under way. A much-needed smile pulled at her.

"What?"

Kelly peered out the windshield at the pristine yards of snow, all viewed over a sludge-covered hood. "Why in the world would someone own a car this expensive and never wash it?"

He adjusted the rearview mirror, an air freshener shaped like a pine tree swaying. "Lesson number one in field craft. Sometimes the simplest tricks are the most effective."

"Having a car with Wash Me scrawled across the back is field craft?"

"Actually it is." He turned another corner, downshifting. His legs flexed as he worked the clutch, brake and gas pedal. "Think about it. What happens if someone rubs away those words?"

"It leaves a big smudge," she answered absently, admiring the impressive play of muscles beneath faded denim.

"And if someone tampers with other parts of the car..."

His words sank in, pulling her attention back to chilling reality. "Their handprints will be noticeable—or smudged."

"Exactly. Sure, ARIES provides plenty of the high-tech gadgets. But sometimes simple works well, too."

He existed in a world of constant threats and car bombs, and all for a higher good. How could she not admire him? Even his freshly shorn hair reminded her that every facet of his life bowed to the demands of his job.

Her plan was not going well at all. Time to dig deeper into his real life for those flaws.

"How long have you lived with your aunt?" she asked, envisioning some teenage rebellion that led him to being shuffled to another relative.

"Since elementary school."

"That young?"

His hands clenched around the steering wheel. "My parents died in a car accident."

How did she not know this about him? "I'm so sorry."

"Me, too."

Much more of emotion-tugging Ethan and she'd leave this assignment with a marshmallow heart. "I'm sorry for laughing earlier, about you living with your aunt, I mean. It's really sweet that you stayed on to take care of her."

"Take care of her?" Ethan snorted. "Better not let Aunt Eugenie hear you insinuating she needs help for anything. She's sixty-five going on twenty."

"Oh, okay." Was his aunt some kind of socialite poster-girl for plastic surgery? Panic tickled her lungs. She might like herself just fine the way she was. That didn't mean she wanted to spend the next two weeks with Ethan's aunt questioning what he saw in such a quiet wallflower. "She knows this is just a working relationship, right?"

"Yes."

Her panic faded. "Good."

"But the servants don't."

"Servants?" Kelly pulled her gaze away from Ethan and looked out the window. Sprawling houses loomed on either side of the road—brick, columns, even the occasional turret. Plots of land acres large spread between gates and towering homes. With every block, the houses grew bigger and Kelly grew more uncomfortable.

"We need to protect the cover," Ethan continued. "The servant network is tight in my aunt's world. We don't want them wondering and passing along their doubts. If we expect to pull this off, they need to think we're a couple and we can use the practice."

A couple? How had she gone from getting over him to pretending to be his girlfriend for two weeks? "What have they been told?"

"That you work for an embassy as a translator. I met you through a friend. We fell for each other, and you're taking an extended vacation to meet my family."

The sense of having been maneuvered washed over her and she didn't like it. If he'd told her this the night before, she would have shot down his plan.

And he probably knew it. "When were you going to tell me?"

"I'm telling you now."

Kelly stared out the window and counted passing houses to calm her temper. Of course she didn't get to count very many since the yards were so darned big. No snowmen littered these lawns like in her Nebraska hometown.

She'd realized he was wealthy. But this neighborhood wasn't just rich. It was filthy rich. Beyond-her-comprehension rich.

He obviously didn't have to work. She recognized his thrill-seeking need, but he could have channeled that into any number of expensive hobbies. Instead of swimming with sharks in Aruba, he dodged bullets to make others safe.

Damn. He grew more admirable with each passing Mercedes.

"This didn't have to be so complicated."

"It isn't," Ethan insisted. "If anything, there will be fewer questions and more acceptance than if I'd just shown up at the summit ball with you. People would have been curious about you, which would attract too much attention. This gives everyone two weeks to become accustomed to the idea."

"And afterward?"

"We break up."

Breaking up with a guy she'd never gotten to enjoy. That depressed her as much as the loss of his longer hair, the lost chance to test the length and texture with her fingers.

Ethan turned off the road, pausing at a security gate to punch in a code. Kelly peered through the metal bars.

This wasn't just a *big* house. It was a mansion.

A white-columned palatial home sprawled before her. Towering evergreens with snowcapped branches proclaimed age and heritage. An iced-over fountain bigger than most pools perched in the middle of a horseshoe driveway.

All of Ethan's altruistic qualities aside, he came from a different world. He might as well reside on a different planet. She'd harbored dreams and fantasies about this man for two years, and yet she didn't know the first thing about him.

No doubt, their break up would be completely believable.

Steering up the drive, Ethan thought through the round of introductions he would have to make—housekeeper, chauffeur, cook. Thought of all the times he would touch Kelly like an attentive boyfriend. Like a lover.

His great plan had a serious flaw.

Too late now. Bottom line, this would protect Kelly on a number of levels. Not only would she be better prepared by his aunt, but Ethan also fully intended to follow through on the plan to teach her self-defense. Who knew what their digging into foreign embassy workings might stir? All the more reason to have her close by where he could guard her.

At least her voice wasn't tormenting him anymore since she'd started clamming up four blocks ago. The tension emanating from her had increased with the size of the houses. He dreaded the moment she would turn and look at him differently, when she wouldn't be able to see past the stacks of money to the man anymore.

The house might be his but it wasn't *him,* and for some reason it became important that Kelly understand that.

Forget front-door welcomes. He didn't want her first impression of his home to be some three-story winding staircase and a cathedral ceiling. He sped past the horseshoe driveway and circled around to the back. Pulling into the five-car garage, he parked between his aunt's Mercedes and the housekeeper's VW Beetle.

Ethan shut off the engine as the door slid closed behind them. "Leave your luggage. I'll bring it up later when I take you to the main house. First, we're going to head upstairs to the apartment."

"Where I'm staying?"

"No."

"Your Aunt Eugenie has a suite over the garage?"

"No. I do." The surprised lift to her brow brought a rush of victory. He'd find his footing with this complex woman yet. "I thought you could use the time to ask any more questions before you meet everyone."

"You mean questions about how you set me up." Her eyes probed him with quiet censure.

She couldn't have already figured out why he needed her here, could she? Heaven help him if he'd been too obvious about the socialite polish.

He reached behind the seat for her laptop computer to give himself a reason to look away. "Set you up?"

"By not telling me about the real reason for coming here."

He twisted forward with her laptop and lapsed into the foolproof method of answering questions with questions.

"Suppose you tell me since you do such a good job at spelling things out."

"Because even with everything I said yesterday, you still don't trust that I can keep my head on straight while posing as a couple. So you've planned this 'lover practice' in front of your servants for the next two weeks."

Lover-practice. Now that had a tempting ring to it. "Kelly, I'm not doing anything more than I said. We're here to work through leads in hopes of finding Alex Morrow before someone tortures him to death. And maybe we'll be able to stop the whole heist attempt before the summit so a room full of people won't be in danger. And if that doesn't work, we're going to make damned sure we both have every tool available so no one gets hurt."

So Kelly wasn't hurt.

He ignored the nagging voice that insisted he was already hurting her by not being honest. But he'd abandoned scruples long ago in favor of winning, and he wanted that thirty-year-old file on his parents.

Kelly threw her door open. "Then let's get started."

Ethan led her up the stairs, punching in the alarm code onto the pad outside his door before pushing inside. As always, he made a quick sweep through his barnlike studio apartment. He held up a hand for Kelly to stop while he took the six steps in three strides up to his loft bedroom. Closing the door behind him, he jogged up another half set of stairs to the open gallery computer area. Loping back down, he nodded. "All clear."

"Do you always check your own house this thoroughly?"

She thought that was thorough?

"Yes." He tucked his hands in his back pockets and cruised to a stop in the seldom-used kitchen area.

Kelly trailed a hand along the back of a gray leather sofa, her gaze sweeping the sparse furnishings. "So you brought me to your bachelor pad, after all."

"I've never brought anyone outside of family here."

Her gaze snapped up to meet his. Solemn brown eyes

studied him with confusion and an odd sort of expectation he knew he couldn't fulfill.

Ethan turned his back on eyes that threatened to become as tempting as her voice. "If we're going to work together, this is the only truly secure place." He swept an empty pizza box off the kitchenette table. "You can set up your laptop here today. I'll arrange something better by tomorrow."

Shrugging out of her coat, she strolled through the cavernous room. Her tennis shoes squeaked on the bright tiles his Aunt Eugenie had ordered from Italy. She'd insisted he needed something lively in his dark world.

"There's certainly plenty of space. My apartment would fit in here twice."

"I like how open it is." Easier to watch. Even at home, he never relaxed his guard, probably hadn't slept through the night since he was five.

Ethan pitched his jacket over a kitchen chair. He opened the refrigerator and pulled out a can of orange juice for himself. "Want one? Or something more substantial—like a two-day-old burrito?"

He earned her genuine smile for the first time in twenty-four hours, a heady victory.

"No, thanks. I had breakfast already."

Ethan elbowed the refrigerator closed and planned his next move for relaxing her. His computer system upstairs might not make a bad start.

Footsteps sounded in the stairwell. Ethan tensed a second before—

"Yoo-hoo, Ethan?" His aunt's voice floated up the hall. Eugenie Williams charged through the door and across the room. The sleeves of her mummy-covered caftan, a souvenir of her latest trip to Egypt, fluttered from her open arms. "You're early! Why didn't you come into the house?"

"Because we're early."

"Like manners have ever mattered to you." She folded him in a hug.

He dropped a kiss on her head. "You tried your best."

A soft smile creased her round face. "I certainly did."

Ethan couldn't stop his smile in return as she stepped back. He loved his aunt, eccentricities and all. She'd been the only constant during his childhood after he lost his parents. He would never forget how she'd put her own jet-setting life on hold for him.

Well, not exactly on hold, but she'd carted him along on one extended field trip after another, giving him purpose, just as ARIES had done after Celia. "Aunt Eugenie, this is Kelly Taylor."

She spun to face Kelly, stirring a drift of flowers and some kind of spice. No doubt his aunt had been knee-deep in aromatherapy this morning. Every time Ethan turned around, she sported a new mood-enhancing scent concocted by her masseur.

Eugenie studied Kelly with keen eyes, before nodding. "Ethan, go put her things in the Jefferson suite. And don't blow out the candles the way you always do. I ordered a special blend of sweet marjoram, lavender and ylang ylang for serenity." She flapped her hands to shoo him away. "Now scoot, so we can talk."

The tension Ethan hadn't even realized gripped him eased. There might be something to all Eugenie's mood oils and fragrances after all.

He should have trusted his instincts, which had told him he'd made the right decision in handing Kelly over to Aunt Eugenie's tutelage. The woman was a miracle worker. She'd actually made something halfway productive out of a screw-up rebel like himself.

This would come together. Aunt Eugenie would not only transform Kelly, but she would also be the perfect buffer for any awkwardness.

And while they worked on hairstyles, he could figure out who the hell had been following them.

Chapter 4

Kelly trailed Ethan's aunt to the sofa. Not that she had much choice unless she wanted to stand in the middle of the room pinned by the woman's curious eyes and the gaze of all those gold mummies on her muumuu.

Why didn't Ethan hurry? She wanted to work, not chit-chat with his eccentric aunt. She would prove herself a worthy partner, not a woman who had to practice something as simple as pretending to be a girlfriend.

At least she wouldn't have to pretend when she was alone with Eugenie Williams, since Eugenie knew Ethan and Kelly were working together. Kelly relaxed onto the sofa, grateful she didn't have to hide her lack of polish for the next few minutes.

Her crush on Ethan, however, Kelly intended to keep well hidden around his aunt.

Eugenie swept across the room toward the gray leather couch, her steely bun twined on top of her head adding two inches of height. As she drew closer, the older woman's vitality radiated through despite the tiny lines around her eyes.

Eugenie Williams sat.

Well, sort of. Just *sitting* seemed too ordinary a word to describe any motion from this woman. Her imposing presence made a simple stroll across the rug seem as if it deserved a diva spotlight.

Apparently Ethan had learned to command a room from a master.

Her caftan settled to rest around her, revealing strappy yellow sandals. Those snow-encrusted spike heels would have sent Kelly sprawling. "Tell me about yourself, dear."

"Well…" Kelly couldn't imagine anything about her upbringing on a Nebraska wheat farm that would be of interest to this woman. "I work with Ethan."

"So I hear."

Kelly searched for a safer topic. The woman might be a fountain of information for the quest to learn more about Ethan, but those shrewd eyes would be onto her in a heartbeat. Kelly tapped an edge of the woman's caftan. "This is lovely."

The pattern of Egyptian sarcophagi on silk stared back with eerie voids for eyes. "No, it's not."

"Pardon me?"

Eugenie fluffed her silver hair with her fingernails. "It's a godawful eyesore I bought with the sole intention of shocking the Chanel right off those pastel suits worn by the country-club set."

"Oh."

"But it's comfortable."

Kelly snuck a quick glance at the door. Still no Ethan. "That's important."

"Essential. Life should be lived. Enjoyed." She whipped the air with her bejeweled fingers. "Savored."

Kelly agreed a hundred percent. She inched back farther on the sofa. "How wonderfully liberating not to worry what others think."

"Oh, I do care. Very much." Eugenie's hands fell to rest on her lap. "I absolutely cannot tolerate the thought that someone might think I'm bowing to the god of status quo."

Not much chance of that. "Where did you find this, uh, comfortable eyesore?"

"In Egypt, of course."

Kelly's soul soaked up the thoughts of travel. "Did you buy it at one of the street markets?"

"Oh, I like to tell most people I haggled with a vendor in the old Turkish bazaar. *Ba Kum?*"

Kelly searched her memory for the translation— "How much?"

"Excellent. Ethan always struggled with languages, no matter how many informal field trips I took him on abroad. Of course he did get an A on his volcano science project after our weekend jaunt to view one in Italy."

Kelly smiled at the image. What had it been like for Ethan being brought up by this unconventional woman?

The answer came to her in a flash.

Fun.

No doubt spelling drills for Ethan hadn't consisted of sitting in a straight-backed chair until his legs fell asleep. "So you got your deal on the caftan at the market?"

"Actually I bought this in the airport on my way home. I just said I like to *tell* people it came from a vendor. Without the story, my caftan has no allure for them."

"Of course," Kelly agreed, rather than admit she'd lost the thread of Eugenie's reasoning back at the bazaar.

Where was she going with this rambling? Or was Eugenie Williams one of those people who just liked to talk? Either way, Kelly knew she didn't stand a chance of stepping off the roller coaster. Not that she wanted off just yet. "What a, uh, fascinating concept."

The older woman waggled a bejeweled finger. "Ethan didn't tell me what a diplomat you are. Not one of his strong points, I might add. Diplomacy. I missed the mark in teach-

ing him that one. But I did a fair job in showing him how
to savor life.''

Kelly decided she would pass on hearing about Ethan's
exploits.

Eugenie twisted rings around her fingers with her thumb,
one sapphire set in platinum, a double ruby and an emerald-
cut diamond. ''In the interest of savoring life, I want you
to come with me to my spa.''

It sounded heavenly, but she didn't have the time. The
story of her life, but a price worth paying to rise to the top.
''I'm here to work.''

''You can't work for every waking minute. We'll go after
hours.''

''Thank you, but I really can't—''

''We'll have mud wraps and a massage. My masseur does
the most wonderful relaxation therapy with river stones
along the back to ground and center you.'' Her eyes drifted
closed, her fingers wavering down in front of her face as
she exhaled deeply.

Kelly twitched her foot. How long should she wait for
Ethan's aunt to come to?

Eugenie's eyes snapped open. ''After that, we can indulge
in a pedicure, and maybe even work in a hair trim.''

''A hair trim.'' Realization trickled over her like the
stinging bite and stench of the home perm solution her
mother had squeezed onto her head in the eighth grade.

Kelly stared at the woman with a new understanding.
She'd dodged her mother's mall salon gift certificates often
enough to recognize a makeover offer when she heard one.

Ethan had set her up again.

And that royally pissed her off.

Why hadn't he just told her? She could have handled
hearing she needed a new wardrobe to make this work. She
wasn't so socially inept that she expected to wear tennis
shoes to an embassy ball.

But he'd obviously worried about hurting her feelings,
and that reeked of a pathetic air she could not stomach. ''So

that's why I'm here. For you to concoct a cover story. Like with your caftan, you'll set up an allure to your social set so they'll accept me.''

A part of her wanted Eugenie to deny it, but she knew better. Those extra IQ points carried the burden of being right quite often.

Eugenie's bittersweet smile confirmed the scenario before her words. ''Sadly, my dear, I'm afraid there are people in this world who don't trust what their own eyes tell them. They can't believe something has beauty or worth unless it conforms to their standards. I'm sorry about that. But most of all, I'm sorry you had to find out this way. Ethan should have told you.''

''Yes, he should have.'' She couldn't stem the anger in her voice.

''Remember, he is a man. And when it comes to second-guessing what women want, men can be the most clueless creatures since the Komodo dragon.''

Kelly couldn't help but be affected by the woman's whimsy. A snort of laughter slipped past her anger. ''He should put you on the payroll for damage control, as well as makeovers.''

''My nephew can be an insensitive ass.''

''It's not your fault. He's just doing his job.'' Her frustration redirected itself all onto one, all-too-deserving target. Ethan.

''Consider it a cover, like Ethan's ever-changing hair length. We'll drape you in Versace and diamonds. Then we'll tell people your parents are Nebraska land barons.''

''They're wheat farmers.''

''No, no.'' Eugenie batted the air as if whipping up her story. ''They launched an exclusive brand of hybrid organic wheat germ that's all the rage in Paris.''

''Wheat germ? My father is somewhere right now cringing over his cholesterol-laden breakfast and doesn't know why.'' No doubt this woman would have her way. Kelly surrendered to the inevitable. "I guess I can live with Versace and the wheat germ. But no feathers."

"I wouldn't dare."

The wicked glint in cerulean eyes so like Ethan's made Kelly doubt the woman's word. She picked at the hem of Eugenie's caftan. "And no sarcophagi."

"Brat."

Kelly relaxed into the sofa with an exaggerated sigh. "Okay, then, maybe one chiffon diamond-studded turban."

Eugenie's face smoothed, no laughter in sight. She lifted a lock of Kelly's hair from the sofa back. "Oh no, my dear. I wouldn't cover this glorious mane for anything."

Her hair?

She'd never thought of her hair as anything other than an obnoxious tangle. Kelly looked for signs that Eugenie might be flattering her just to win her point and found nothing of the sort. The woman meant it.

Not that it should matter in the least.

But it did. After years of waiting for even one affirmation from her mother, Kelly soaked up that single comment. If this woman ordered a torturous combo of a seaweed wrap and bikini wax, Kelly would be first in line.

Ethan, on the other hand, would pay big-time for his latest deception.

"It's all about deception, Kelly. Make your attacker believe you can't defend yourself." Ethan stood across from Kelly on the exercise mat in his private gym. He hoped like hell this hand-to-hand combat lesson would end soon. He'd had enough of flipping, tripping and *touching* to last him two lifetimes. "Use your smaller size to your advantage by lulling him into a false sense of security. Then blast him with an explosive surprise shot."

Security? He wanted the security of a mission in, say, Taiwan. Yeah, Taiwan, where he could kick butt against a pack of bad guys.

Instead, he was stuck in the mansion gym serving as Kelly's personal trainer.

Much more body tangling and he would lose his mind. Please, Lord, he hoped she'd absorbed today's self-defense lesson and they could move on to weaponry. He could use some time with his 9mm to blast holes in a target, a safe outlet for his frustration.

"Remember, Kelly, it's all in the hips." He did not want to think about her hips. "Lower your center of gravity so the power of your punch comes from your body and not just the body part."

"Right." She nodded, her ponytail bobbing. "Sling hips into the punch and follow through."

"Good. Now roll out the moves we reviewed. Got it?"

"Got it." A stray lock of hair whispered across her damp brow. Kelly braced her feet apart, her sweat pants pulling taut across her hips.

Ah, hell. Not her hips again.

He forced his eyes up to her face. Not that it offered his libido any relief. Her swept-back hair revealed high cheekbones models paid big bucks to create with implants.

The Nebraska State T-shirt showed a lot more than her bulky sweaters. Even a sweaty mess, she looked damned good inside that T-shirt—and felt good underneath it.

He wanted to crawl into a cold shower.

Not wise when he still didn't know who'd followed them or why. His review of the security camera footage from when they'd arrived had revealed zip, nada, zilch. The tail could have been a fluke—except he didn't believe in coincidence.

"Ethan?"

Kelly's voice kicked through his thoughts.

"Huh?"

"Are you ready?"

"Of course." He advanced a step and ignored the perfume of Kelly's shampoo mingling with perspiration, so close to the scent of sex. "Just waiting for your go-ahead. Let's try it again."

Friendship was more important, he reminded himself.

Says who? his libido asked.

"Shut up."

Kelly looked up. "What?"

"Nothing." Too much of nothing at the moment.

Friendship did count, especially for a man who didn't allow many into the inner circle of his life. The fewer people he let in, the less chance he had of losing them.

And no way in hell did he intend to lose Kelly on this mission. He would train her until she dropped. "Envision someone you want to hurt."

She blinked once and nailed him with her gaze. "Done."

"No time for sympathy."

"Got it."

"Focus. Pull your mind in tight. You have to quit thinking about all those pretty kicks you see on TV or in whatever class you took. This is about street fighting, blending techniques that work for your body." He'd spent the whole night before putting together a Kelly plan, a mix of women's defense courses and Krav Maga used by elite forces around the world.

Ethan stepped closer, crowded her space to emphasize the differences in their size. Recognizing limitations was the first step to overcoming them. "No rules. Fight dirty. Fight to win because losing means you're dead. List target zones."

"Vulnerable tissue areas—throat, eyes, inner arm, inner thigh. And of course the cro—"

"Yeah, I'll let you slide by without practicing that one." Technically, it didn't qualify as a soft tissue area at the moment, anyway. "Run the strikes."

"The palm strike, eagle claw, bear strike," she paused, flexing her hand into the proper form for each, "and my favorite, the double dragon." She swung her hand forward as if tossing something, two fingers jabbing toward his eye.

He blocked her wrist. "Well done."

His fingers curved around her and held a second beyond necessary before he dropped her hand.

"I have to admit," her voice whispered through the air, husky bedroom tones gliding over him as she circled to his back, "the tiger claw seems so violent."

Her breath stroked across his skin. Ethan swallowed. "That's the idea."

"How can I know I'll be bloodthirsty enough to go for the throat like that?"

The husky catch in her question caressed the skin on the back of his neck. "Instinct to live."

"But to pinch through the Adam's apple…" She crossed to his other side, a full-out attack on his senses. Her hand fell onto his shoulder, curved around. "I think I prefer to just—"

His world rocked.

Whoosh. Air abandoned his lungs.

The ceiling stared back down at him as he lay flat on his back.

Kelly leaned over him. "—do something like that?"

Damn. She'd lured him with a pretended weakness and then flipped him. Tripped him, actually, but a minor technicality since either way, he'd met the mat.

"Yeah, Kel, just like that." He pushed the words out with minimal oxygen left in his lungs.

His head thunked back and he stared at the ceiling. When the hell had someone painted stars up there?

Never mind. The last one faded.

Kelly smiled, hands on both her knees as she leaned closer, nearly nose-to-nose, her ponytail swishing like a pendulum over his chest. "I took you down. Flat on your back. Oh, yeah."

She swung upright, dancing around him in her victory trot, her eyes laughing as much as her full, luscious mouth.

Ethan just lay on the floor and watched her come alive. He hadn't been dropped since early training, only to be taken down by a woman in bobby socks. He wondered if maybe he needed some self-defense courses of his own before those dainty sneakers danced right over his focus.

No more hand-to-hand, body-to-body combat today. "Time for target practice."

Maybe she'd miss and put him out of his misery.

She couldn't shoot worth a damn today.

Kelly clicked away on her new computer in Ethan's loft, the man himself absorbed in his own keyboard three feet away. The locale may have changed, but apparently her role was still the same. Desk jockey.

Aim low. Aim low. Aim low. She chanted the too damned rudimentary advice Ethan had given her every time her arm bucked and her shots went wild.

Her victory in the exercise room had been short-lived once they'd shifted to his private shooting range. Okay, so her poor aiming could have had something to do with the fact that she'd spent the hour prior tangling her body up with his on exercise mats.

Talk about exercise—more like an exercise in self-torture. He'd stood so darned close to her, smelling so *damned* awesome. Which made her shots go wild.

Which made him stand even closer.

Bottom line, she needed what he could teach her about self-defense. Sure she'd been given entry-level defense courses upon joining the agency, and she'd learned some basic moves after her grab-happy ancient languages professor had started stalking her. Her regular Pilates Method exercise and relaxation training kept her toned.

Not that she planned to let on about those and give away her miniscule edge. Besides, she'd learned more in the hour with Ethan than in her six-week course at the campus community center.

At least here at the computer with Alex Morrow's final transmissions in front of her, she could be certain of her footing.

She snuck a glance at Ethan at his computer. A miniature ivory elephant perched on top. A gift from his Aunt Eugenie, no doubt. How sweet that he'd kept it.

Kelly shoved the sympathetic thought away. The rat bastard had set her up and hurt her feelings. Twice in one week. One simple flip onto an exercise mat didn't come close to canceling that debt.

Although it made a decent start.

What was he doing? His computer screen split into multiple images of the mansion grounds. He clicked keys. Angles widened.

Kelly spun her chair for a better look. She hadn't considered there might be a threat behind Ethan's fortress walls. She understood the risks involved in setting a trap the night of the embassy gala. But why would there be safety concerns prior to that?

She hoped his grounds perusal was only routine.

He tapped two more keys, then leaned back. His chair squeaked a slow call almost as lengthy as his legs. "Whatcha got there, Taylor?"

The warm glow of lamps over the desk cast an umbrella of privacy in the darkened apartment, almost as if they were suspended in air together. Every detail of his face called to her for study, for touching—the thick arch of his dark brows, the strong jaw with an enticing cleft in the chin, and a thin scar on the side of his neck. Only about two inches long, it had faded so much she might not have noticed except it contrasted with his tan.

Kelly tore her gaze away and back to the safety of her translations. "I'm working through Morrow's references to overhearing about a *stein*."

"A brewsky?" He quirked a brow.

Kelly smiled under the shield of her hair. "I doubt it. Although it's still unclear. Many words in the German, Gastonian and Rebelian languages overlap, but the shades of meaning can differ. That can make interpretations difficult. *Stein* basically means stone. But what kind of stone? Rock, gem, jewel? It serves as a root word for so many variations. Look here." She keyed in a list of words. "*Gestein* means rocks. But *edelstein* is jewel or gem. And this, see, *feuerstein*."

His eyes fell to her mouth as she formed the words. "*Feuer?*"

"Fire stone." She resisted the urge to bite her lips. "It's like they're trying to confuse the issue."

"Or bury the meaning." He cleared his throat and pointed to the screen. "What about this?"

"*Ein herz aus stein.*"

Ethan shut his eyes as if concentrating on the phrase for interpretation. The process must have pained him since his brow furrowed.

"*Herz* means heart." A heart she wanted to protect.

"Stone heart?"

"No." Although she wished for one when dealing with this man. "Heart of the stone."

He stared at her with eyes so blue she'd only seen them on a precious newborn. No man should have eyes that beautiful.

His gaze held hers, wouldn't let go any more than he'd been willing to cut her slack on the exercise mats earlier. Although now, she had no edge. No defenses. She battled a deep yearning to press her lips to that scar on his neck and taste his skin.

A drone startled her. A buzz? Kelly jerked back into her chair.

Ethan scrubbed a hand over his chin. "The door."

He pointed to the surveillance images on his screen and Kelly grasped the distraction with both hands. The screen displayed a young woman waiting at the base of the stairs, holding a tray with a cloth draped over it. Kelly sifted through the countless introductions from earlier and placed the girl as the cook's granddaughter, around nineteen or twenty, a college student working part time at Williams Manor.

Ethan rolled his chair away from the desk and stood. "Supper. I'll be back in a second."

"She must know what the inside of your refrigerator looks like."

His low chuckle floated up for a sneak attack on her senses. She'd barely recovered when he popped into view on the security camera. Kelly couldn't resist leaning closer to listen.

Ethan took the tray from the blond teenybopper in a snow parka with white fur. "Thank you, Brittany."

"You're welcome, Mr. Williams," she crooned, bouncing on her toes like an overeager kid.

Kelly jabbed a finger at the screen. "He's old enough to be your father, Brittany."

Well, almost.

And who was she to talk, only twenty-four herself? Eleven years younger than Ethan.

He slid from the camera's angle, but Brittany stayed. Watching. Her face so open and lovesick that compassion swept aside Kelly's jealousy.

She chewed a nail and studied the screen until it blurred. Did she look at him like that, too, so young and hungry and full of longing for something she knew full well could never happen?

God, she hoped not.

The door snicked, then swung open.

"Prepare to feast." Ethan kicked the door shut again and set the tray on the kitchenette table.

Kelly hooked her arm on the back of her chair and looked down onto the too-intimate dining setup. It was just dinner, she told herself and started to stand.

An image of Brittany's face doused those thoughts.

Kelly sunk back into her chair. "How about bringing it up here so we can keep working?"

"Hatch doesn't pay overtime, you know." Ethan reached into the refrigerator and pulled out two long-neck bottles.

Alcohol and Ethan at the same time? Unwise.

She needed to keep her inhibitions firmly in place around him. Time to shut down the hormones and get to work before she turned into a Brittany. "Water for me, please."

Ethan reached into the refrigerator and let the cool blast wash over him. Like it actually made a dent in his over-heated body temp.

He'd already had enough. Frustration churned through him and he still had two more weeks left shut up in a suddenly too-damned-small apartment conjugating German verbs with Kelly.

He wanted to pick a fight, feel something other than this damned destructive need to lead Kelly into his bedroom and discover how the stars shining through his skylight would play on her pale skin.

Ethan waggled a bottle at her and pressed. "It's imported."

"I'm working. And it's from the supermarket. I can see the sticker on the six-pack carrier from here."

"Busted." He swapped one beer for bottled water, keeping the other long-neck in hand. He carried the food up the stairs, past his room and up to the open loft. Kelly didn't even acknowledge his presence, instead presenting him with a view of her back. Her hair shimmered half way down only to be captured by the back of the chair.

Lucky chair.

He ached to gather up a fistful of that hair, see it spread over his pillow in stark contrast to silver-gray sheets. Tension wound tighter within him.

He slammed the tray on the stretch of desk between their workstations and grabbed his beer. Kicking back in his chair, he tipped the bottle for a long drag.

Kelly's fingers never hesitated on the keyboard, but her mouth pulled tight. Even pinched, her lips tempted him to tease them to fullness again. Ethan nursed another swig off his bottle while watching her through amber glass.

She shot a disdainful sniff his way.

He rolled the bottle between his palms. "You might still

be on the clock, but I'm finished. I'm tired and I'm sore since someone beat me up today.''

"Poor baby."

Ethan's face twitched with a grin. He liked that most about her, the way she never seemed impressed with him, always called his bluff. More than once she'd booted his butt off her desk, chewing him out for wrinkling a report. He didn't excel at being there for other people and the thought of letting Kelly down soured the beer in his mouth.

This wasn't the sort of job for Kelly if she turned prim at controversy and boundary pushing. He raised his bottle to the light. "You know, this is nothing. One time I was undercover to bust an arms-selling ring down in Central America. Late one night, the guy was so close to talking, but he kept pouring rotgut tequila shots. If I didn't toss 'em back, he would have walked. Christ, I could hardly see straight, and I'd dumped half of mine on the floor. But the recorder worked, and I knew I could shoot straight even in my sleep—no offense."

"None taken," she answered without pausing or looking up.

He nudged the tray toward her. "Eat before you drop."

She shrugged and snagged a grape from the fruit bowl.

He couldn't condemn her for not understanding. What sort of life had she led to prepare her for this anyway? "Hey, Kel, is there a reason anyone would be following you?"

Her eyes snapped up to him.

She pulled a napkin off the tray and shook it out with exaggerated care. "No. You've probably guessed that I lead a pretty tame life. Why?"

"Someone tailed us through town on our way here."

Her napkin crumpled in her fist. "You're sure?"

He didn't even bother to answer.

"Of course you're sure. Sorry." She folded her napkin in half, smoothing the wrinkles before placing it precisely on her lap. "Why didn't you tell me then?"

"No need to worry you. Nothing you could have done about it anyway and I figured I could track it down later."

"Worry me?" Her spine straightened until she grew at least two inches in height and burgeoning anger. "You didn't want to worry me? I'm your partner, not some little woman to cosset."

Whatever she wanted to think. "Uh-huh."

"I mean it, Ethan. We're supposed to be working together, sharing responsibility and risk."

"Okay, partner." Lying didn't bother him in the least if it kept her safe. "Now eat so you can hold up your end of this operation."

Kelly's eyes stayed on him for five measured seconds before she grabbed a roll stuffed with thinly sliced beef and nipped off a corner.

Wonder spread over her face with each bite until finally she paused to say, "Ohmigosh, this is incredible. Now I'm not so surprised you don't keep anything in your fridge with Brittany bringing up this kind of food every night."

How did she know the girl's name? He glanced at the screen. Kelly had watched him and listened, Brittany's juvenile crush bothering her.

Here was his easy out. He'd pick on her about being jealous of Brittany. Or he'd let her assume the worst about him and a co-ed who didn't even remotely entice him.

Damn, he felt old today.

And Kelly looked so young and vulnerable at the moment that he couldn't do it. He would likely hurt her enough before this case ended. He couldn't bring himself to heap on more when he had a choice otherwise. "Her grandmother cooks. The kid just helps sometimes for extra money."

"Okay." Kelly looked away too fast, dipping the roll into a bowl of broth and staring down into the juice so long her bread turned to mush. She shouldn't care about his personal life. And he shouldn't care that she cared.

The last thing he wanted was to care about anyone again. Damn. Ethan rubbed the kink in his neck that had nothing to do with being slammed onto a mat and everything to do with the woman who'd put him there.

Kelly's eyes zeroed in on his hand working out the kink. "So during that drunk-fest bust—is that when you got the scar on your neck?"

She tore off another bite of her soggy sandwich.

He scratched the thin line where his beard didn't grow anymore. "Bad shaving accident."

With a drunken gunrunner determined to shave fifty years off his life.

Ethan had bolted awake to find a knife at his throat, the wild-eyed gunrunner certain his wealthy houseguest had betrayed him. It had only been six months after Celia's death, and Ethan hadn't cared much about the risk in daring the man to finish it. Ethan had lived. The gunrunner had ended up dead since Ethan truly could shoot straight half drunk and nearly asleep.

He'd considered it a fifty-fifty victory. Back then, living had hurt a hell of a lot more than the nick to his neck he'd taken fighting off his attacker.

Kelly's gaze glided down the long healed scar with such perception Ethan feared she might detect deeper scars still raw.

No question, he wanted Kelly. And if hormones had been the only factor, they'd both be in his bedroom right now. But he respected her. Even more important, he liked her, which presented a potential tangle he wanted no part of.

He'd clawed out of that pit once and knew he'd survived only half the man he'd been before. Even if he wanted to risk a relationship that could send him there again—which he sure as hell didn't—he wouldn't shortchange any woman by offering what little he had left. He would grit his teeth through the next two weeks of playing the attentive boyfriend and ignore his libido urging him to make it real.

Flicking on an extra overhead light, Ethan dispelled the intimate haze with a fluorescent flash. He returned his attention to the spread of screens in front of him and focused on locking up security as tight as his nonfunctioning heart.

Chapter 5

Kelly's heart stopped for five dizzying seconds.

Standing in the Williams Manor weight room four days later, she tugged the voluminous robe closed as she left the massage room. "Geez, Brittany, I must not have heard you knock."

The teen slouched against a bench press. "Didn't mean to sneak up on you. Sorry."

Not that she looked it.

Kelly's muscles twisted back into knots again. So much for the soothing effects of an early-morning massage Peter had just given her. She stepped deeper into the exercise room. "No harm done."

Other than the risk of a coronary. It also offered a reminder that she sure as hell needed to brush up on her awareness of her surroundings if she expected to watch Ethan's back. Kelly tightened the belt on her white robe and nuzzled deeper into terrycloth, hints of massage oils lingering on her body. "Did you need something?"

Attitude slumped her shoulders. "Mrs. Williams wanted

me to let her masseur know she's running a couple of minutes late.''

"Peter's cleaning up the table in the next room if you want to peek in and tell him.''

Brittany looked longingly back at the other door leading to the breezeway into the garage—and thus Ethan's apartment. Finally, she dragged her feet toward the massage room. Kelly wanted to tell the girl Ethan wasn't around so she could take her drooling self elsewhere, but wouldn't lend credence to her jealousy by voicing it.

The master plan for getting over Ethan Williams was turning into a big bust only a few days into operation. The more she knew, the more intriguing he became. She'd been mesmerized by his brash, bad-boy smile back at ARIES. Now, she was entranced by his tenderness to his aging aunt. The contradictions intrigued her—a Jag owner never washing his car, a man with more money than many foreign governments choosing supermarket-brand beer instead of vintage wine.

Something had to give soon, or she'd be in worse shape than when she'd buckled into his sludge-covered Jag.

Kelly slid a hand into the collar of her robe and rubbed along a kink returning to her neck. Taking advantage of the mansion's luxuries seemed frivolous, but Eugenie had insisted. And her back truly was wrecked from so much time at the computer, as well as in the gym.

Or maybe from so much time at the computer and in the gym this week *with Ethan.*

They'd both worked until three in the morning to accommodate time changes in overseas communications about banking transfers linked to terrorist groups. Brainstorming through security measures for the gala. Researching experimental advances made by the Marines in nonlethal weapons for use in a crowd of civilians.

Given the long night, they wouldn't be starting until ten this morning. Of course she couldn't sleep in thanks to a certain too-hunkish-for-his-own-good partner.

The outside door swung open, admitting a blast of cold air and a hundred-percent-hot Ethan in running clothes. Apparently he couldn't sleep, either.

He whipped the sweatshirt hood off his head and dusted snow from impossibly broad shoulders. Before the door slam finished echoing through the gym, Brittany popped back into the room. She breezed over to Kelly—that much closer to Ethan.

The girl melted at his feet.

Mitts off. Kelly didn't bother to stop the possessive thought. Brittany had better keep her little paws to herself.

For the good of the case, of course, Kelly reminded herself. Her country was counting on her to present a convincing act.

Kelly flashed an apologetic smile. "Excuse me, Brittany."

Three bold steps took Kelly chest-to-chest with Ethan. She flattened her hands on his shoulders.

Really nice shoulders. "Hi, sugar."

Sugar? *Ewww.* Her ineptitude was showing like a too-long slip.

Muscles beneath her palms contracted into a sheet of pure metal. Suddenly Brittany's melting seemed understandable.

Then he cupped her face. "Hey, Kel."

Snowcap liquefying. Flood alert!

She needed to remember his attentive boyfriend gig was just an act for their audience. But, man oh man, his gaze scorched over her face and down to the V of her robe with such convincing power the man deserved an Oscar. Even she believed he wanted her, and she knew better.

Her fingers curled to grip the warm cotton of his sweatshirt. "Why are you here?"

"To see you." His hands dropped to her waist, searing through her clothes to her skin. "I missed you."

"We just had breakfast together an hour ago," Kelly improvised.

A gasp sounded behind them. Hell's bells. She hadn't meant to insinuate a shared three-egg omelet in bed.

"Is my aunt around?" Had he pulled her forward or had she swayed? Not that it mattered, since her hips brushed his either way.

She was drowning in her own meltdown. "Eugenie's on her way over to meet up with her masseur, uh, Paul?"

"Peter."

Who could think anyway? "Right."

He glanced over her shoulder. "Brittany? Did you need something?"

"No, sir. All done." She sashayed past, blasting Kelly with a glare behind Ethan's back, before flouncing away. The door thudded after her.

Ethan's hands slid from Kelly's hips.

Ohmigosh, did they ever slide in a tingling stroke that seemed to take forever. She wanted…she wanted…

More.

He stepped back. "Sorry about all that."

"No problem." Liar.

"Let Aunt Eugenie know I'm looking for her when she's through." He jammed his hands into the stomach pocket of his sweatshirt.

Footsteps sounded in the hall. "Yoohoo," Eugenie called. "Peter! I'm on my way. Hold on."

The wiry masseur stepped from the back room, a dark pump bottle in hand. A spa and salon owner, Peter Miller still made special trips out for his best client.

"No need to rush, Miss Eugenie," the man enunciated with a news-broadcaster-style boom, sounding more like Peter Jennings than Peter-the-masseur. "The oils are warming."

Ethan's aunt bustled inside wearing a tomato-red kimono. "What's the blend of the day?"

Peter cradled his concoction like a carnie sideshow salesman. "For Miss Eugenie, a centering mix of atlas cedar, sandalwood and frankincense to promote inner peace."

Eugenie flattened a hand to her chest, her long exhale ending with a smile. "Perfect."

"But first…" He thrust the bottle toward Kelly. "A welcome gift for you, my dear. Use three capfuls in your bath water."

She clasped the cool glass in her hands. "Thank you, Peter. The serenity blend you used earlier smells lovely."

A grin multiplied his wrinkles. "No-no." He sidled between Kelly and Ethan. "This is a special romance blend for the young lovers. Sweet orange for happiness. Sandalwood to relieve loneliness, dwelling on the past and cynicism."

Did the guy have some kind of crystal ball tucked under his massage table?

"And finally," he pinched the air, "ylang ylang, imported from Indonesia."

Okay, that might not be so bad since it had been an element in her welcome candle.

Eugenie clasped her hands together. "Yes, ylang ylang, for euphoric union."

Kelly willed herself not to wince. Apparently the guy did have some kind of insight into her psyche. "Thanks, Peter."

"Kelly, dear," Aunt Eugenie called, halting her at the door. "Why don't you enjoy the hot tub or have a swim?"

Kelly smiled without actually agreeing. Somehow she suspected her tense muscles wouldn't be cured by any amount of massages, hot tub stints or ylang ylang.

Standing beside his smirking aunt, Ethan planned to flush every ounce of Peter's ylang ylang straight back to Indonesia.

He did *not* need images of Kelly in a scented hot tub.

Judas-freaking-priest. He was already more frustrated than a sixteen-year-old-boy watching cheerleader tryouts. Thank you very much, Aunt Eugenie and Peter.

Ethan led his aunt into the privacy of the supply room, all the while trying his damnedest to stifle fantasies of Kelly wearing a heated blush and nothing else. He shut the door. "How's it going with Kelly?"

Eugenie strolled from shelf to shelf, her fingers trailing over stacks of bleached towels and industrial-sized jugs of antibacterial hand soap. "You tell me. How do you think she looks?"

That loaded question held more firepower than his 9mm. "The clothes look…nice."

Understatement of the year. Every day, Kelly sported a new adjustment, minor alterations that sent his head spinning.

Pierced ears one day, with tiny pearls drawing attention to delicate skin he'd never noticed before. Another day, the arms of her sweater tied around her waist, leaving a silky shirt out there for him to see and want to touch. But the white robe was his favorite, hands-down. Or hands-on would sure as hell be nice.

Aunt Eugenie was a serious masochist.

"I'd like to introduce her around a bit, give her some familiar faces for the night of the gala." Eugenie adjusted the sash on her kimono without looking at him. "Nothing fancy. Just some friends of yours around the pool."

Ethan leaned back against the refrigerator stocked with sports drinks. "You remember this isn't real, don't you?"

"Of course. A dinner will smooth her way at the ball since she'll know more people."

"So you think she'll be ready?"

"Tomorrow we have an appointment with the hairdresser."

Panic kicked him at the thought of all that magnificent hair on the floor. "You're not going to cut it?"

A Cheshire-cat smile creased her round face. "No."

The woman knew him too well. Damned good thing she wasn't the enemy or his ARIES status would have been busted long ago.

Something he wouldn't let happen, especially not now. He wanted that information on his parents.

"What really happened the day my parents died?" The question fell out of his mouth.

His aunt blinked, just once, but enough to surprise him with how a single question had shaken her.

She turned to the shelf of bottled oils and nudged them in line. "What do you mean?"

"It was an open-and-shut case, right?" He waited, not that she seemed inclined to offer anything up before she had those bottles in regimental order. "My au pair sold me out to kidnappers. The actual attempt went to hell when my father tried to evade the car chasing us and my parents died."

Long-ago echoes pounded through his memory, sounds of crunching metal, screaming tires. The burn of the seat belt digging into his waist as the car slung to the side. The betrayal of seeing his au pair, Iona, watching from the car beside.

Finally, Eugenie faced him, eyes sheened with tears now as they had been when she'd picked him up in Switzerland after the accident thirty years ago. "Thank God the authorities had already been alerted so we didn't lose you, too."

"How did they know to come?" Ethan shot straight for the hole in the story that had niggled at him through a sleepless night. "There wouldn't have been a ransom request yet."

She didn't blink. Didn't move. Didn't answer, not right away. Not more than four or five seconds passed, but more than enough to make Ethan wonder.

Then his aunt patted his face. "Your parents were late with a promised call. I was worried, so I called the authorities."

"That makes sense." So why the hesitation?

"Of course it does, since that's what happened. Why all the questions now after so long?" She tucked her trembling hands into her robe pockets.

Those shaking hands shut him down faster than any anger

or frustration. This woman had been through enough grief for two lifetimes.

"No reason." He slung an arm around her shoulders and dropped a kiss on her silver head. "Go enjoy your massage."

When had her shoulders started to curve forward? She was growing older, sixty-five now. She deserved to be bouncing grandchildren on her knee...or taking them kayaking in Alaska.

He felt damned bad that he couldn't be the son she deserved. He would do just about anything for his aunt.

Except that.

He couldn't pull off the family gig, even for her. Memories of the childhood kidnapping attempt dogged him as Ethan tried to piece together childhood impressions of speed, his mother's screams, his father's hoarse shouts— and blood, so much blood.

How could he subject a wife and kid to that possibility? A very real possibility, given his career choice and bank balance. He'd give away all the money in a heartbeat if it would make a difference. But there were people who would always believe he'd secreted it away.

None of it mattered anyway since he wouldn't be marrying. He understood the fragility of life too damned well.

Hell yes, he intended to make sure Kelly Taylor was in tiptop condition before that gala. He trusted that her sharp mind could wrap around anything that came their way. But physically, she would be at a disadvantage and that, Ethan couldn't allow. He would continue to be her personal trainer nonstop, whatever it took to turn a desk jockey into a primed and ready agent.

Kelly's feet pounded the sidewalks in day nine of Ethan Williams's Operative Training School of Torture. With forty-degree weather melting away the snow, Ethan had insisted on an outside run. The man was a machine.

She saw another massage in her future. Adding Aunt Eugenie's formal dancing lessons on top of all the other physical fitness training left Kelly with muscles twisted in more knots than were on that hundred-year-old oak in her path.

She didn't even dare relax in the hot tub anymore since she'd almost scalded herself. Sure she'd fallen asleep, but she could have sworn she set the water temperature lower. Thank heavens Ethan had woken her before the accident resulted in something worse than red toes.

Her only respite from the physical exhaustion came in the form of meetings at ARIES with Carla Juarez and Robert Davidson to coordinate security for the embassy ball. She'd never thought she would see the day she would long for an afternoon at a desk.

Jogging a sloshy pace around another oak, Kelly focused on one foot in front of the other. She forced her hands to unclench inside her woolen gloves.

She wasn't a couch potato by any stretch, having already compiled a personal exercise regimen in preparation for the time she would be called up to serve in the field. She'd thrived on surprising Ethan with her endurance, something he obviously hadn't expected to encounter.

Of course, then he upped the pace again. But she would prove she had something more to offer to this operation than her knowledge of languages.

One foot in front of the other, she distracted herself by drilling Ethan on basic European greetings. Even though her lungs threatened to burst from his killer pace, she had to admit the open spaces offered less temptation than the privacy of his loft apartment or the gym. He also seemed to comprehend the nuances of the language better conversationally than when she presented him a written list.

Kelly adjusted the wooly band over her cold ears. "Forms of good evening or hello. Spanish?"

"*Buenas tardes.*" He exhaled steady puffs of white. "Christ, Kelly! This is rudimentary crap."

And repetitious *crap* gave her something to think about

beside the burn in her legs and an attraction that wouldn't quit. "Italian."

"Ciao."

"German."

"Guten Tag."

Didn't the man ever tire? She inhaled another icy gasp. "And my favorite of all languages—the language of love—French."

He stumbled. *"Au revoir?"*

"Bonsoir," she corrected. "Rudimentary, huh?"

"Yeah, yeah. Whatever." The white clouds of air exploded faster as he pounded around a corner. "I'll bet you dream in multiple languages."

"On occasion."

Ethan's steps slowed. Kelly wanted to shout her relief, but didn't have the energy. He'd probably quit early for her and she didn't care.

She slowed her steps to a cool-down pace. "Different languages seem conducive for different activities."

He kicked aside a chunk of sludge, trailing behind. "How so?"

"German has a strong, guttural sound. It's good for focus and punch in a run. Run. *Lauf. Laufend.* Jog. *Trotten.*" A gust of wind dipped the temperature. "Cold. *Frostig.*"

Her feet slowed to a halt. Kelly bent over to grab her knees and suck in icy air. She huffed through at least ten chilly breaths waiting for him to answer before calling, "Ethan?"

Where had he gone?

"Ethan?" She looked behind her.

And found him doing the last thing she would have expected. The one thing guaranteed to throw a whole new, confusing, frightening…dangerous complexion on their working relationship. She found Ethan Williams…

…checking out her rear view.

Ethan tried to drag his eyes from Kelly's backside. Wind pants had never looked so good.

He told himself fifty times over he had no business staring at a fellow operative that way, regardless of how perfectly curved, soft, inviting…

Damn it, time to move to a safer language. Ethan stepped level with her again. "How about cooking?"

Kelly searched his face for two gusting bursts of wind before straightening. "Italian, of course."

"What about Spanish?"

"Is for dancing." She started walking again toward the entrance to the mansion's gym.

He didn't want to think about what she did in her favorite language. Even the idea made him burn to dive into a half-melted snowbank. The mere mention of her "love language" had sent him bungling basic foreign greetings.

Ethan walked faster, past her, turning to face her as he jogged backward. "So which was your favorite country to tour?"

"I haven't been overseas." Some of his disbelief must have shown because she rushed ahead. "There never seemed to be the right time. I almost made it to Portugal for a couple of weeks in one of those high-school travel packages."

No wonder she'd hung on to an Eiffel Tower paperweight souvenir. A pang of regret stabbed through him that he'd never known she hadn't seen the real thing. He'd probably spent their time together talking about his latest mission instead of finding out more about a woman who intrigued the hell out of him. Had he been blinded by her quiet air, her baggy clothes to a certain extent, too?

He wouldn't make the same mistake now. "What happened to keep you from going to Portugal?"

"My folks wouldn't sign the permission form. They were a little overprotective."

A surge of gratitude for what he owed his aunt charged through him. She'd had every reason to coddle him after the way his parents had died, but she never had. They both enjoyed traveling—although his reasons differed from his aunt's. "And later?"

"College was a crush to finish early so my folks could retire. I didn't have the time or money to schedule a trip abroad. But I'm on my own now. Someday soon, I'm going to use all my vacation days at once and do every one of those things in all those languages in each of those countries."

He wanted to call his travel agent and start booking the tickets. Damn it, he wanted to go with her and see all those places through her eyes.

Ethan cruised to a stop outside the gym door. "Make sure you send me postcards."

"Who knows, maybe now that I actually have a shot at upgrading to full operative status, the government can foot the bill for my travel. That was my original plan."

"Join the agency. See the world." He yanked open the gym door. "There had to have been an easier way."

She paused in the open doorway. "But I don't want easy. I never have. I want a challenge while I'm making my difference. You of all people should understand that."

Ethan recognized the resolve in her set jaw well since it mirrored his own determination. She was going to do this. Come hell or high water, Kelly Taylor would be a full operative.

What language would she curse in the first time she had to kill someone?

His gut twisted until his breathing constricted. That was a language he hoped she'd never have to learn.

With any luck, no one would ever suspect this woman was an operative. That innocence could prove to be her ultimate cover to keep her safe.

Until assignments took their toll and jaded her as they did other agents.

Then she would need every bit of expertise to stay ahead of the next bullet. Time in the field was often short for agents. Eventually they either died or blew their cover. He'd already pushed it too close with his last assignment.

How long would Kelly last?

Ethan looked at her sweet face and mourned the day she would lose her innocence. "You're so damned young."

She slumped back against the door. "Then why do I feel so very old?"

He braced a hand over her head. He resisted the impulse to drop it just an inch lower and toy with her hair. Strands fell loose from the ponytail, swaying against her cheek.

Framing her eyes.

Vulnerable eyes.

Worse yet, disillusioned eyes.

Ethan frowned. Had that always been there? He looked deeper and realized that while she might be inexperienced, she wasn't completely innocent. Someone had hurt her. And that stirred a surge of anger so strong it scared him.

Why had he never noticed before?

Because he'd been too much of a selfish jerk to look. In all those lunches, he'd never once asked her about herself. He'd just gone with the assumption someone as shy as Kelly would rather not be pushed.

A convenient excuse to keep things superficial.

Even now, all this soul-searching made him itchy. Ethan shoved away from the wall and ushered her inside the gym. He shrugged out of his jacket and pitched it over a StairMaster before charging over to the weight machines. "Are you up for a few more reps before we quit for the day?"

She draped her jacket over his, flinging her wooly white mittens on top. "Bring it on, Williams."

Ethan started for the ThighMaster, then decided his libido couldn't take the reality of Kelly in any kind of suggestive position. He opted for the leg press instead.

Kneeling, he set the weights at one hundred and ten pounds, twenty pounds lower than earlier, but she'd withstood a hell of a workout like a real trooper.

What other surprises did Kelly Taylor have tucked under all her clothes and hair? "Tell me about where you're from."

"Not much to tell." She slid onto the padded seat. Feet flat on the press, she pumped, exhaling on the exertion as he'd taught her. "You probably already know most of it. I'm an only child, born late in my parents' lives, so they had lots of time to spend with me. The whole perfect childhood thing."

"What about college?" Ethan snagged two sixty-pound weights off the rack and began alternating bicep curls. "Did you go all wild and crazy when you broke away from home?"

He'd raised more than his share of hell at the University of Chicago with his three best buds. The Blues Brothers, they'd been labeled by women for their taste in music and track record with relationships. Christ, that had been so long ago, back when he let more than a handful of people into his life.

Back when he knew better than to think the miniscule amount of friendship he'd offered Kelly counted. "Well, Kel? Did you cut loose like most freshmen?"

She continued the steady reps, but a smile flickered across her face.

Ethan's arms slowed in time with his seeping realization. "You did! You had your great rebellion." Still she didn't answer. He dropped his weights back onto the rack with a clang. "Spill it, woman, or I'm increasing those weights."

"I got a tattoo."

Thank God he'd put the weights away or he'd have dropped them on his feet. "No way."

Nodding, she swooshed the weights higher, faster.

"Where?"

She smiled.

Ah, hell.

He searched for a safer subject. "What did you get? A kitten, maybe?"

"Nope."

"A rose?" Yeah, a pretty pink bud, rosy tipped... Sweet heaven.

She shook her head.

He lamented the loss of the rose. Probably for the best. "What did you pick?"

Her sultry grin made her look as old as Eve. "Wouldn't you like to know?"

More than he wanted air. "I guess that means you're not going to tell me. You're a wicked woman, Kelly Taylor."

"Not hardly." She jammed the weights up with vicious force.

Ethan focused on the rise and fall of the weights and pulleys to keep his attention off checking out her body to catalogue possible locations for that not-a-rose tattoo. Even thinking about it set his world off-kilter. Tipped the whole damned room until even the machines...

Tilted?

"Kelly!" Adrenaline flamed through him as he flung his body between her and the weights tumbling toward them.

Chapter 6

Air rushed from Kelly's lungs. From the force of her fall or the bulk of Ethan's weight, she didn't know or even care since she couldn't breathe yet.

Her ears echoed with the clang of metal.

Clang of metal?

Her head anchored sideways, she slowly opened her eyes. Weight disks lay scattered over the floor.

Fear slammed into her, heavier than the hundred and ninety pounds of muscular man on top of her. Those blocks of metal would have rolled over her if Ethan hadn't acted so quickly.

A new fear cranked within her. She grabbed his shoulders. "Are you all right? Did any hit you?"

"I'm fine." One hand cupping her head, he skimmed his other hand down her arm. "And you?"

"I'm okay."

"The maintenance crew responsible for the weight room can be damned grateful, because I'm already going to have their—"

"Ethan!" She silenced him with her hand over his mouth. "I'm fine."

Totally fine. Feeling far too good at the moment with his hot hands searing an even hotter brand onto her skin. His leg pressed between her legs so firmly she couldn't tell if the throbbing pulse came from him or her.

Her hand slid from his mouth, but the heat of his lips lingered until her body flamed like in the overheated hot tub. He moved his leg. Not much, just a firmer pressure, closer. Her breath hitched. His pupils dilated with unmistakable arousal, an arousal echoed by the increasing need pressed into her belly.

He wanted her.

Ethan Williams wanted *her*.

Not Kelly with her Eugenie-chosen clothes she would wear for the dinner party tomorrow, but Kelly in bulky work-out pants, hair a mess and any hint of makeup sweated off hours ago.

"Kelly."

"What?"

His eyes heated over her with a blue flame. "Just Kelly."

Uh-oh. Somebody must have given her a straight shot of IV ylang ylang because sweet longing pulsed through her veins. The near miss with the weights had her heart pounding against his. "What are we doing?"

Damn, she should shut up. But if she reached for him, she feared he would pull back and the desire in his eyes would disappear.

"I don't know," he growled. His forehead fell to rest against hers. "I do know I feel like I'm going to die if I can't see your tattoo."

"You want to see my tattoo?" Which would involve quite a few less clothes.

He nodded without ever taking his eyes off hers. "I want to know what it is. Why you got it." His fingers toyed with her hair, along her scalp, stirring as much heat as his other hand on her hip. "Where it is."

She couldn't deny him his answer, feared she might not be able to deny this man anything. "You're touching it."

His hand tightened around her hip. She watched his throat move in a slow swallow.

Ethan's chest pumped against hers, drawing in air. "Tell me what it is," he demanded.

She slid her hand from between them to trace the pale line on the side of his neck. "If you tell me how you really got this scar, because I'm not buying the shaving accident story."

His skin chilled beneath her touch. Ethan's fingers convulsed in her hair, pulling almost too tight until she couldn't stifle a wince.

Slowly, his fingers relaxed their grip as shutters closed over his eyes, shielding any further glimpses of the man inside. "On-the-job hazard. I made a mistake and lowered my guard."

The terrifying reality of a knife at his throat doused her passion. But then what had she expected when she asked that question? She'd known full well the sort of answer she would receive.

Had she subliminally sabotaged the moment? And still she couldn't stop herself. "What were you doing?"

Please, Lord, she hoped he wouldn't say he'd been with another woman. "Ethan?"

"Sleeping. I was sleeping."

Only sleeping. The lone word punched through any glorified dreams of fieldwork. Not some even-odds knife fight at all. He'd been ambushed in his sleep.

All his self-defense training the past week came crashing around her like those disks raining down. Rules and precise form didn't count. Only fighting to win.

He carried a scar, and somehow she knew the other person hadn't lived long enough for his wounds to heal into any such marks.

Chilling realization prickled over her. Forget hormones and tattoos. These were actual life-and-death stakes with her as his partner. And apparently Ethan had remembered exactly the same thing.

He rolled off her and to his feet, visibly shutting down the desire that had been in his eyes only moments before. "We're done for the day."

Kelly suspected they were done for a lot longer with that. Thanks to her need to know more about Ethan and her penchant for asking questions, she'd just stripped away any possibility for seeing where the desire in his eyes might lead.

For the best, since her intent was to get over the man. Right?

Ethan stood at the edge of the indoor pool and nudged a candlelit lily pad with the toe of his shoe. Over twenty-four hours since his tangle with Kelly on the weight-room floor and he still hadn't been able to wash away the feel of her body pressed to his.

The last thing he wanted was to sit around at some dinner party and make nice. Of course his life seemed to consist of nothing more than wheel-spinning lately. He'd wasted hours on the phone with one of his old Holzberg contacts—a guy who obviously knew nothing about Alex Morrow and even less about a long-ago kidnapping attempt on Ethan in Switzerland.

Ethan shook the water off the tip of his shoe. He wanted a quick ending to this case and his life back in order.

He wanted to strip Kelly down and find her tattoo.

Instead, he had to suffer through some lame social engagement to solidify his cover.

He paced around the kidney-shaped pool, the entire area encased in a glass solarium with thriving plants. Fluorescent lights and moonbeams streamed through the glass roof, glistening off the water.

His aunt had planned the evening to include two other couples. People he socialized with more than anyone else but who knew nothing about the real Ethan. Not like Kelly.

What would his old college buddies Matt and Jake think of her?

Ethan's restless feet carried him to the corner bar. No doubt White House advisor Matt Tynan would fall over laughing at seeing Ethan brought down. Of course, his old frat brother couldn't understand why anybody would want to commit to one woman.

Commit.

Where the hell had that come from? Not out of him. He must be falling victim to sinking too deep into his cover.

Ethan snagged a cracker off a silver platter and scooped through caviar, reminding himself to keep perspective. Chewing, he rubbed a hand over his shoulder and worked to ease the ache from where the weight had grazed him. He needed to check in with Hatch about all Kelly's recent "accidents" that Ethan's gut insisted were nothing of the sort.

Agents who believed in coincidences died.

The defective weight machine. An overheated hot tub. And a tail during one of their runs that Kelly didn't even know about.

What the hell was going on?

Whatever it was, he had enough on his plate finding Alex Morrow, stopping a jewel heist, and figuring out what the hell one had to do with the other. He didn't need to waste brain cells trying to uncover Kelly's tattoo.

An outside door to the pool area clicked, then swung open, admitting a cold blast of air and a bundled duo. Matt Tynan and Samantha Barnes made a damned striking pair, even if they were friends rather than a couple.

A rogue thought snuck into Ethan's mind. How could he know these people well enough for them to be comfortable letting themselves in the back entrance to his home, when they knew so little about him personally? What kind of life had he set up for himself, keeping secrets beyond what even ARIES demanded?

Matt strode toward him with urbane assurance, brushing

snow off his shoulders. "Good Lord, it's as cold out there as the mother-in-law I'll never have."

Ever the charming playboy, Matt played hard, worked hard and lived large. He might be fickle as hell in the romance department, but the guy made a fiercely loyal friend. He'd jumped right in to support Samantha, ambassador pro-tem to Delmonico, after her ambassador husband had died…six or so months ago? Matt made a better friend than Ethan ever had.

"Thanks for driving out." Ethan reached to take Samantha's coat. "Jake and his fiancée are running late."

Samantha smiled over her shoulder, tugging her auburn hair free of the overcoat. "That will just give us first dibs on dishing out all the Ethan stories to this mystery woman."

What would Kelly think of Matt's stories of their college days at the University of Chicago? He, Matt, Jake and Eric, the fourth member of their Blues Brothers group, hadn't come close to living the same sort of bookworm existence Kelly had.

Maybe Samantha might be a safer companion for Kelly for the evening. Given her new position in the embassy, Samantha knew Ethan had CIA connections, just not about his operative status or about ARIES.

Ethan squeezed her shoulder. "Hey, Samantha. How are you hanging in there?"

Samantha drew in a shaky breath. "Better today than yesterday. Maybe not so great tomorrow, but I know eventually the day after will be easier. Standing in as ambassador pro-tem keeps me busy. And there's solidifying the economic treaty between Delmonico and the US before I head back."

She'd been working nonstop since her husband had died, leading Matt to insist on bringing her along tonight as his date while she was in the country. Matt had worried she wasn't giving herself time to grieve. Ethan knew time didn't necessarily help.

Who did she turn to for support? He should have offered more than superficial condolences. "Call if you need to talk.'' He forced himself to offer more now. ''I know where you are right now and it's not a good place.''

Eyes wide, she kept tears back by not blinking and nodded. ''Thank you.''

But he knew she wouldn't. Indomitable Samantha Barnes never needed anyone.

Matt gravitated to the caviar. ''So where's this Venus who brought down our fleet-footed Ethan?''

''Kelly and I are just dating.'' Why the defensive answer? Convincing them guaranteed success.

''Yeah, right.'' Matt nudged the tray toward Samantha. ''Like he brings all his dates to stay with his aunt? I don't think so.''

What could he say? Matt had a point.

Ethan tucked behind the bar and poured drinks for his guests from memory. ''Kelly will be down in a minute.''

Matt winked at Samantha. ''Women and their makeup rituals.''

She elbowed him. ''Brat.''

''Princess.''

''Bite your tongue.''

He grinned at her. ''So you want me?''

Samantha snorted. ''Not in this lifetime, Tynan.''

''Ah, then I'll just have to hold out hope for the next incarnation.'' Matt jabbed a finger toward Ethan. ''Quit laughing. She turned you down, too, pal.''

Ethan shrugged. He and Samantha had gone out a couple of times. She was a gorgeous woman, a statuesque redhead, but chemistry was a damned unpredictable beast and it hadn't been there for them.

Not like it was with Kelly.

Ethan glanced at his watch. Kelly was never late. The woman's Palm Pilot told her when to eat, for God's sake. Aunt Eugenie was probably plastering some kind of makeover magic on her face. He hoped he'd chosen right in trusting his aunt with this project.

A surge of protectiveness swelled within him. He wanted

this evening to go smoothly for Kelly, as well as for the investigation. He knew Matt and Samantha would charm her, but Jake's fiancée hadn't struck him as the empathetic sort. With any luck, she would be obsessed with the purchases from her prewedding shopping spree in New York and DC. He still couldn't figure what his friend saw in the woman, not that it was any of his business.

Friend? His thoughts cranked back to Kelly being his friend. Except what he shared with her seemed different from what he experienced with these people.

Surely it had to be because he could let down with Kelly since she knew about his ARIES connection.

And then there she was. Kelly. His friend. Looking so like her but not at all that he forgot to breathe. He had to give Aunt Eugenie credit. She'd done her job well with subtle strokes of understated elegance.

A creamy blouse glided over Kelly's skin, rippling a sheen of enticement with her every step. Silky black pants enhanced her dark eyes. Why had he never noticed her eyes before? He'd only seen the innocence, never the smoky temptation as she looked up through long lashes at him.

Her hair was gathered low at the base of her neck, the tail trailing over her shoulder in stark contrast with her pale shirt. Much like that same hair would look caressing her bare skin.

Rein it in, pal.

Ethan clasped her hands in his. "Hi, Kel."

He meant to kiss her cheek.

Meant to.

But didn't.

His mouth brushed hers. Not long. Not open. Damned platonic for that matter. And more arousing than anything he could remember.

Hell yeah, chemistry was an unpredictable creature.

His hands fell to rest on her hips. "You look great," he growled, then wondered why he hadn't said it louder for the benefit of other ears and the cover.

''Thank you.''

''Although those sweats of yours have their appeal.'' He squeezed her hip right over that elusive tattoo. Taking advantage of the luxury of his cover, he lost himself in the smoky depths of her eyes until a throat cleared behind her.

Ethan glanced over Kelly's shoulder to find Jake Ingram and his willowy blond fiancée, Tara, who was holding onto her man with a death grip.

''Well, fella,'' Jake taunted with just a hint of Texas drawl to soften the edge, ''the big ones do fall hard.''

Kelly slipped around to Ethan's side. ''Introduce me to your friends.''

Ethan searched for the right words to explain the woman at his side and found simply, ''This is Kelly.''

How could he describe her any more fully when he barely understood her himself? Forget the adjustments in clothing, he'd found more layers to this woman the past week than all those sweaters she used to wear.

Samantha stepped forward and extended a hand with the gracious elegance Ethan had counted on her showing. ''So pleased to meet you, Kelly. I suspect we'll all be seeing a lot more of you in the future.''

Ethan watched Kelly slide into conversation with ease.

They had somehow convinced these people after not more than one close-mouthed kiss and a simple greeting. It shouldn't have been that easy, given how commitment-shy they all knew him to be since Celia.

Yet they'd bought it all the same. Had he and Kelly looked that convincing as a couple? So much so, Samantha immediately plopped Kelly into the prospect of any future gatherings.

The future.

Ethan hadn't thought beyond finishing a mission in years and yet, he found himself imagining how much Kelly would enjoy outings on Jake's yacht. Or how she and Samantha would discuss European politics and brush up on foreign languages together.

The future. With Kelly in it outside their roles at ARIES.

As much as an operative tried to distance himself from his cover, the lines blurred. He'd been around long enough to accept that. Except right now the lines seemed a hell of a lot more than fuzzy.

For the first time in over ten adrenaline-packed years with the CIA, Ethan Williams was in serious trouble.

"Thank you for going to the trouble to come over." Kelly walked Ethan's guests toward the sunroom door, tension twisting within her until she felt ready to snap.

She'd made it through with no social gaffes, rounding out their dinner party with after-meal drinks by the pool. So why the unrelenting tension?

Because that kiss had knocked her off-kilter for the whole evening. The heat of his lips, his breath, his words lingered.

Why did Ethan stir her when both of these other men left her cold? All three tall, dark and studly men could have stood in front of a camera—Matt for a *GQ* cover spread, Jake for a cowboy calendar pin-up, and Ethan for *Biker's Monthly*.

Kelly definitely favored the Harley.

Matt helped Samantha into her beige suede coat and winked over her shoulder at Kelly. "I wouldn't have missed this."

Jake's pampered fiancée Tara smiled her farewell. Kelly suspected if they'd met without the endorsement of Ethan's arm and hefty bank account, the woman wouldn't have considered Kelly any more important than Aunt Eugenie's brass bull doorstopper.

Jake clasped her hand. "Nice to meet you. Have Ethan fly you out to the ranch for the weekend sometime soon."

Matt thumped Jake's back. "Yeah, looks like these two may beat you to the altar if you change the date again."

Tara's smile turned brittle. "I wouldn't count on it."

Apparently Matt's White House position bought him

courtesy points since she let him off the hook with only one comeback.

After the couples left, Kelly sagged onto a poolside lounger. She stretched out, wiggling her toes inside her shoes and staring up at the stars.

Their kiss had left her too restless to call it a night. They would have to debrief the evening anyway. She would just keep a safe distance on her lounger.

Ethan dimmed the overhead lights until only the moon-light above and lamps inside the pool illuminated the glass room. He cruised to a stop beside her. "What did you think of them?"

He snagged a deck chair and flipped it to face her before he dropped to sit. Close. Too close.

So much for distance.

His elbows rested on his knees, a drink clasped in his hand. Muscled forearms flexed, a dusting of dark hair along tanned skin showing beneath his rolled and cuffed shirt.

The heater purred to life in the already too-warm room.

"I liked Samantha." Air swirled around her, saturated with the scent of chlorine and Ethan's musky soap. "She had some fascinating insights on the current political unrest on the Delmonico-Rebelian border. Delmonico should kiss her feet in gratitude if she gets that economic treaty hammered out with the US."

Ethan tapped her chair with the toe of his wingtip shoe. "What were the two of you saying about us when you swapped languages?"

"Nothing much." Except for Samantha's friendly warning about Ethan's commitment-shy ways and a confusing reference to a woman named Celia. Somehow the mere mention of that name carried more weight than a pack of Brittanys.

"And what do you think of the others?"

She turned her head to look at him, to enjoy the play of the starlight along his coal-black hair. "Jake's a good guy. I'd trust him."

"You're right on with that. Solid intuition will serve you well in the field." He rolled his glass between both broad palms. "What about Tara? You didn't seem to say much to her."

"I've learned that quiet can be good, too." She toyed with the edge of her ponytail. "I discover more about people that way. You'd be surprised what I pick up around the agency because people don't notice me."

"Kelly—"

She didn't want to hear his protest. "Or if they do notice me, they're so convinced I must want detailed descriptions of their exciting lives since mine must be so boring." Kelly smiled. "Listening to Tara go on, I got such a kick out of knowing that 'astute' corporate attorney didn't have any clue who she was talking to."

"You're ten times the woman she is."

"Thanks." The draw of the admiration glimmering in his eyes proved as heady as his touch.

"I apologize for any awkwardness, all the same."

"It's not your fault she and I didn't have much in common to discuss. Makes me glad you and I aren't really a couple so I don't have to put up with her for the rest of my life."

Their eyes met, held, heated, until his gaze dropped somewhere around her ponytail dangling over the side of the lounger.

Ethan rattled the ice in his glass and knocked back the last swallow. "It took a determined woman to rope Jake."

"Some don't fall easy, I guess."

"Guess not." He scooped a melting ice cube from his glass and pitched it in the pool. "What about Matt?"

"He says you cheat at poker."

"He's just pissed because I beat him last time." Ethan angled his head to the side. "So what did you think of him?" he asked again.

Kelly smiled at the memories of Matt ribbing Ethan throughout the night. "He's fun."

Ethan's face blanked.

What? Did Ethan actually think she was stupid enough to chase after the guy, even if she was attracted to Matt, which she wasn't. "You can quit the jealous boyfriend act since no one's around. Mighty dog-in-the-manger of you anyhow since you only want me for the job."

"Who says I don't want you?" He lifted a strand of her hair and caressed it between two fingers.

Kelly held herself still, willing away the shiver of awareness at his touch.

He twisted the lock of hair around two fingers. "That doesn't mean it's right. Knowing I'm the wrong kind of man for you won't turn off the attraction. Men's minds and, uh, libidos aren't necessarily in synch with each other."

"Oh." The power of that single kiss tingled back over her like a near-miss with an electrical socket.

"Yeah, oh. But your objection is duly noted. No more jealousy." He dropped her hair. "Good luck chasing Matt around the White House when this is over if that's what you want." He started to stand.

She dropped her hand to his knee, halting him. "It's not. Not what I want, I mean."

Ethan sat down again without speaking.

"Just ask the whole office. I told them all how I feel, didn't I?"

His pupils dilated until the black nearly pushed past the deep blue, like storm clouds chasing through a clear sky. The electric tingle spread into something more like an unharnessed lightning bolt.

Samantha's words came back to haunt her. Not because she harbored any thoughts of settling down with this guy. But because he seemed so far out of her league at the moment she wondered if an encounter with him would leave her fried to a crisp.

She needed to think, and she couldn't with him so close. So gorgeous.

So wanting her, too.

Kelly sat up. "I told the office this is about business. In spite of your..." she paused to let her eyes rake him in a bold maneuver she would have never managed a couple weeks' prior, "...charms, I will do my job."

She shot to her feet and made tracks away from him before all her bravado abandoned her in favor of returning for another round of Ethan's kisses.

The house echoed like an abandoned tomb from one of Aunt Eugenie's sightseeing jaunts. Sure the place usually reminded him of a crypt with all its ghosts, but he'd been willing to wade through them to find Kelly. No luck. Ethan took the stairs two at a time back into his apartment.

Where had Kelly gone after she'd run out an hour ago? He still wanted to punt Jake's fiancée on her liposuctioned butt for being condescending to Kelly.

Although Kelly seemed to have held her own damned well.

A newfound respect for her swelled within him. He'd thought she was insecure. What the hell had he known? Kelly didn't need to flaunt her importance to make herself feel good. She'd let Tara condescend without ever once setting her straight or putting her down.

So, if she wasn't upset about Tara, what the hell had gone wrong to make Kelly run away? Whatever it was, he had to fix it and ease the tension between them.

If only he could find her.

Unease threatened the edges of his reason. He wanted to believe nothing could happen to her behind the walls of his home. But he knew he couldn't count on that.

Part of him shouted to run the grounds. Find her. Now. But logic argued he could search faster with his surveillance system.

Ethan jabbed the code into his lock and swung into the main room. Five steps in, he realized he hadn't taken time for any of his usual precautions.

Hell. He'd get them both killed this way.

He wasted twenty-three heart-pounding seconds checking his apartment before he leaned over the computer desk. Forget sitting. He punched codes, clicked through locations…

The empty industrial-sized kitchen.

The library. Aunt Eugenie and her cat curled up and napping in a wingback by the fireplace.

The camera made a slow sweep of the front grounds before he swapped to the rear-grounds angle.

"Come on, Kelly. Where the hell are you?" She wouldn't leave without telling him. She might not be experienced in the field, but she knew better than that.

A flicker sliding off the screen snagged his attention.

Ethan reversed the camera. Adjusted the angle. Narrowed. Closer, until he locked in a close-up of the greenhouse.

A light shone through the thick panes.

His heart rate regulated back down to only time-and-a-half. He clicked through keys, searching for the camera inside the greenhouse.

Nothing?

He hacked into regular security…and still nothing.

Why the hell hadn't any of them thought to install cameras inside the greenhouse? Ethan swiped his 9mm off the desk and sprinted down the stairs. Damn it, Kelly was inside. He knew it.

And heaven help anyone responsible if she'd had another one of her "accidents."

Chapter 7

Kelly reached to brace a hand on the glass pane beside the spidering ferns. Sleet pinged the greenhouse roof with hypnotizing regularity. She secured her headphones and let the CD sounds of *Ocean Serenade* soothe her.

She straightened into the delicious stretch until her spine reached perfect alignment, and then she began the series of controlled movements. She didn't have the equipment for her Pilates stretches and exercises available, a price she would have to pay as she didn't want to risk interruption in the gym. So she improvised, the solitude and scenery being more important to her. Her feet never tangled when she was alone.

Inhale. Stretch. Exhale. Inhale. The fragrant bouquet of hothouse roses, gardenias, lilacs and lush fertility swirled through her with every breath and conditioning exercise. If only she could capture this scent and setting to take home with her, so much more deeply transporting, sensually exotic than her window garden.

Tension melted from her a layer at a time as she directed

energy to one area at a time, while relaxing the rest of her body. She put all worries of investigations and deadlines and criminals out of her mind.

Excising thoughts of a certain agent tempting her to bare more than her tattoo proved a little tougher. What had happened to getting over him? Their whole evening together as a couple had felt real. Too real.

Too right.

Inhale. Stretch. Exhale. Focus on the rushing waves flowing through the earphones.

Her connection crackled. Wobbled. Kelly secured the cord on the headset. She should have just bought a new one. It wasn't like the things were even expensive, but frugality became second nature in her quest for travel.

The soothing sounds steadied. Kelly nodded and pulled herself straight again. On a whim, she reached to snap an orchid off the plant. Eugenie had issued an open invitation to help herself to anything in the greenhouse, and right now she couldn't resist treating herself to at least one sensual indulgence.

Kelly savored the heady scent before tucking it behind her ear. A frivolous gesture, but who would know here in the shadowed darkness?

Moving shadows.

Outside the window.

Apprehension stung her like the sleet sheeting the panes. Ethan had never uncovered who had followed them. She might be behind secured walls, but that didn't mean she should let down her guard for a minute. She dropped into a crouch, cursing that her new SIG-Sauer lay locked and useless inside a secret compartment in her suitcase.

Hadn't she learned threats could lurk in the safest of places? Her professor hadn't respected the sanctity of school grounds when he'd lured her into his office under the pretense of discussing a test grade.

Her pounding pulse throbbed in her ears. At least no one skulking outside would be able to see her. She inched farther to the side. Think. Stay out of sight until she could find a weapon and ID who it was.

She stifled suffocating memories of a hand on her mouth, blunt fingers pinching her nose until she stilled beneath him rather than pass out from lack of air. Her hands fisted.

More than her safety depended on keeping a cool head. Alex Morrow was somewhere, waiting, hoping his government would retrieve him.

What if Ethan had been the one lost overseas?

Determination fired within her. She made a quick visual sweep of the greenhouse.

Snaking a hand up, she snagged a miniature garden rake from the shelf. The lethal three prongs on the hand-sized cultivator would make a weapon more deadly than any dragon-eye slap. As long as she didn't lose control of it.

Kelly crouched, crept toward the door. Adrenaline burned the sweat from her skin, the spit from her mouth. It was likely nothing, she reassured herself. Just some animal rustling through the snow. There certainly wasn't much noise.

The knob turned.

Not an animal. Kelly's grip tightened around the plastic handle. The door swung open, the entryway empty. Pressing her back against the wall by the door, she waited. She wasn't stupid. She wouldn't strike unless necessary. But if she did—

"Kelly?"

Ethan's voice rumbled through the opening even though he didn't show himself. Relief surged through her and she shot to her feet.

Her body slammed against the wall. Ethan pinned her, his face looming over. Where had he come from so fast?

"Kelly?" His hand vise-locked her wrist to the wall.

Her fingers numbed. The three-pronged rake clattered to the ground. "Geez, Williams, way to stop a girl's heart."

He didn't laugh.

She glanced down at the 9mm in his other hand. Suddenly

the abundance of flowery scents made her nauseous. Thank God for his fast reflexes in lowering the weapon.

Harsh lines marked his face, his skin pulled taut along angular bones. "Don't ever, ever jump out at me like that. You're damned lucky I didn't shoot you."

Residual fear made her ornery. "I didn't jump out. You snuck up."

"That's what I do in order to stay alive, take my time entering an unsecured area." Water glistened on his hair like the sparks flecking his angry eyes.

"I waited until I knew it was you." She nudged the gardening rake with her toe. "And I had a weapon."

A smile kicked through the harshness hardening his face. "Good, making the most of what's around."

Pride flowed through in a warm rush that eased her fear. Slowly, her heart rate returned to normal.

Only to speed right back up again.

His long lean body pressed flush along hers. His hand lowered her arm, bringing them closer still until her breasts flattened to his solid chest in an exchange of heat that conversely sent shivers through her.

He stared back at her. Then down. His slight shift allowed a whisper of air between them.

Ethan's eyes cruised every inch of her leggings and sports bra. The fire of his gaze threatened to melt Lycra clean away from her skin.

Not that she could feel any more exposed than she already did.

She scrambled for composure. A sweatshirt to yank over her skimpy getup might help. Her increasing breaths threatened hyperventilation, not to mention too-damned-enticing brushes of her breasts against his pecs. "So glad you've decided to apologize for what you said earlier about Matt," she babbled.

"I'm not here to apologize."

"Oh. Then please leave." Please, please, please. "I'm busy."

He braced an arm over her head. "But I will apologize for scaring you just now."

Kelly sagged against the wall, farther from him and the temptation to rest her hands on his shoulders. "I'm fine. Just startled."

"Couldn't guess by that yell."

"I never yell."

"Tell that to the office full of operative-support folks."

"It's called projection. Not yelling. There's a difference." She knew she was rambling to cover her nerves, but couldn't make herself stop. "You can go now."

He pushed away from the wall and strode down the row of plants, tapping along each one with careless leisure, while the 9mm dangled from his other hand.

"What are you doing?" She scooped her sweatshirt from the floor and yanked it over her head.

"Taking inventory."

She grabbed her jacket from a hook by the door. "Then I'll leave you to it."

"Stay," he called over his shoulder without turning.

She shouldn't. But suspected she would anyway. "Did we forget to discuss something?"

He shook his head.

"Okay. Then I'd like to go." She clutched her parka in her hands without moving.

"Soon." The length of the greenhouse separating them, he pivoted on his heel to face her. "Right now, I need to look at you for another minute."

"What?"

He set his weapon beside a potted topiary of miniature roses. "You may have only been startled, but I was damned scared."

"Of what?"

The harsh lines of his face hardened into a man she barely recognized, but she'd bet those he'd taken down in the field would know well. "You scared the hell out of me, disappearing like that, Taylor."

"I did?" Kelly clutched her coat to her stomach in direct pressure against a dangerous yearning blooming faster than the orchid stretching toward the sunlamp.

"I'm responsible for you."

And then he wilted those tender feelings as quickly as if he'd pulled the plug on the lamp. "We're responsible for each other."

"Whatever."

Damn it, they had to start working together as partners or they would end up maiming each other with garden tools by the end of the week. She accepted responsibility, as well, knew she should have kept him informed if she intended to wander off.

But he wasn't being straight with her, either. Sure his ego might sting if this assignment didn't shake down right, but he would still have a future in the field. Unlike her. She needed to close this case.

Alex Morrow needed them to close this case.

No more holding back. No more secrets. Finally, Kelly asked the question that had knotted her muscles all night, necessitating her relaxing escape to the greenhouse.

"Who's Celia?"

Ethan planted his feet to keep from staggering. Damn, the woman knew how to stage a hell of an ambush. "What?"

Kelly flung her coat on top of bags of potting soil. "Who's Celia?"

He stalled for more time to find his footing. His head still buzzed from the outright fear that something had happened to Kelly. He didn't need this conversation, not now when he just wanted to look at her and reassure himself she wasn't somewhere bleeding out.

Or already dead.

Ethan braced a hand against a support beam. Yeah, he would just hold up this wall for another few minutes. "Where did you hear her name?"

"Samantha mentioned Celia as if I should already know

about her.'' Kelly trailed a hand down a table of empty clay pots, her sweatshirt doing nothing to disguise her curves now that he knew what rested beneath that cotton.

"Who's acting dog-in-the-manger jealous this time?"

She met him toe-to-toe. "This has nothing to do with jealousy and everything to do with the integrity of our cover. If I'm going to convince people we're a couple, you can't hide important parts of your dating history from me."

She was right, damn it. He pulled the words up and out. "Celia and I were engaged. She died."

Kelly deflated. "Oh, Ethan. I'm sorry. How? What happened?"

"Still working to get our stories straight?" he asked with bitter precision.

Her hand settled on his arm with a gentle reassurance he didn't want.

"Ethan, be fair, please. That's not why I'm asking now, and you know it."

He stared down at her wide-open face, so full of emotions and caring and giving. The eleven years difference between their ages stretched in front of him. The world he'd made for himself would suck her innocence dry in a heartbeat.

He held still, only an inch of air and miles of experience separating them. "In case you haven't noticed, life isn't fair and I'm not a nice guy. Whether it's poker or basketball or my job, I fight to win. I learned fast and early there are too many damned times you can't control losing, so you'd better fight like hell to win the ones you can. No rules. No boundaries."

She didn't move, didn't stop him, just listened with her typical Kelly understanding that wore him down faster than any amount of questioning.

Ethan jammed his hands in his pockets to keep from reaching for her, holding her close and stealing some of that sweet innocence, and damn it, yes, comfort, for himself. The sooner he told her about Celia, the sooner they could move on. "She caught hepatitis on a trip to Mexico. It destroyed her liver. She died before an organ donor became available.''

Kelly stroked his arm. "I wish you'd told me."

Anger steamed through him, mostly at himself. "Damn it, I know I should have briefed you."

"No." Silky hair straggled free from her ponytail, but not enough to hide the sympathy he didn't want. "Before this case. I wish you'd told me."

And watch her eyes turn soft and compassionate the way they were doing now? Not a chance would he have risked that. "Talking about it won't change anything. It happened six years ago, right before I joined ARIES. I was a regular CIA operative then, so most people in ARIES don't know. I should have considered that Samantha or Matt or Jake might mention her."

He defied her to ask more. Hell, he would have. But then Kelly was a better person.

"Okay, that subject's closed." A bracing sigh later, she asked, "But is there anyone else I need to know about?"

He shook his head. "No one. There haven't been more than passing relationships since then. Never anything serious."

Never.

The word hovered between them in the silence, only the watery hiss of the plant mister answering his one statement that told more than he'd wanted to relay.

Time to stem all the sympathy pouring from her like water from the ceiling. "You know I go out, but only with women who want as little as I do. The smart ones like Samantha punch out of any relationship with me damned quickly."

Her gaze probed him, luring him to share more than if she'd openly asked. He needed to distract her before he started spilling his guts in some pathetic display that would land him right up against the comfort of those incredible breasts. "So what were you doing out here anyway in this getup?"

"Pilates."

Pilates Method exercising? Good God, he'd expected any answer but that. "How does a girl who grew up on a Nebraska wheat farm pick up an affinity for Pilates?"

She stared at him so long he wondered if she would let him off the hook, but her sweeter side obviously won out against her pit-bull determination. "Nebraska isn't the boonies."

He held up his hands. "Sorry! No offense to Nebraska."

"None taken." Her shoulders relaxed their defensive arch. "Actually, I started out with meditation first, looking for some kind of relaxation. It takes a lot of late nights to become fluent in seven languages. That doesn't leave many hours for sleep."

"Seven, huh? I wondered what the count was."

She packed a big-time IQ under all that hair. No secret since Hatch had plucked her from the CIA ops support for ARIES so fast.

Kelly rested her hip on the center row of plants, facing him while he held up the support beam for a while longer. "If I wanted to maintain the pace, something had to give. One day in eleventh-grade gym class, I fell asleep standing up on the volleyball court. I didn't wake up until the ball clocked me on the head."

Eleventh grade? He expected that kind of drive in a college student, but not in a high-schooler. He kept silent though, so she would keep talking. Kelly didn't share often and he needed distraction from the unwanted emotions talk of Celia had raised…the old fears of losing someone close to him again. Only Kelly hadn't gotten that close. Had she?

She swept wisps of dark hair off her face. "My gym teacher took pity on me. She was a real health nut who mastered meditation in the sixties before she fell for the farm boy standing next to her at Woodstock." A smile played with Kelly's full lips. "That day after the volleyball game, she gave me an icepack along with my first meditation lesson. Once I realized how much rest I could cram into a power nap, my world changed.''

What kind of social life could she have had with such overprotective parents and nothing but academics? None, of course. In her sweatshirt and leggings she looked more like a cheerleader on her way home from practice. Except he suspected she'd never had the star quarterback appreciate the fullness of those luscious lips of hers.

She should have.

And dog-in-the-manger be damned, he was glad she hadn't.

"So, Kelly Taylor." Ethan hooked a finger in the hem of her sweatshirt, the back of his hand brushing the warmth of her thigh. "Is there anything more I should know about you? In the interest of seeming like a couple, of course."

Her hand fidgeted with a watering can, turning it so the spout faced inward. "Can't think of anything that'll come up in conversation."

"I don't know about that." He let his hand sweep around to the side where her tattoo waited a mere scrap of Lycra away. "It's probably important I know what that tattoo is."

She abandoned the watering can, but didn't move his hand. "You're certainly a focused man."

"That I am. So?"

An impish smile teased at her lips. "No one we come into contact with will know."

Which hinted that someone else did know, and he didn't like the surge of possessiveness chugging through him at all. He wanted her, damn it. And he didn't want to want her.

He needed space. Good thing he'd made a morning appointment to meet with a retired agent specializing in gems. Kelly would insist on coming along, but at least their jaunt to North Carolina would take them out of close quarters.

He'd never been any good at denying himself what he wanted. And right now, with his emotions still raw from worrying about her and dredging up ancient history, he couldn't find the will to do the right thing and push her away. Tomorrow would come around soon enough.

He accepted he would probably never see that tattoo of hers, and he would regret it for the rest of his life. But he damned well didn't intend to go to his grave without the memory of tasting one long, thorough kiss from Kelly's beautiful mouth.

Kelly felt Ethan's eyes on her mouth as surely as if he'd kissed her. And she did so want him to kiss her, this hard man who'd never touched her with anything other than the gentlest of hands.

Ethan tugged her forward by the waistband of her sweatshirt. "I can think of another thing we need to work on in order to pull off this couple cover story convincingly."

Her heart tripped over the next beat, then forgot altogether about another beat before jump-starting a double pace. "You can?"

"It's important we look comfortable together—physically."

Oh, geez. "Uh-huh."

His hands skimmed up her arms to rest on her shoulders. "We need to lock in that familiarity with kissing."

"Wouldn't want to bump noses." Was that husky voice hers?

"Not a chance." He angled his head toward her and found her lips with ease.

The scent of musk drifted down around her, mingling with the crisp freshness of melting sleet on his hair. The lingering taste of their chocolate dessert and something distinctly Ethan seeped into her senses with such ease it had to be right.

Part of her insisted the perfection of the meeting of their mouths had more to do with his experience than any pre-ordained rightness. Then his mouth opened, his tongue touching hers for the first time, and she knew there *had* to be a second time, as well. "Ethan. More."

He growled his agreement into her mouth.

A desperate need built within her to explore more of him than just his mouth. She combed her fingers through his damp hair and mourned the loss of its length. Desire lending confidence to her inexperienced hands, she tore his shirt from his pants, flicked buttons open, found the incredible chest she'd felt through cotton earlier in the gym.

While he stroked down her arms, over her belly with bold possession, her hands reveled in the undiluted sensation of honed man under her palms. The cut of whipcord strength bulged under her touch. Flexed in response to her caress. A moment's trepidation shivered through her as she considered why he needed such strength, followed by a thrill from the pleasure the gentleness of that restrained power brought her.

His hands trekked a deliberate path to her hips. One bold callused finger hooked in her waistband, on the same side as her tattoo. He eased back from their kiss until she looked into his eyes. She knew what he wanted and waited for him to find it.

Holding her gaze with his, he dipped one long finger into her leggings, along her hip, exploring until he landed on the patch of skin where the texture would differ. His low growl of appreciation, of possession, sent her up on her toes and into another kiss. He insinuated his whole hand in to cup her bare hip.

She tugged his head down to her and surrendered to the fiery heat of his hand, his mouth, her need.

Again, he traced the patch of inked skin on her hip. Would he guess its pattern? Somehow this sensory investigation of his sent tendrils of desire smoking through her more powerfully than if she'd bared her body to his eyes.

Tingling need pulsed lower with almost painful intensity. She arched into him, closer, rocking her hips against his. Desperate for release after a lifetime of abstinence. Desperate for beautiful memories to overlay the bad. Her hands grabbed his shoulders, gripped, pulled him to her until he winced under her touch.

Winced?

Reality forced its way through her need. She'd been working out, sure, but no way was she strong enough to hurt him yet. "Ethan? Is something wrong?"

He pulled her hand from his left shoulder and pressed a kiss to the center of her palm before replacing it on his chest. "Forget about it."

He canted toward her.

She jerked her wrist away. She wouldn't let him steamroll her. "Tell me what's wrong?"

"Damned pit bull," he mumbled, pulling his hand from her leggings.

She ignored his comment since he probably only meant to distract her with it anyway. Stretching up on her toes, she tugged his shirt down his shoulder. Purple, green and black bruising stained down his shoulder blade. Her hand fluttered to rest on top. Carefully. "Did this happen yesterday in the weight room?"

He shrugged his shirt back up and flashed her a vintage Ethan grin. "Doesn't matter."

She wouldn't let him distract her with that killer smile this time. "Yes, it does. You were hurt protecting me."

He cupped her face. "You'd have done the same."

"Damn straight. Have you seen a doctor?"

"I'm fine."

She gripped the open V of his shirt to keep herself from shaking him. "Why didn't you tell me?"

"You didn't need to know."

"Why do you get to decide that?"

"I have more experience." He silenced her with a lingering kiss before backing away. "Finish up your Pilates. I'll be watching the security cameras until you make it safely back into the house."

Ethan swiped his 9mm off the table and disappeared into the night.

Experience.

The word lingered in the air, heating it with the knowledge he had in another area, a knowledge she suddenly found herself wanting to learn.

From him.

The thought blindsided her. For two years, she'd spun fantasies about the man, resenting the crush while wanting the fantasy all the same. Right now, the longings and dreams felt very real. And very possible.

She wasn't one bit closer to getting over her infatuation. Instead, need for him burned deeper, hotter, threatening to overtake her concentration if she didn't do something about it.

He'd made it clear he wanted her, too. Why not pursue that? She certainly couldn't be hurting any more than she already was at the moment.

Twenty-four years of abstinence sprawled out in her mind. She'd been waiting for someone she could trust. And as much as she knew Ethan wouldn't be the man in her tomorrows, she could trust him with today.

He would treat her body and her friendship with care.

A scant fragment of rational thought insisted she might well be influenced more by her hormones than her brain. Too bad. The force of her desire might be causing an edgy ache and reckless decisions, but she welcomed every ounce of frustration because she felt normal.

She might not be as experienced as the other women he chose, but she knew with unquestioning certainty that he wanted her. Badly. She intended to follow through on the promise in his eyes. In his touch.

Ethan Williams would be her lover.

Before this case ended, she intended to broaden her horizons in more than just field craft.

Chapter 8

A flash sparked across the horizon outside the airplane's windscreen. Ethan gripped the yoke and flew into the light, piloting his twin turbo toward their North Carolina destination with Kelly sitting beside him.

Granted any damned luck at all—and they could use some—the retired agent who'd opened a mining museum would have insights into the underground European jewel trade. They would spend the morning quizzing him about his legendary gem-cutting skills. Time well spent since they needed to widen the scope of their investigation.

Ah, hell, he needed some breathing room from the attraction dogging him, and an airplane winging its way to North Carolina made a fairly decent start.

His private plane also made for a secure location to brainstorm about their investigation going nowhere fast. Sure, they'd lined up top-notch security for the night of the ball, but he wanted answers for Alex Morrow before then. Every day missing increased the chances the agent had died. Or was surviving God only knew what kinds of torture.

Actually, Ethan knew well. Had in fact been through a few such instances in deep-cover situations that placed him in dark corners of the world, places that never saw light.

So far, he'd been able to shield Kelly from that. Today's informal interview would offer her a chance to stretch her wings in a safe environment.

Although at the moment, he wished he'd opted for a more formal venue so she would have to slap on additional layers of sweaters along with those long skirts she used to wear.

Kelly twirled the end of her ponytail between two fingers, denim looking sinfully good plastered against her curves. "How long's this guy been out of the agency?"

"About fifteen years." Clyde Hanson had earned his retirement working his way out of one of those hellholes. Ethan made a visual scan of his instruments, then the clear sky ahead of them. "Word has it he knows everything about jewels and gemstones. Picking his brain may help us find a new direction for why someone's targeting the summit display."

"Couldn't they just be after the monetary value?"

"Maybe. But then why not hit something like Lord Stanfield's private collection? Or the Cairo exhibit next month. Even the Smithsonian has less security. With all the dignitaries flown in for this, safeguards will be thick even before we implement our extra carpeting of manpower."

It was one thing to bring down scum in a sting, but keeping that entire mass of people safe hamstrung many of the methods usually open to him. Keeping everyone alive would take creativity, luck, and some serious thinking outside the box.

Given all the current war situations with noncombatants so heavily mixed in, turning to the military for unconventional methods of crowd control made sense. They'd opted to use the cutting edge breakthrough Laser Dazzler—its benign name meant to emphasize the weapon's nonlethal means. Nonlethal, but effective as hell with intense, rapid bursts of light that disoriented, stunned and even temporarily blinded attackers. "Any word back from Carla on her meeting with the Marines over in Quantico?"

"Their Urban Warfare Battle Lab is still working up the stats on using the Laser Dazzler in this sort of setting. No doubt, it would be easy to lace in with all the equipment in place for the laser show to highlight the jewels. They just need to work on better eye wear to protect the security personnel from being disoriented, as well." Kelly fished a hand into her purse and pulled out her Palm Pilot. "They've made improvements since using it in Somalia, but it would still look odd if the security folks are all wearing goggles. Hopefully, they'll have something worked out soon with contact lenses that diffuse the light."

"God knows we don't need bullets flying and one side claiming someone assassinated their ambassador. Could start a world war."

Kelly stared down at her Palm Pilot, flipping it in her hand without turning it on. "Samantha's negotiations for economic relations between Delmonico and the US have stirred fires in more than one nut-case faction."

Ethan peered out his windscreen at the miniature landscape below. A haze of mist blanketed the ground. Trails of steam and smoke from power plants rose, not yet dispersed or dissipated by winds—early morning peace, deceptively calming before the launch of a day that could hold anything. "There's no simple answer to wars generations old. Even if we avert a jewel heist, we'll be lucky to get through the evening without an old-fashioned fistfight."

Kelly twirled the stick to her keypad between her fingers. "You really used to date her?"

"Who?"

"Samantha Barnes."

So she'd picked up that slip back in their conversation in the greenhouse after all. He'd wondered why she hadn't commented on it during the discussion of Celia. "If two dinners count as dating, then yeah. Matt introduced us years ago, back in our twenties. Nothing serious. Nothing for you to be concerned about.''

''Who said I was concerned?''

''Concerned about our cover.''

She clicked on her Palm Pilot. ''I trust you to do your job.''

Not that he deserved her trust elsewhere. His relationship track record sucked. He never cheated, but he didn't stick around long, as Kelly should well know since he'd spilled all about his latest breakup more than once during their lunches. Before he'd known about her feelings for him. Before he'd seen her stand up on a chair and blaze with magnificent fire as she talked about what an ass he'd been.

Before he'd seen her in a sports bra and leggings.

Down, boy.

Eyes on the sky and mind on the mission. He'd invert the plane if he let his mind wander that Lycra-clad path. ''Someone's targeting these jewels at this occasion for a reason. They want something in particular.''

''I'm surprised they don't have Tara's engagement ring on display.''

Discussion of engagement rings sent a prickling down his spine like St. Elmo's Fire crackling through the airplane. Not particularly lethal in and of itself, but potentially deadly in its ability to distract. ''That rock of hers might blind people during the laser show.''

Kelly's laugh swirled through the cabin.

He wanted to open a window. ''Read over the inventory list again.''

She keyed the tiny pointer along her PDA. ''The ambassador of Gastonia has donated the world's largest sapphire for viewing.'' She tapped her lips with the pointer. ''Hmm. Sapphires. Funny, but mystics hold that sapphires banish fraud.''

''No kidding.'' Good. Talk that had nothing to do with engagement rings.

Celia's engagement solitaire had been buried with her.

"Sapphires are supposed to alleviate depression by lightening tension. Historically, they were even used as an energy source for curing boils."

"And you learned this where, Nebraska farm girl?"

"From my gym teacher, of course."

Damn. Vectoring too close to those meditation thoughts again. "Any more mystic lowdown on the other jewels on display? What about emeralds?"

Kelly played with the zipper tab on her parka. "Emeralds are said to increase inspiration and patience. Rubies, on the other hand, deal in more volatile emotions and can bring out anger. Centuries ago in Burma, soldiers embedded rubies under their skin to make them invincible."

"And to think Carla Juarez and the folks over in ops support have been spending millions developing embedded tracking devices to keep us safe," Ethan joked, cutting his eyes toward Kelly.

A smile dimpled her cheeks. "Maybe we should tell Carla so she can include them in her next study."

Ethan tore his eyes away from the temptation of Kelly and back to the sky. Silence echoed between them, broken only by the low drone of the engines, the tap of the stylus against her PDA.

Eventually, Ethan's gaze gravitated right back to the woman beside him, her brow furrowed, every line of her body taut with tension as she focused on the work in front of her. She looked as if she could use one of her meditation power naps right about now.

Ethan kept his mind damned well off what she would be wearing and reminded himself today's mission had a dual purpose. More than tracking leads in the European jewel market, he planned to work in some fun for Kelly into the mix. A rundown, gemstone mining park in North Carolina wasn't Rio, but he intended to make the day memorable for her.

Starting now. "Wanna have a go?"

"At what?"

He nodded to the controls.

Her eyes widened, sparked, then glowed with definite interest. "Me? I don't know anything about flying."

"Taking off and landing's the tough part. This is easy. Just like a car, keep the direction and speed steady. Feel the adjustments in the yoke like you do with a steering wheel. I'll even put the autopilot on altitude hold for you. Take the throttle if you need to adjust airspeed. Throttle up is faster. Throttle back for slower. Otherwise, hands on the yoke, point her straight and level. If you have the least doubt, watch the artificial horizon on the instrument panel."

"Or you could take over."

"Not a chance. You're on your own." He raised his hands.

"Ethan!" She grasped the yoke. A slight yaw, bump, jolt and she leveled the wings again as they plowed past the clouds. "Ohmigosh." Her breath huffed in faster gasps as she flew. "This is incredible. Why would you ever want to land?"

"Gotta refuel eventually."

Her hands loosened around the yoke, her shoulders dropping into a more relaxed angle. "Have you ever thought about doing this professionally? The CIA has pilots on their operative roster."

"Nah. For those folks and active-duty service people, it's more of a calling-to-the-skies. For me, it's just a cool way to get from point A to point B, like the Jag."

"Really cool way."

Her adventurous spirit matched to his own with a power he couldn't miss.

Couldn't resist. "Yeah. Next time I'll take you flying over the ocean. With the Gulf Stream IV, we can make London in less than seven hours. Maybe even wrangle an invitation to look at Lord Stanfield's jewel collection while we're there."

What the hell had he just said, committing them to time together after the case? Still, the idea took shape in his head

with appealing clarity. Too easily, he could envision touring
Europe with Kelly—climbing around Stonehenge, making
out at the top of the Eiffel Tower.

Making love on a private beach in Monaco.

Hell, he was thinking like some damned kid. Someone
closer to her age. She should enjoy those kinds of courting
rituals from someone still young enough to possess a few
illusions.

For as long as he could remember, he hadn't wanted anything except the thrill of the next case. No matter how much
slime he sent away, it was never enough to satisfy the hun-
ger inside him. He always wanted more.

Except now. He only wanted one thing.

He wanted to see if Kelly's eyes would spark with all
that life and vitality when she unraveled in his arms, a thrill
beyond any he could imagine.

An addictive thrill that could lead him into forgetting that
his self-indulgence would eventually hurt her.

Kelly peered through the rental-car windshield at the deserted, snow-filled parking lot outside Crazy Clyde's Cavern. The tourist trap had pretty much shut down for the
winter. Clyde Hanson could well have agreed to see them
out of boredom rather than any residual patriotism.

Reaching for her car door, Kelly stopped short when
Ethan pulled it open like some guy on a date. The quaintly
old-fashioned chivalry tickled her whimsy. "Aunt Eugenie's
training, I guess."

Ethan grunted.

Not an encouraging sign from a man she hoped to lure
into an affair.

Rows of cabins sprawled dark and bare, puffs of smoke
only rising from one chimney in the brown clapboard building labeled Clyde's Country Store. Kelly trudged through
the ankle-deep snow past a thirty-foot neon statue of an old
miner with a cheesy searchlight inserted in his helmet where
a mining lamp normally resided.

Who'd have imagined the owner of this two-bit pit stop had once been a driven agent?

She knew Ethan thought she lived in some innocent ops-support bubble, but she watched and listened, always trying to pick up as much as she could in preparation for her turn. Rumor had it, Clyde had lost more than half a finger when a friend turned on him. Some said he'd gone a little crazy. Others said he'd wised up and gotten out.

The job allowed so much latitude in obtaining justice, it cultivated a ripe environment for corruption. How hellish not knowing how far to trust even fellow operatives. Ethan lived with the dark underside every day. Alone.

She slid her mittened hand into his, and he didn't pull away, this complex man with wandering feet but the gentlest touch. This man who saw into the secret yearnings of her soul enough to give her impromptu flying lessons.

Ushering her past a frozen pond and up the slick steps, Ethan shot her a quick smile and squeezed her hand. Nothing big. Or overt. Just a simple gesture of reassurance.

Who saw into his soul and soothed his innermost hurts? Of course he would laugh at her if she even insinuated he needed anything from anyone. Maybe through today's interview she could show him having a partner wasn't so bad, teach him there were some people who could be trusted.

He could trust her.

Ethan stepped ahead of her. He rapped on the glass pane just over the Closed sign.

The door swung wide. A burst of dry heat swelled through and warmed her face while the cold chilled her back.

"Welcome!" boomed the Santa Claus of a man with hands far too large for the intricate gem cutting he performed. "Thank God someone saw fit to drive up here and talk to me before my brain froze."

"Hello, Clyde." Ethan tugged his gloves off and stuffed them in the pocket of his ski jacket. "This is Kelly Taylor."

"Well, hi there, Kelly Taylor." Clyde kicked the door

shut behind them, sealing out the howling wind. "I never lucked into a cute little partner like you back in my day."

A day long before political correctness, as well, but she couldn't help but smile at his bluster. "Thanks for seeing us on short notice."

"Nothing else to do."

Kelly unzipped her jacket and let it flap loose as she strolled around the gift shop made to resemble a nineteenth-century store. Jars of candy canes perched in front of the old register. Wooden display boxes lined the counter and inside the display case. She let her hands sift through labeled box after box—garnets, rose quartz, citrine, topaz. Moonstone?

So cool to the touch.

Her eyes traveled ahead of her hand to the next box, clear blue stones glistening, and a sigh whispered free.

Clyde's beefy hand shot past her. "You have a good eye, Miss Taylor." He scooped a handful, the smooth perfection making a startling contrast as they trickled back through his nicked and scarred fingers. "The hue will accent your pale skin nicely."

"I'm just trying to remember what qualities this is supposed to posses."

"Ah, well, actually a perfect choice for a lady agent. Aquamarines are reputed to weed out unnecessary information. They clarify thought, banish evil sprits and promote light. Here. Feel."

He passed her a grape-size stone with a necklace hook soldered on the top.

Kelly let it roll around in her palm. "Maybe I should take a dozen."

"It's also said to be a symbol for chastity."

Suddenly, she wanted to pitch it back in the bin.

"We'll take it." Ethan tugged a folded clip full of cash from his pocket and peeled off two one-hundred-dollar bills, obviously purchasing information along with the simple gemstone, even if Clyde did throw in a handful of peppermint sticks for good measure.

Kelly tucked the candy in her pocket while Ethan slid into interrogation mode. Hooking a casual elbow on the counter, he began quizzing Clyde and the old agent soaked up the chance to revisit his days with the agency. Kelly listened to Clyde explain the intricacies of cutting gems for decorative versus more practical purposes. She catalogued everything he shared to sift through and analyze later.

Somehow she knew the cost of purchasing this information and the use of Ethan's plane wouldn't go onto his agency expense account. This man gave so much of himself and his resources for his country, shrugging it all off as nothing more than a way to pursue thrills.

If that were the case, then he would be scaling mountains in the Andes. Instead, he channeled those thrill-seeking ways into a higher good.

How could she not admire him for that?

How could she not want him?

The mention of Rebelia jerked her from her ridiculous daydreaming. She needed to keep her mind on the job. Her quest to land in Ethan's bed would have to come later.

"In fact," Clyde leaned back in his chair, peppermint stick dangling from the corner of his mouth, "there's an old Rebelian saying that goes something like, 'He who owns the gem of power owns the world.'"

Kelly inched closer. "Oh, really? How so?"

"About four hundred years ago, a Rebelian ruler gave his new wife a bridal gift, an exquisite stone set in a necklace. Shortly after the birth of their son, she died. Some said she mourned herself to death because her husband only married her for her royal connection to a neighboring country."

Kelly's hand tightened around the cool weight of her rock. "The poor woman."

"The necklace was passed on to her son to give to his wife. A wife who also mysteriously died. Three generations of bumped-off brides later, this one savvy queen-to-be decided she didn't want any part of that cursed stone. She sold it to a merchant who wanted to exchange his older model spouse for an eighteenth-century trophy wife. The stone disappeared. No one knows for sure what kind of gem it was, but its power over life and death became legendary.''

Ethan snorted. ''What a load of crap.''

Clyde waggled half a finger in Ethan's face. ''Don't dismiss it out of hand. Even if you don't believe it, other people do and that gives it power. Think about it, son. Leaders have been screwing with people's minds, twisting core beliefs and cultural customs into propaganda since the beginning of time. Take a starving group of peasants and play on that, and the mix is rife for an uprising.''

''Valid point,'' Kelly interjected before Ethan could dismiss the mystical implications out of hand again. ''So jewels collected for any number of purposes could be useless if there isn't someone on hand to assess or cut them.''

Clyde nodded. ''Exactly.''

Which gave cause for nabbing Morrow, a geologist with a renowned interest in gems.

Kelly and Ethan exchanged glances before Ethan tugged a second round of bills free as payment for information received. ''Thanks for your time, Clyde. You know how to find me if you think of anything else.''

''Stay awhile.'' Clyde crunched a candy cane that was wrapped in his three-fingered grip. ''Look around if you want. The mine's closed to the public for the winter, but I can fire up the generators. My handyman, Johnny, is out back. He can show you around some if you'd like. Just follow the fluorescent arrows painted along the wall. Stay clear of roped-off areas and you'll be fine.''

Kelly hesitated. The warmth of Ethan's hand earlier and the weight of his gift lured her into wanting to steal more from this day. A stroll through the mine would give her the perfect chance to get closer to him. ''Ethan?''

''Sure.'' He nodded to the door. ''We can play tourist, soak up some more of your woo-hoo stuff about crystals.''

Kelly jabbed a finger in his arm. "Better watch it, big guy. Don't diss the crystals." She tugged the zipper up on her jacket and pulled on her gloves. "Thanks, Clyde."

"You bet," he called as they stepped back into the blustery cold. "And listen to the lady, son."

The door swung shut behind them.

"Yeah, yeah. Whatever." Ethan palmed her back down the stairs.

"You'll be sorry," she warned, smiling back at him.

He scooped his gloved hand along the rail. "I'll show you who's gonna be sorry."

"Hey? What are you doing?" She inched away from the growing mound of snow in the palm of his glove. "Don't even consider it, Williams. I'll drop you again."

"I'm scared." He packed the snow as he stalked toward her.

"No!" Kelly squealed in protest, already reaching behind her to make her own retaliatory snow bomb. He'd warned her to use whatever she could. Too bad for him if he didn't prepare.

He advanced the last seven feet between them, his every crunching step launching a delicious thrill of anticipation through her.

Nose-to-cold-nose, he stopped in front of her. Goosebumps sprinkled her skin beneath her parka as she waited for him to shove the snowball down her jacket.

He raised his hand.

She clenched her fingers around the packed snow in the palm of her glove.

Ethan lifted his snowball higher, chest level, face level, and—

—took a bite. "Always loved this stuff as a kid."

She watched him down another bite. Ethan as a kid, now there was an enchanting image full of motion and mischief.

Although he looked a hundred percent adult male at the moment.

Kelly wrapped her fingers around his wrist, urged his arm

toward her face until the snowball reached her mouth. As deliberately as Eve taking a bite from the apple, she nipped a section of the packed ice free, swirling her tongue out to catch the crumbling flakes.

She could have sworn Ethan's hand shook in her grip. But that wasn't possible. Not from something so simple.

From her.

His eyes dilated. Her breath puffed clouds between them. Ethan dropped his snowball to the ground and gripped her arms. Her hand slipped around his neck.

He startled under her touch. "What the—"

Snow cascaded down his jacket from her forgotten snowball. Kelly looked at her glove, compacted crystallized snow gleamed back at her like tiny diamonds.

He dusted powder off his neck. "Guess you got me, Taylor."

Yes, she had. But she knew it would only be for a short time, a much safer prospect than risking some broken heart of legendary proportions yearning for anything more.

She turned away from the tempting image of Ethan smiling at her. Only her. "Let's go find that Johnny fellow and see the mine."

Lights lined the narrow tunnel, carved earth with jagged holes winding ahead of them. After spending just ten minutes alone with Kelly since Johnny pointed them on their way and went back to work, Ethan questioned his own intelligence in going along with the impromptu tourist gig. Sure, he wanted to show Kelly a good time, help her relax and enjoy life the way he had with piloting the plane.

But not at the expense of his sanity.

He sidestepped a decorative mining cart. The shadowy recesses of the mine felt too much like total solitude. He and Kelly—alone. Completely.

Kelly strode across a planked observation deck and pressed her gloved hand to the chiseled earth, pulling her parka taut across her breasts. Her fingers explored embedded crystal chips. "How depressing to think of the hours, days, months people spent in here away from the sun."

An image of her at her cubicle flashed to mind. Windows weren't allowed in the deeper bowels of ARIES for security reasons. Did she yearn for light?

If only he could make her understand there wasn't any light to be found outside her ARIES office. Just a deeper darkness that sometimes swallowed the soul. "People do what they have to do to survive."

"I guess so." She turned to face him, leaning a hip against the metal railing. The yellow glow from the strips of light overhead cast shadows along her perfect cheekbones. "Well, partner, what do you really think of Clyde's insights on the mindsets in the region?"

He thought he wanted to listen to her talk some more, those sultry Kelly-tones echoing all around him in triplicate. "What's your take on it?"

"There's some validity in all of it. People act for any number of reasons. That portion of eastern Europe sports plenty of rebel factions trying to finance an overthrow. Jewels would pay for that. Others act from their belief system. For those people, finding the right jewel would be crucial to establishing a blessed reign or good luck."

"Or maybe like the legend, some guy's collecting jewels for a woman, to entice her, persuade her to take on someone who's wrong for her." Was he any different? Damned if he hadn't been subconsciously trying to lure Kelly all day with private planes and trips, all to cover up for the ways he knew he fell short of being the kind of man she deserved.

Damn. Not such a selfless gift of friendship after all. Ethan dragged his mind back to work, a safer, more reliable topic. "Who do you think's responsible?"

She shrugged. "Certainly Rebelia is a possibility with that nutcase DeBruzkya trying to secure his position. But then Gastonia isn't the most popular kid on the block now, either, since it's rumored to harbor terrorist camps. And of course Morrow disappeared in Holzberg. How the hell do they sleep at night with so many enemies around them?''

He advanced a step closer to her, his hiking boots thudding against the wooden deck. ''Better get used to it, Kelly, because that's the world you're going to be living in if you commit to being a field operative. What we do is necessary or innocent people die, but that doesn't make what we do any prettier. You can learn all the self-defense moves in the world and they won't mean a damn if you forget the most basic element of self-preservation in this job.''

Ethan leaned until he could see the light glinting in her honey-brown eyes. ''Don't trust anyone.''

''What about you?''

''Not even me.'' Especially not him. As selfish as he was, he could so easily take everything she had to give. She deserved better. Anyone other than him, except the image of her finding that man tore him up inside.

Christ, he wanted her. Right or wrong, he wanted her for himself. Ethan canted closer, wanted even closer still to see if the taste of their shared snowball lingered in her mouth. ''We should head back.''

''We should,'' she agreed but didn't move. He could already taste her from just the air they shared as they stood so close together.

He forced his feet to carry him backward, away from her. ''The airport will probably be ready to clear us for take-off by the time we get back.''

''Probably so.''

He spun on his heel to leave.

''Ethan?''

He glanced over his shoulder. ''Yeah, Kel?''

''Thanks for the aquamarine.'' She leaned her elbows back against the railing and smiled at him.

Her warm eyes shone with so much gratitude over a cheap little rock, he wanted to detour to Cartier and buy out a display case. She would make a hell of an image in her workout clothes draped with diamonds. "Glad you liked it."

Kelly pushed away from the rail and stepped forward. The rail wobbled. Ethan's stomach clenched.

He grabbed her elbow. "Hey, Kel, careful there." He reached behind her to test the rail. "Clyde needs to make some repairs or he could have a major lawsuit on his hands."

Kelly shuddered. "Let's get out of here."

"Sounds like a plan to me." Ethan turned back toward the exit tunnel, boards creaking under his feet.

Kelly's arm jerked free a second before she screamed, "Ethan!"

The wooden deck shifted. Broke apart. Started an avalanche slide downward with Kelly slipping out of sight as the ground fell away from under him.

Chapter 9

Kelly plummeted down the sloped embankment. Rocks, wood and debris skittered past her. Battered her.

She grappled for something, anything to halt her fall. Found nothing.

Kept fighting anyway. She wouldn't give up until she met ground. Soon, she hoped.

Dim light flickered from above, barely penetrating the abyss under her. She swallowed a scream. Dust clogged her nose. She wouldn't let it choke her, too.

Below, the blanket of black thinned, muddied. The ground rose up to meet her.

She slammed to a stop.

Pain jarred through her. Air huffed from her lungs. Rumbling sounded above her as more debris cascaded down. Ethan. She scrambled back. Out of the way.

"Ethan? Ethan!"

She peered up toward the glow above. Ethan skidded on his back in a swirl of sliding mud and boards. He landed at

The Silhouette Reader Service™ — Here's how it works:

Accepting your 2 free books and mystery gift places you under no obligation to buy anything. You may keep the books and gift and return the shipping statement marked "cancel." If you do not cancel, about a month later we'll send you 6 additional books and bill you just $3.99 each in the U.S., or $4.74 each in Canada, plus 25¢ shipping & handling per book and applicable taxes if any.* That's the complete price and — compared to cover prices of $4.75 each in the U.S. and $5.75 each in Canada — it's quite a bargain! You may cancel at any time, but if you choose to continue, every month we'll send you 6 more books, which you may either purchase at the discount price or return to us and cancel your subscription.

*Terms and prices subject to change without notice. Sales tax applicable in N.Y. Canadian residents will be charged applicable provincial taxes and GST. Credit or Debit balances in a customer's account(s) may be offset by any other outstanding balance owed by or to the customer

If offer card is missing write to: Silhouette Reader Service, 3010 Walden Ave., P.O. Box 1867, Buffalo, NY 14240-1867

NO POSTAGE
NECESSARY
IF MAILED
IN THE
UNITED STATES

BUSINESS REPLY MAIL
FIRST-CLASS MAIL   PERMIT NO. 717-003   BUFFALO, NY

POSTAGE WILL BE PAID BY ADDRESSEE

SILHOUETTE READER SERVICE
3010 WALDEN AVE
PO BOX 1867
BUFFALO NY 14240-9952

Play the Romance Crossword Game

and get...
2 FREE BOOKS
and a
FREE GIFT...
YOURS to KEEP!

Scratch Here!

to reveal the hidden words.
Look below to see what you get.

Yes!

I have scratched off the gold areas. Please send me my **2 FREE BOOKS** and **FREE GIFT** for which I qualify. I understand that I am under no obligation to purchase any books as explained on the back of this card.

345 SDL DRTT   **245 SDL DRUA**

FIRST NAME   LAST NAME

ADDRESS

APT.#   CITY

STATE/PROV.   ZIP/POSTAL CODE

Visit us online at
www.eHarlequin.com

ROMANCE	MYSTERY	NOVEL	GIFT
You get **2 FREE BOOKS** PLUS a **FREE GIFT!**	You get **2 FREE BOOKS!**	You get **1 FREE BOOK!**	You get a **FREE MYSTERY GIFT!**

Offer limited to one per household and not valid to current Silhouette Intimate Moments® subscribers. All orders subject to approval.

her feet with a thud. A fresh shower of debris rained after him.

Kelly swiped her wrist across her gritty eyes, blinking to clear the dust and adjust to the minuscule light filtering from above.

"Ethan?" She crawled across jagged rocks and chunks of wood. One knee snagged on a fresh splinter that tore into the designer jeans Eugenie had helped her choose. She ignored the stab of pain. "Are you okay? Talk to me!"

He groaned. She almost groaned, too, relief slamming through her harder than any of the boards.

He rolled to his back. "Judas-freaking-priest, Kelly. That hurt." He pushed up to sit. "You okay?"

"Fine." Scared spitless, but damned well not going to show it. "A little banged up, no doubt. But everything's working."

Ethan swept a hand over his dust-encrusted hair. "Same here."

Renewed relief punched an exhale from her that stirred a fresh swirl of dust and mustiness. Her eyes attuned enough to discern earthen walls around them in a six-foot-wide cavern with no way out but up. She rubbed her hands along her arms. "What happened back there?"

He squinted, tipping his face up to where they'd started. An oozing scrape glared along his cheek. "Ground gave way beneath the deck, I'm guessing. We're lucky there was a slope rather than a sheer drop off."

She stared all the way up the steep incline, at least a hundred feet. "Guess we should climb back out." When he didn't answer, she turned to him. "Right?"

Ethan braced one arm on his knee and pointed at the remaining pieces of deck, twisted and hanging on by a splinter. "See that? Too much jarring will loosen it. I don't want to scare you, but we need to be realistic here. There's also the chance of starting an avalanche of dirt."

The thought of being pummeled, then buried alive, sent smothering fear clogging her senses. Kelly steadied her breathing, and slowly her heartbeat, as well. "What would you do if I wasn't here with you?"

"That's not the point."

"What would you do?" she insisted.

He relented. "Since there's light, I would climb."

She set her teeth and ignored the fear. "Then let's climb."

"Hey, now." He raised his hands in surrender. "Just because it's what I would do doesn't make it the smart move. I'm a reckless idiot and there's no reason for you to be the same. I could go without you—" Her glare silenced him. "Or we can park our butts here and wait. Clyde will come looking when he sees the rental car's still out front."

"Unless that wasn't an accident. You said never to trust anyone."

Ethan stayed silent.

Of course he'd know that. Johnny's directions and convenient timing to return to work took on a sinister tone. "I'll let you decide who's going up first. But as long as there's light, we're climbing. We can spot each other."

Ethan studied the slope, then Kelly, and shook his head. "If this wasn't an accident, who the hell knows how many more traps have been set. We'll sit tight. Aunt Eugenie doesn't know details about my job, but she has a number to call if I don't return. A direct line to Hatch. Once she does that, they'll activate the tracking chip in my shoulder and locate us."

A chilling thought settled in her too-damned-logical brain. "Which shoulder?"

"What?"

"Which shoulder is your tracking chip embedded in?"

"The left."

The one with the bruise smeared across it from his tango with the weights. She almost didn't want to know, but had to ask, "Do you think it's still working?"

Ethan's jaw set as if he was already planning to bar her way up that wall of dirt. "Carla designed it to withstand stress. It's fine. If not, we'll just jam your stone under my skin.''

''I told you not to diss the crystals.'' If there was even half an ounce of truth in those mystic possibilities, they'd no doubt maxed their bad luck for the day.

The light overhead dimmed, flickered. Went dead.

End of bad luck? Apparently not.

Just his damned luck. As if it wasn't bad enough he'd been trapped in an unstable cavern with a ton of debris waiting to crash down on their heads. As if he wasn't already beating himself up over not finding a way to drag Kelly out of this dank hellhole.

The fates had decided to punish him by submerging him in complete darkness with Kelly's voice echoing around him for the past hour.

Of course if talking kept her calm, then fine. He would keep listening to her recounting of every childhood holiday since birth while they shared peppermint sticks.

She racked up serious points in his book for grit. Kelly hadn't complained once of the damp cold that chilled to the bone. And there wasn't a chance she'd survived that plunge without some injury. His arm was throbbing like a son-of-a-bitch. He was used to shrugging it off, but Kelly—what a job initiation.

He hated the helplessness of the situation, waiting for the chip to activate once Aunt Eugenie reported them missing. There wasn't a damned thing he could do to get them out. The inky darkness posed countless hazards, even if they somehow made it up the slope without releasing an avalanche of rubble. Too many sheer drop-offs waited on the trail back.

On his own, he'd chance it. But the risk was too great to gamble with Kelly in tow.

Give him an enemy to bag. A crook to down. A target to shoot. Anything but depending on fate and luck to pull them through when he knew fate could be a heartless bastard.

Kelly's light laugh broke through the darkness. She paused midstory, somewhere around dyeing eggs or baking cookies. "As much as I'm sure you're enjoying hearing the details of my fifth Easter, maybe I should teach you some meditation instead. We could alternate power naps."

Ethan massaged his aching arm. At least the pain would keep him awake. "I need to stay alert."

"Or we could take turns keeping watch."

"Okay. I'll go first."

"Mule." She slugged his arm.

He stifled a wince along with a curse. He didn't need her turning into Florence Nightingale on him since there wasn't a thing she could do to help him anyway. "What kind of cookies were they?"

"Sugar cookies. Cut out shapes with colored spr-sprinkles." Her chattering teeth clacked through the last word.

Knowing he would regret it, he called to her, "Come here."

"Why?"

"It's only going to get colder."

"I'm f-fine."

And the little pit bull dared call him stubborn! He rolled out the only excuse he could conjure that would lure her into accepting what she needed. "Well, good for you, but I'm freezing my ass off over here."

"Oh." Rustling sounded from a few feet away as she scrambled closer. "Ethan?"

"Right here."

Her hand landed in his lap. No chance she would miss the furnace of heat there. Damned inconvenient that the libido didn't turn off even in life-threatening situations. Just the opposite. His body screamed *procreate before you die*.

Kelly's hand slid away. He stifled a groan, tougher than withholding sound when she'd slugged his arm. He tucked his good arm around her and drew her closer until she dropped between his legs. He locked his arms around her waist and tucked her back against his chest. Her bottom nestled against him.

No way could she miss the obvious.

"Uh, Ethan?"

"Ignore it, Kelly. I am." Not.

"Maybe we should talk about—"

"Nope. Don't think so." He had enough trouble resisting her voice when she talked about Santa Claus and the Easter Bunny. He'd damn well explode if she switched to discussions about his too-obvious arousal. "Let's move on to Halloween number five."

"Tell me about yours instead."

Her question sideswiped him. Leave it to Kelly to zero in on his first holiday without his parents. He couldn't wait to get his hands on Hatch's mysterious file about their deaths.

He'd thought he'd squelched the pain from their accident years ago. But now that he had reason to believe it wasn't just an accident, old ghosts of the past came back to bite him on the butt when he least expected. As soon as he closed this case, he would make it his personal mission in life to find out what the hell had really happened that day.

"Ethan?" Kelly pulled him back to dank, cold present. "Your fifth Halloween?"

He slammed the door on the past and focused on surviving in the present. "Just like any other one, lots of popcorn balls and Pixie Stix."

"No fair." She sagged back against him, her hair tickling his nose. Deprived of light, Ethan found his other senses honing tenfold by the second. The scent of her. The feel of her softness.

The sound of her. Especially that.

"Come on, Ethan. I told you all about the year Mom dressed me up like a mini Marie Curie. At least tell me what you wore."

"I was a clown."

"A clown?" Her breathing evened out against his chest in a reassuring pattern.

Good. She was relaxing. If he kept talking, maybe she'd fall asleep.

"I wanted to be a cowboy, but Aunt Eugenie had already flown to Paris and bought me this renaissance clown costume." He'd been so hell-bent on not causing her any trouble so she would keep him, he hadn't argued. He'd just slapped on the pointy hat and trick-or-treated his bells off.

"I'd love to see the pictures."

"They all magically disappeared the next year when I dressed up as Houdini." He'd wanted as few memories as possible of those first months without his parents.

Kelly traced a finger along his hands linked over her belly. "So was Houdini your choice or Aunt Eugenie's?"

"Mine. Of course she made sure I had some kick-ass tricks to go along with the costume." He'd realized by then she wasn't going to send him anywhere. She might not have been the most conventional of parents, but then he'd have driven a conventional parent to the nuthouse inside a year. "The lock pick and handcuffs were a huge hit for this CIA agent in the making."

Kelly's yawn echoed. "What else did little Houdini do?"

"Let's just say I'm not sure Peter ever got over the chemicals I put in his oils."

"Poor Peter." Her finger slipped up past the cuff of his jacket. "What kind of chemicals?"

Who'd have thought a wrist could be an erogenous zone. Of course, his whole body felt like one big erogenous zone at the moment. "Stuff that changed colors the warmer it got. He walked around with blue hands for a month."

Kelly's whisper-soft laughter filled the cavern, swirled round and came back to tempt him with every echoing repetition.

She snuggled under his chin. "I'm so glad she was there for you when you lost your parents."

"I was lucky. She stepped in full tilt to take care of me.

Strange to think she was my age then, bringing up a five-year-old hellion. My parents didn't even make thirty-five.'' Neither did Celia. His arms convulsed around Kelly. "I won't let anything happen to you.''

"I'm not afraid of dying.'' Her fingers wrapped around his wrist with surprising strength from a woman who'd seemed three seconds from snoozing off. "Just afraid of dying without making a difference.''

"Damn it, Kelly.'' He gripped her shoulders and twisted her round until she sat sideways on his lap and could face him, even if he couldn't see her. "You're not going to die. And you've already made a difference or Hatch wouldn't have promoted you to this job.''

Determination radiated from her in waves so strong he almost expected it to light the air. How had he ever thought her timid?

Her hand fell to his hair. "I wish you could let it grow again. Will you do that, after we're out of here?''

"Sure.'' He'd promise her anything right now to give her hope—and if she'd keep touching him.

Kelly feathered her fingers along his scalp. "There are so many things I wanted to do with my life and I'm just sitting here wondering if I was making excuses to keep from going after what I want.''

"What do want, Kelly?'' He'd make it happen.

"I want you.''

Those three simple words wielded a sledgehammer to his already diminishing self-control. Thoughts of losing his parents, losing Celia, possibly losing Kelly, too, had left him too damned aware of how precarious life was. Even on a good day he didn't excel at denying himself.

And this sure as hell wasn't a good day.

"Kelly.'' He savored her name a second before he savored her lips, savored the taste of peppermint and Kelly.

Her soft moan echoed through their darkened chamber. The world closed in on them. There might never be anyone else if they didn't get out of this alive.

Ethan anchored her to him as if that would keep her safer. Her tongue met his with more confidence this time than in the greenhouse. She'd taken note of how he liked it when she slid those soft hands under his shirt, around to his back. Even gloved, her touch aroused.

But he wanted to feel undiluted Kelly under his hands. He tore his mouth away to tug his gloves off with his teeth.

"Ethan?"

He was back to her before she could finish her protest, a smart move since just the sound of her voice charged his libido too much, too soon. He nestled her more securely on his lap, felt the warmth of her soft hip against him, wanted to plunge into her softness but knew this wasn't the time or place. For now, he had other plans for her. Starting with memorizing every inch of her he could touch in their constraining clothes.

Ethan tunneled his hands under her jacket, higher, over skin so silky he could almost see its pearly color. Higher still until he found her breasts. The taut peaks welcomed him, teasing him with what he couldn't see but damned well intended to explore.

Kelly swung her knee around until she straddled him. Ethan's hands shook, not that he let it stop him from finding his way into denim to cup her bottom.

"Ethan?" Silky tones caressed the air.

Her voice. God, what a voice.

"Yeah, Kel?"

"Please say you have protection in your wallet."

He did. But they weren't going to get in a position to need it. He wasn't so far gone that he'd lost sight of keeping her safe. "We're not going to do anything."

A small whimper of protest slipped free.

"I have something else in mind for you."

"What—"

"Shh." He silenced her with his mouth, or maybe it was the stroke of his fingers gliding forward in her jeans,

flicking her snap and zipper free to give him easier access lower. Much lower where he discovered her hot, wet, ready.

For him.

The surge of victory made his self-denial worthwhile. "Kelly?"

"Don't talk. Don't stop."

An easy enough order to follow. He sought, found, circled with two fingers, her breathy sighs guiding him until he learned her pace. He stroked, soothed, teased her closer, the increasing pressure of her hands digging into his shoulders offering all the encouragement he needed.

A moan started low in her throat. Heaven help him, he should have known she would be vocal. That incredible voice of hers so perfect in her pleasure. Hearing her desire build was the hottest damned thing he'd ever experienced and he hadn't even had sex with her yet.

Yet?

Yet.

Her back arched against his supporting arm. Her cry rolled up and out of her throat with a force that charged through him, leaving him conversely physically frustrated and mentally satisfied. Before the echoes of Kelly all around him faded, she collapsed against his chest.

Soft, pliant and for the moment—his.

Kelly rested in Ethan's arms, her world hazy until she could only be certain of one thing. The guy wasn't budging on the issue of completing what they'd started. The pig-headed, honorable man had it in his head he would be taking advantage of the adrenaline from danger.

Like she didn't know her own mind.

Of course, until about fifteen minutes ago, she hadn't known her body could feel so incredible. She wanted more than ever to get out alive. Now. So they could finish what he'd started. She'd been right to pursue Ethan.

He tucked her closer to his side. "So tell me how you got that tattoo."

Peppermint-scented words drifted down.

"Single-minded son-of-a-gun, aren't you?"

"Focused."

And she'd benefited well from his focused attention on her. "You may have noticed I'm not the most outgoing of people," she stated. He stayed diplomatically silent while his hands stroked over her back. "Well, once I started college, I decided the time had come to assume control over my life. I was hell-bent on doing something daring. So I packed an overnight bag, and took a bus to Reno."

He kissed the top of her head. "And got a tattoo."

"Eventually, but that wasn't my original intent." The dark made it too easy to slip back to that time, to relive the frenzy that had driven her to lash out in rebellion since she couldn't tell her parents she was tired of trying to be the perfect daughter they wanted. Seemed ridiculous now, but so very real then. "I planned to go to the casinos and pick up a guy."

He stilled against her, so silent only the sound of his heart thudded in her ears.

"Stupid, I know. Don't worry, I chickened out in the end and realized I was doing it for all the wrong reasons. After I lost fifty bucks, I decided I was going to have *something* out of that weekend. So I spent my last forty on a tattoo."

Ethan raised her hand to his mouth and pressed a kiss to her wrist. "You still haven't told me what it is." The heat of his words branded her skin.

"I wasn't going to get a rose or the cute little mouse they tried to sell me. I was out to make a statement."

Ethan's laugh rumbled against her chest. "I've found from experience that when you decide to speak up, it's impossible not to listen."

She wished she'd had that power then. Kelly scratched her fingers through the dirt beside her. "I know now it was just a knee-jerk reaction. I was striking back at my parents for years of pressure. Sort of like how I tossed on a few extra layers of sweaters and pitched out my lip gloss after the attack. I needed to regain control of some portion of my world.''

''Whoa.'' Ethan's hand found her leg and squeezed. ''Back up. Attack?''

Had she told him that? She hadn't meant to, didn't want that between them or in his mind when he thought of her. She wasn't a victim anymore and refused to let anybody think of her as one. ''Oh, uh, I guess I left out that part.''

''Yeah, you did.'' His grip tightened on her. ''Kelly, what attack?''

She knew he wouldn't back off until she told him. What he imagined was probably worse anyhow. ''My ancient languages professor in grad school. I was so young, only twenty when I started graduate school and beyond innocent. I didn't have a clue what he was after until it was too late. There were eleven other people in that class, nine of us women, and for some reason he targeted me. I guess I didn't realize guys like that prey upon vulnerability more than beauty.''

A burning need blistered Ethan's brain, a need to escort that son-of-a-bitch straight to hell and then spend a few years torturing him.

Before he killed him.

He needed to lash out at the person who'd dared hurt her. He hadn't been able to fight the disease that had ravaged Celia, but the threat to Kelly had been tangible. Real.

Soon to be in pain, if Ethan ever got his hands on the guy.

Ethan regulated his breathing, tucked those dark thoughts away and focused on what Kelly needed. ''Talk to me. Tell me everything.''

His arms tightened around Kelly as if he could protect her from that long-ago threat.

Long ago? Just four years.

''Most of all, I hated the lack of control. Other than a powerful set of lungs, I was pretty much at his mercy. But the minute I convinced him to stop covering my mouth, campus security heard me scream."

The thought of her beautiful voice racked with terror sliced him clean through. But he couldn't let that show now. He swallowed bile. "Did you ever talk to anyone about this?"

"I am now."

"I mean before now."

"Why?" Her hair tickled his chin as she tipped her face toward him. "He didn't actually, uh, penetrate. I'm still totally a virgin."

While Ethan thanked heaven and a thousand patron saints that the cops had showed up in time, he still knew she had to carry some emotional scars. "You were attacked. Whether or not he," Ethan blinked back the red haze of anger, "penetrated, he assaulted you and you deserved to have support."

"It was his word against mine, so there wasn't much chance of a conviction in court. But I put enough pressure on campus for him to retire early. I took self-defense courses." A whisper of a laugh escaped. "Bet you didn't know about my edge that day in the gym."

"No." But he admired her for using it.

"I've done everything in my power to make sure I can defend myself."

The woman hadn't joined ARIES to see the world. She'd done it out of self-preservation. They had more in common than he could have ever guessed. "You're an amazing woman, Kelly Taylor."

She laughed. "Who me? I'm just a farm girl from Nebraska who knows what she wants from life and finally has decided to go after it."

Left unspoken were the words now understood.

She wanted him.

And he knew.

He couldn't be with this woman because it *would* mean something. If he let himself crawl into her bed and slide into her body, he might well want to stay. The thought of giving anyone that much control over his emotions again sent his heart pounding so hard she must hear it.

A hum started. Flickerings in front of his eyes with a second's warning before light flooded their hellhole of a cavern.

The power had returned.

And in the middle of hell, a halo of light streamed across Kelly's dirt-smudged face. Hair straggled over her eyes, chocolate-warm eyes that called to a man when shining from the face of this so-damned-pretty woman. A woman he didn't dare claim, because he knew something she didn't.

He could stand down a renegade drug runner packing heat without wincing. But when it came to giving his heart, Ethan Williams was a coward.

Wrapped in an Aztec-patterned blanket, Kelly pumped her canewood rocker into motion in the back room of Clyde's store while the last rays of the day filtered through the frost-speckled window. What thoughts churned behind Ethan's stark face, the hard lines illuminated by tauntingly romantic firelight? Her own emotions still swirled with a mix of passion and the adrenaline buzz of having survived death.

Clyde had started searching after a couple of hours, quickly discovering the blown generator. A tampered-with generator. And a missing handyman. The aging agent had immediately alerted headquarters, then charged ahead to the rescue on his own.

Those lights coming back on had illuminated more than their way out once Clyde had tossed down a rope and re-assurance. They'd cast a spotlight on the harsh reality of Ethan's panicked expression.

She wasn't naive enough to think he didn't want her. She could tell she turned him on, could see it in his eyes even now. And he hadn't been repulsed by the attack, just predictably protective.

But any tenderness from her? Forget it. He didn't want it.

She should be happy, right? She didn't want anything long-term from Ethan Williams anyway. She wanted to focus on her career. And when her days in the field ended, she would find some scholarly guy to converse with in French for the rest of her life. She wanted a nice, reasonable man who would let her control her own world.

She was through having people tell her what she wanted. She wanted an affair with Ethan. She'd walked away from that casino all those years ago with nothing more than a tattoo to show for her efforts. This time, she wouldn't stop until she'd tattooed herself on that man's memory.

A man who looked like more than an avalanche of dirt and boards had crashed onto his shoulders. Waiting around like delinquent children for their boss to arrive obviously didn't sit well with Ethan. By the time Clyde had pulled them from the mine and they'd checked in with ARIES, Hatch had already been airborne.

Ethan rolled a stoneware mug of coffee between his hands. "About last night in the greenhouse, about what happened a couple of hours ago."

Kelly halted her rocker. "Ethan—"

"Let me talk." He set the steaming mug aside. "I want to apologize for taking advantage of the situation."

"There's nothing to apologize for. There were two of us down there." Even the memory sent fresh shivers through her, and more than a tinge of embarrassment. "Even if only one of us finished."

A smile picked at the corner of his mouth. "Still, I know you haven't spent time undercover. When you're working a deep cover 24/7, it's easy to get caught up in the act."

He thought she was that gullible? That she didn't even recognize her own feelings? "Pretense becomes reality?"

"Something like that."

Maybe he spoke from experience, a thought that stung more than the scrapes from falling down a hundred-foot slope. "So you always roll around on greenhouse floors and abandoned mines with your partners, James Bond style, and I shouldn't let myself get carried away."

Irritation stamped his lean face. "That's not what I meant."

"What did you mean?"

"Just that I know it happens."

"To you?"

He stared at his hands, hands that had brought her such an incredible release. Silence echoed in the paneled room. The fire crackled in the grate, a log popped, snapping in two to release a shower of sparks. "We're already friends. I think that makes us both more susceptible."

A blaze of renewed hope glowed to life in her with more warming power than the heater vent pumping underneath the dormant potbelly stove. "So you haven't—rolled around with your partners before."

His head jerked up until he pinned her with a laser-blue stare. "No. You're special, damn it. Is that what you wanted to hear? Well, there it is. I tell myself I'm too old for you and an honorable man would leave you alone. But damned if being honorable has ever been my strong suit."

He flung his head back, eyes closed. "Judas-freaking-priest, woman, you've blown my concentration to hell and back with no more than your voice for two years."

Two years? Those words opened the door on a possibility she hadn't considered, one she wasn't sure she wanted to ponder because it rocked her. Scared her.

His eyes iced into the determined agent who never gave ground. "But does that mean I plan to do anything about it? No. No. And hell no. Because you *are* my friend, and I know a relationship with me is the last thing you need. If I were even a relationship kind of guy. Which I'm not."

She couldn't stop herself from asking, "Why would that be?"

He plowed his hands through his hair. "For some damned reason I can't fathom, women seem to think when a man says he isn't the marrying sort, that becomes an invitation to prove him wrong.''

With a few words he had slammed that door shut again and she refused to acknowledge a sting of loss. She had her personal and professional wishes clearly lined up in her mind, and she wouldn't let Ethan Williams distract her from any of them.

''Marrying sort? You actually think I'm expecting you to whip some princess-cut diamond out of your pocket?'' She let her snort of disbelief roll free and reveled in being the one to surprise him for a change. ''Believe me, if I go fishing in your pocket, it won't be for a wedding ring.''

Chapter 10

Ethan choked. Coughed. Struggled for air.

What else could he do with words like Kelly's pinging around in his head? Sizzling through him like embers taking flight from the fireplace.

Demanding that he finish what they'd started in the mine.

He tipped back in his chair, as if that might give him some much-needed distance, and studied her through narrowed eyes. Fading rays of sun through the window speckled over her, highlighting every exhausted line, every smudge.

And every ounce of her determination sparking from her eyes with more vibrancy than the display cases of gems littering the walls.

She wanted him. He wanted her. So why the hell was he so pissed off at her statement?

Kelly had obviously decided to find someone with experience to relieve her of her virginity with no ties. Well, hell. There were men out there who would leap all over that offer. *He* should leap all over her.

Instead he wanted to shake her, tell her not to sell herself so short. She deserved better than that. Better than him. "What do you mean you don't want a ring? Don't you want to get married and have kids some day?"

Damn. Damn. Damnation! He needed to shut the hell up before he landed himself in a monkey suit, chowing down wedding cake. He'd been tied into more knots than a rope on a Boy Scout field trip. And all by one woman.

He would zip his yap shut—as soon as he heard why someone as giving as Kelly didn't want to settle down with a happily-ever-after of her own. If that bastard professor of hers had scarred her so much... Ethan cut the thought short before it fired the red haze of anger in his brain again. "Well, Kelly?"

"Of course I want to get married. And I'd love to have children of my own." Her face softened with a timeless Madonna glow that warmed the room.

He searched for the answer and wondered why it had become so important to know. "You want to have your career first?"

"I understand I'll need to stay out of the field during pregnancy." She tucked the Aztec blanket under her chin and kicked the rocker into motion again as if already soothing her first baby to sleep. "But afterward, I don't see any reason I can't do both."

Ethan disagreed with her there. "Field agent work is dangerous. What if you left a family behind? What if someone threatened you?"

She cocked a gently arched brow, her rocker creaking against the wooden floor. "Abiding by that logic, no cop, firefighter, lawyer or military person could ever get married."

Bingo. He found the hole in her argument about no ring. "So you *are* ready for a ring."

She shrugged.

He enjoyed three seconds of smug satisfaction. Until realization sucker-punched him with a brutal blow to his pride—and some deeper part of his emotions he didn't want to consider. "You just don't want to marry me."

Kelly picked fuzz balls off the blanket. "You said it yourself, Ethan. You're not marriage material. Don't worry. You're off the hook." Her hands fell to her lap. Her spine straightened until the woolen blanket fell from her shoulders. "But I want you to be my first. I trust you, and you want me. Let's have an affair."

"No." *Yes. Yes. Yes!* his libido insisted.

Frustration puckered her dirty brow. "You sleep with women all the time without commitment. Why not me, too?"

He commanded his brain to take over before his body accepted her offer. With the scent of her still on him, not that he could ever erase it from his memory, he would be damned lucky to get out of here with his pants zipped. "Do you really think we could have a no-strings affair, Kelly? I don't know about you, but I have no intention of throwing away two years of friendship."

"Haven't we already done that?" She tossed aside the blanket and crossed to kneel at his feet. Her hands fell to rest on his knees. "I want to have something to show for it."

Damned if she wasn't right, and the thought bit. Too much.

He struggled for something, anything to keep distance between them. Control slipped a little further away every time she put those soft hands on him. The warmth of her touch filtered through his jeans to his skin. If she inched even a hint higher, he would lose it. He would toss her on her back and finish. He had to protect her from making a mistake.

And sex with him would be a colossal mistake. He wouldn't be able to walk away from her. He had enough trouble pushing her away after just kissing her, touching her. If he slipped inside her, he could damned well lose himself in Kelly Taylor for good.

If he hadn't already.

Pure panic slapped him like a cold palm. He could love this woman. This woman who wanted to throw herself into a career full of daily risks and evil he understood too well. The realization popped sweat along his brow.

Hell, he wasn't just the wrong man for her. She was the wrong woman for him, and not because of her innocence.

He didn't want to love anyone like that again, not after he'd barely survived losing Celia. He most definitely didn't want to love Kelly, not now. Maybe if she still worked in her cubicle and kept herself safe. Maybe.

Meanwhile, they needed distance. Fast. He had to get through the next few days with his sanity intact. Then he could volunteer for an assignment somewhere in the far reaches of the universe.

Where he would sit and worry about Kelly.

For now, he had to wade through the next three days with enough mental distance to keep Kelly from getting killed by some screw-up of his own.

Ethan tossed out the first argument that came to mind to keep Kelly safe from the greatest threat of all. Him. "Maybe you're capable of seeing this mission through in spite of how we..." he searched for a safe word, any word other than the one pounding at his brain, "...feel about each other, but I'm not risking it. You mess with my mind, and I can't afford that right now. You said back in the mine that you've got more to lose here. I wouldn't be so sure of that."

Kelly studied Ethan through narrowed eyes and wondered what churned around in that gorgeous dark head of his. No doubt, he was running scared. And rather than upsetting her, it sent a rush of feminine power tingling all the way to her grit-filled hair.

What excuse would he roll out to protect her this time?

She sank back on her heels, her hands falling to her lap. "What do you mean?"

He hesitated so long she wondered if he would answer

her. He toyed with the old rotary phone on the dormant potbelly stove beside him. "I told you my parents died in a car accident."

His choice of topics stilled her. "Yes, I remember." She remembered every word this man had ever said to her, knew she always would. Could she be as indelibly stamped on his memory?

"That isn't the whole story." He scrubbed a hand along the scrape on his cheek. "There was a kidnapping attempt made on me. It went to hell during the car chase and my parents died."

The chill from the wood floor and his words seeped into her. Thoughts of seduction faded. He'd only been five years old. What must those young eyes have seen? How much had he understood? Regardless of how much he consciously remembered, the loss of his family would have scarred a part of his soul. Combined with losing his fiancée, my God, no wonder the man had fears about the danger of his job. He understood too well what it was like being the one left behind.

"How awful for you." She twisted her hands in her lap to keep from touching him, regretting that her bold approach had robbed her of offering a comfort she would once have given him easily. This assignment and their out-of-control attraction had damaged, if not ruined, their friendship. The years stretched out ahead of her with a strange pall without him in the picture.

Ethan scrubbed a hand along his five o'clock shadow that had slipped somewhere closer to a seven o'clock beard. "The guy in the other car died, too. I've always been told my au pair, Iona," a tic twitched his eye at the mention of the name, "was responsible for selling information, and that she died along with the other driver. Now, it seems there was more to it."

As if that wasn't enough. "How did you find out?"

"Hatch has more information on my parents' deaths. For some reason, the CIA was involved in the investigation.

That information is mine when this case is finished." His elbows on his knees, he leaned toward her. "I want it, Kelly. More than anything. I have to know the rest of what happened that day."

The intensity of his need seared her. She'd focused on her own goals in this investigation, never once considering why Ethan might be so driven. "Of course you do."

"I've tried to find out what I could on my own, but without whatever Hatch has, I'm stuck."

A dangerous thought entered her mind. "You've tried to find out on your own?"

"On my own time."

"Oh, I didn't doubt that." How long had he known? Her sympathy for him began a slow disintegration. "Did you ever consider asking me for help?"

"No."

"Of course not." The rush of surviving their fall into the mine, the afterglow of what they'd shared faded as reality intruded. They'd worked together for almost two weeks and still he didn't value what she had to offer.

Maybe her anger had more to do with the sting of rejection and a physical frustration bordering on pain. Her voice rose and she didn't bother reining it in. "I have access to things in that office. Believe it or not, I'm actually damned good at chasing a paper trail."

"Well, yippee for you." Anger seeped into his rising voice. "And did you ever think of telling me about that…" his jaw flexed, "…pervert in your past? I'm actually damned good at creep-chasing."

"No," she conceded, begrudgingly. She hated hanging out her old hurts for the world to see, especially when she'd been trying hard to stay on her toes for her first field assignment. "I didn't."

"Guess that doesn't say much about our so-called friendship, does it?"

"Guess not," she snapped.

So much for the afterglow. She took slow deep breaths to keep from hyperventilating on the anger and hurt.

"He's still out there, Kelly." Ethan plowed a hand through his hair, dislodging a shower of dust. "What if he's the one responsible for all these 'accidents'?"

The thought paralyzed her for three heartbeats. Then she remembered she wasn't the same person she'd been then. Her frustration mushroomed. "It's not likely after all this time, but I'll look into that possibility when we're out of here. If so, I'll take care of it."

He grabbed her shoulders. "Like hell you will!"

"Like hell *you* will!" She wouldn't back down.

"If you think just because we—"

The door creaked open—admitting the boss himself. ARIES Director Samuel Hatch strode into the room, followed by Clyde.

She cut off the flow of angry words begging to pour out and rose to her feet in the slow glide Eugenie had taught her for commanding a room. "Good evening, sir."

"Taylor," he nodded to each of them, "Williams. I'm glad my trip out was precipitate and that you're both all right." He shrugged out of his trench coat, shaking snow free.

Clyde tugged at his beard. "Sorry to be an alarmist. Those old instincts die hard. Never know who's out there wanting to put a slug in your back."

Kelly's mind filled with images brought on by two years worth of working files about cases such as Clyde would have seen. Like the one that had taken him out of the CIA. Yes, those experiences would mark a person even fifteen years after quitting the job. And she'd signed on for that.

A high price she was willing to pay. But was there something to what Ethan said about not asking a family to take on the same burden?

Clyde passed her a stack of clothes with a bar of soap and a travel-sized shampoo on top. "I rustled up some clean clothes for you, ma'am. Water heater's all fired up, too.

Y'all can take turns with the shower. Sorry the other water heaters are off in the other cabins for the winter, so there's just the one.'' He pointed with his finger stub. ''Come with me and I'll show you the way.''

Kelly looked from Ethan to Hatch, feeling too much like a shuffled-aside piece of office furniture.

Hatch nodded reassurance her way. ''It's okay, Taylor. We can't talk here anyway. We'll have a more formal debrief on the return flight where it's secure.''

''I look forward to it.'' Kelly backed toward the door, Ethan's eyes meeting hers with none of the warmth or smiles she'd come to recognize, yearn for, the past two years.

She'd botched it big-time.

Kelly turned her back on what she didn't want to see, but couldn't escape. She'd valued their easy friendship, every moment together over the past two years feeding that ridiculous crush. And now she had to face that it had all been an illusion. Some kind of shallow relationship with no basis in honesty or trust.

What kind of person did it make her that she'd wanted nothing more than something so shallow? And what kind of person did it make her now that she would run from the possibility of pushing for anything more?

She'd justified her desire to sleep with him by claiming ''friendship.'' Now she was forced to face two options. Either she was the kind of woman out for sex and sex alone, a thought that unsettled her by what it said about her and the way she would be using Ethan.

Or she truly had some deeper feelings for him, beyond any silly crush.

And that more than unsettled her, because where did it leave her if she was falling for a man who'd been too hurt to ever fall again?

''I want Kelly off the case before she gets hurt.'' Ethan planted his feet on the plank floor and tried like hell to ignore the sound of water shooshing in the background.

Kelly.

In the shower.

The water pipes moaned in the paneled walls. Ethan echoed the sentiment.

Hatch hung his trench coat over a hook on the wall. "Oh, really? Want to tell me why?"

Ethan paced around the rustic room, adrenaline surging, in need of an outlet. "She's had a few too many accidents lately for my comfort level."

"So you've reported. More than once." Hatch nodded, making his way around a sofa to take up residence in the rocker. "Are you saying she's not capable of carrying off this mission?"

Guilt pinched Ethan hard as he thought back to the way he'd questioned Kelly's capability nearly two weeks ago in Hatch's office. "No. Not at all. She's been a surprisingly quick study." Well, hell, he'd be talking her into a promotion into a war zone before long. "I'm more concerned that all these accidents are too coincidental."

The director steepled his fingers against his mouth. "Do you have direct evidence that your cover has been compromised?"

Even one busted cover could sound a death knell to time in the field. Once word leaked out, he couldn't work undercover ops anymore. Neither could she.

Then he could have Kelly.

Except he didn't have the right to steal from her a life he knew she wanted. A life he had been called to live himself. He would resent anyone who took that from him.

A rogue memory whispered of times Celia had begged him to give up agency work, and the risks he'd faced then had been nothing to the ones he saw now in ARIES. Her tender pleadings had torn him in two.

And frustrated the hell out of him.

Ethan scooped Kelly's blanket from the floor and pitched it in the other chair. "There's no concrete indication."

"Well, son, I hate to point out the obvious, but this is what you do. Bag the bad guys. Your job has risks. Taylor knew what she was signing on for. Do you have any thoughts on persons outside the scope of this operation who could be responsible for the incidents?"

"There was a professor who…" Ethan scrubbed a hand over his jaw, steadied his breathing, searched for some of the professional objectivity that had carried him through missions in the past. "Who attacked her in grad school."

Hatch stared back, no hint of surprise showing in his eyes. Ethan stopped pacing beside the stone mantle. "You knew?"

A ghost of a smile flickered across Hatch's face. "I know everything there is to know about all of my people."

Of course he did. Operatives abandoned rights to personal privacy when they signed on with ARIES. He should have realized the same applied for everyone in ops support, as well. The job might come with certain losses of personal freedom, but it also came with some hefty connections and Ethan intended to use them now. "I want him put away."

Hatch's perceptive eyes probed Ethan until he wondered if the old man knew him better than he knew himself. Finally, Hatch released Ethan from the visual interrogation. "Don't you think that's Taylor's call to make?"

"She did what she could. Now I'm going to do what I can. With or without your help, sir."

Hatch nodded. "I'll see what I can do."

"Thank you." A look of understanding that transcended age passed between them, and Ethan could see himself in Hatch, thirty years into the future.

Jaded but not broken. Driven. Alone.

The creak of the water pipes increased until the shooshing sound of water stopped. Ethan turned to leave.

"Williams." Hatch pushed to his feet. "Is there anything else I should know?"

Talk about caught between a rock and a gem mine. If he told of their involvement, it could look bad for Kelly, especially rough at the start of her career.

Ethan opted for the obvious. The truth. His truth. "I've stepped over the line. I've become emotionally involved and it's screwing with my judgment."

The director's face stayed blank. "And Taylor?"

Ethan shook his head. "She doesn't know how I feel. And believe me, sir, she's not looking for a wedding ring from me."

A fact that still jabbed his pride.

"Hmm." Hatch stood. Grabbing a fireplace poker, he prodded the embers in the grate. "And what about you?"

Ethan ignored the question. "I want her reassigned. Let her work surveillance. She's trained well. But my gut tells me things are off-kilter with this one and I want her out of the line of fire."

Hatch replaced the poker and faced Ethan. A calculating look narrowed his eyes. "What if I told you I'll take her off the assignment, but you'll lose access to the file on your parents' murder. What would you say to that?"

Ethan swallowed down a wad of regret and gave the only answer he could. "I'd say okay."

Those probing eyes stabbed clear to Ethan's soul and for once, he let someone look inside him if it would keep Kelly safe. A log fell, popped in the silence.

"Nice try, Williams. But she stays."

"You don't believe me?"

"Oh, I believe you. That answer told me plenty, as if I didn't already know." He closed in on Ethan. "Do you really think I was that clueless about the two of you when I paired you for this assignment? You overestimate yourself, son, and that's far more dangerous than any out-of-control hormones."

Hatch backed a step. "You're the team for this op. People work with partners they're attracted to every day. Do you think you're the only one it's happened to? I can personally guarantee you're not.''

Surprise over the rare peek into Hatch's personal life stilled Ethan for two clicks of the pendulum on the cuckoo clock before he tugged his thoughts back to the problem at hand. Ethan sifted through those thoughts for the words that would force the issue of removing Kelly from the line of fire.

Hatch held up a hand. "Hold on a moment, son. If you push me and I have to move her to another aspect of this assignment, she's going to have someone else watching her back. Do you really trust anyone else to do as good a job keeping her alive?''

So much for being the most Machiavellian guy on the block. Hatch had him beat by a mile. "You win.''

"No. Let's pray Alex Morrow wins.'' Hatch grabbed his trench coat from the hook and draped it over his arm. He paused at the door. "Williams?''

"Yes?'' Ethan turned to look at his mentor, not daring to hope he'd be given a reprieve for Kelly.

"About your parents...you never needed that file from me.''

Ethan frowned. "Sir?''

"Ask your *aunt* about your parents.''

"I already have.''

"Ask her again.'' Hatch's hand twisted the knob and opened the door to the rest of the shop...and to a host of new questions. With no answers. And no closer to getting Kelly any further away.

Chapter 11

Kelly swished her feet through the pedicure soak, wishing her worries could dissolve as easily as the scented beads in the bubbling water.

She sat in the spa chair, the mauve and crystal decor a far cry from the Snip and Curl her mother frequented. The bite of chemicals in the air, however, Kelly recognized well.

Adjusting the heat level on her chair, she wriggled to get comfortable. Cellophane wrapped around her hair while thoughts of Ethan wrapped around her mind. She'd been so proud of the way they'd pulled together a comprehensive security plan with other agents and some ingenuity from the Marines.

Instead, she'd missed a basic element. They couldn't slice away their emotions from the job, and the price Ethan would pay was so much higher than her own if they failed.

The flight back from North Carolina with Hatch the evening before had been blessedly short and filled with discussion of the security measures in place for the ball.

Only two days away.

What would happen afterward?

She sniffled, dragging her wrist under her nose. She wasn't crying, damn it. All the chemicals from other clients were just stinging her eyes.

Yeah, right. She needed to shut down those emotions and couldn't seem to find an ounce of the cool distance Ethan had donned since they left the mine. He needed a real partner, not someone playing out a Nancy Drew Nabs a Hardy Boy fantasy.

She glanced beside her to make sure Eugenie hadn't seen the momentary weakness. The older woman reclined unmoving in her pedicure chair beside Kelly, green cream smeared across her face and a fabric mask over her eyes.

Eugenie had insisted on some serious pampering at Peter's spa and salon after work, vowing the dank mine air could do irreparable damage to Kelly's skin and hair. Kelly had almost kissed the woman's clog-clad feet in gratitude for giving her some much-needed distance from Ethan after a day of terse exchanges at the computer console.

Only two more days and "Cinderella" time would be over. No more dancing lessons. No more torturous seaweed treatments.

No more hot-chocolate chats with Aunt Eugenie.

Aunt?

Eugenie. Eugenie Williams, Kelly reminded herself. Not her aunt, even if she had treated Kelly's feelings with more insight and sensitivity than even a blood relative.

Kelly scratched a finger along the cellophane twisted around her hair. Even though the thing itched like a son-of-a-gun, she appreciated how Eugenie had kept the changes gradual, giving her a chance to become accustomed to each one so she never felt awkward or exposed. A simple trim and conditioning the first time. This time, she'd opted for layers and a cellophane wrap Eugenie vowed would enhance the color without changing it.

Not bad.

Except she had to spend an hour looking like a creature

from outer space to achieve the effect. Kelly crossed her eyes at her own alien image staring back at her from the mirror across the salon.

A door to one of the back rooms swung open, admitting three smocked workers followed by Peter holding two glasses of wine. Smiling and intuitively silent, he placed the crystal wine glasses beside both women, before turning to instruct a stock boy unloading bath beads.

If only life really was this simple.

It would be. For the next few minutes, she would take the Eugenie-road and live in the moment.

Eugenie swirled her feet in the water with a contented sigh. Her hand lifted and fell to rest on top of Kelly's with unerring accuracy. She squeezed.

Kelly squeezed back. "What?"

"Just an old woman reassuring herself again that you're all right."

Kelly patted Eugenie's hand. "I'm fine. And I would never call you old."

"Smart girl." Flipping the mask up, Eugenie sat straighter. "But I'm afraid I'm feeling my age today. Brushes with mortality in the young do that to a person."

"The park owner sent up an alarm before we even had a chance to suffer from mild frostbite." The body heat combusting from her and Ethan had more than compensated for any chill.

"My age provides a host of thoughts on what could have happened on your way down."

Those awful first moments spent wondering if Ethan had been hurt rolled through her mind in a nauseating wave. Their two hours in the mine would have been so very different if she'd been trapped with an injured Ethan.

Or heaven forbid… She shuddered.

Eugenie's grip tightened on Kelly's fingers a final time before her hand returned to her lap. "Once a person has lived through a next-of-kin police notification, she never gets over fearing another."

"I'm so sorry we worried you." Again, those moments of fear for Ethan kicked through her mind, painfully, lending importance to a man she needed to get over.

"I never expected to lose my brother like that. And his wife. It was too much." Eugenie drew in a shaky breath and shook her head. "No. I take that back. Losing Ethan, as well, would have been too much."

Kelly caved. Maybe it was the soothing effect of the footbath, or the lulling strains of classical guitar, or just the lingering remains of her long-term infatuation, but she wanted to know more about Ethan.

And this woman was the best source of information. "Is Ethan like his father?"

"Good Lord, no. My brother was a banker. I vow the man probably had sex with his tie on." Chuckles rumbled through Eugenie until the green facial mask threatened to crack.

Kelly couldn't help but join in, all the while envying this woman's ability to keep life light, uncomplicated. Happy.

Eugenie's face softened beneath her mudpack. "But I loved him."

"Of course you did." She never doubted her parents' love even though their goals for her differed from her own.

"No doubt they're up there in heaven wincing over the way I brought up their boy." She rolled her eyes, her hands smoothing wrinkles out of her tangerine caftan. "But I did the best I could. Believe it or not, I even settled down a bit. I was quite the world traveler before."

"As opposed to now?" Good God, the woman must have been a party animal. Kelly smiled as Peter knelt to dump a fresh capful of crystals into her footbath, then the older woman's, as well.

Eugenie leaned closer to Kelly. "I was a real hottie, too."

Peter smiled up from the footbath. "You still are, Miss Eugenie."

"Why thank you, Peter." She winked, then waited until he rounded the corner into the back room, before continuing,

"He used to have a crush on me, followed me around like a lost puppy. He was all of twenty back then, and I had no inclinations to be his Mrs. Robinson. Besides, I was still nursing a broken heart."

Kelly definitely didn't want to talk about broken hearts at the moment. "What's to stop you now?"

Eugenie's eyes twinkled with a light identical to the one Ethan used to flash so often. "There's a risqué streak in you after all. Having an affair with my masseur, who happens to be fifteen years my junior, would certainly rattle the social set."

"That it would."

Hair dryers and chatter filled the silence between them.

Kelly watched a woman across the salon whip out a wallet full of pictures and couldn't stop herself from asking, "What was Ethan like as a child?"

If Eugenie started with matchmaking ideas, no doubt they would be doused soon anyway. And Kelly wanted as many memories as she could store to take with her when she left.

"What was Ethan like as a child? Intense. All motion. Probably hyperactive, slightly dyslexic. A real handful, and most schools didn't offer much in the way of enlightened compensation for those things back then."

Kelly churned the new layers to Ethan in her mind. She should have recognized the signs. The way he learned better verbally. Always preferred the computer to the written word. Even the surplus of books on tape in the floorboards of his car.

That the sound of her voice had wrecked his concentration for two years. The heady notion tingled all the way to her wrapped roots.

"Many people at the schools we tried saw him as a troublemaker. But he had the most incredible ability to think outside the box, even then. Yes, his imagination took flight in pranks, but never anything dangerous."

Kelly couldn't help but think of how Ethan had orchestrated such an inventive plan for security at the embassy ball. Wrangling a joint operation with the Marines to implement their nonlethal weapons for use in crowds had been inspired. And using Carla Juarez as a liaison so Ethan remained anonymous added to his brilliance. They might well never have to resort to the back-up firepower in place.

Experience counted and Ethan's had shown on this mission.

Eugenie reached for her crystal wine glass, sipping gingerly before sagging back into the leather massage chair. "One winter, he slipped out and jammed sticks into all the neighborhood's electric gates so they wouldn't open. The next morning, dozens of men and women in suits climbed out of their cars in the cold and glared at my house."

That part of Ethan, she recognized. Kelly could almost see him smirking from the bushes.

"He never confessed his reason for doing it, but I always suspected it was his revenge against the country-club crowd for the way they snubbed their noses at me when I moved back to Virginia. I'd chosen to leave the fold and they were going to make me work to earn their acceptance."

The image of Ethan as a child shifted to a youthful avenger, the man who'd taken on the world's injustices. She couldn't help but wonder how many other times she'd misjudged his bad-boy actions.

Suddenly, she wanted Aunt Eugenie to stop. The reckless Ethan was much easier to resist than this boy-turned-man she was learning about. But Eugenie was a mama-figure on a roll about her child and Kelly didn't stand a chance of stopping her.

"He never liked school much. Too many rules and constraints. I tried the best prep schools. His tie always found its way onto one of the statues of saints in the garden."

The grin cracking the crust on Eugenie's face told Kelly Ethan probably hadn't been reprimanded too harshly.

"After Ethan's third expulsion, I gave up on the formalized education route. I soon realized if I wanted any peace, I had to keep him busy. I hired tutors and we traveled. He did better with hands-on learning. So I made life one big field trip. Which suited me fine, since then I could travel without feeling guilty for uprooting a child.''

''It sounds like a wonderful way to grow up.'' One she herself would have wanted. How would her own parents have reacted to a rebellious child? Somehow she doubted they could have been as accommodating had she been the one with the learning disability.

''I must not have done too badly because he was accepted into the University of Chicago. He didn't graduate with honors...not by a long shot. But he finished on time from a prestigious school. He's grown into a fine man, if I do say so myself.''

Maternal pride radiated from Eugenie over the man Ethan had become. Not the grades. Not even his job. But the person. Kelly loved her parents, yet couldn't help but hope she would be able to model this woman's parenting style. Someday.

What kind of father would Ethan make?

Images of him building forts with children in the middle of the sculptured garden filled her mind. Sounds of their laughter echoed.

She shut those thoughts down before they could grow roots in her brain. Kelly peered in the mirror at her alien image covered in plastic wrap and hair solutions for a bracing reality check. ''You should be proud.''

''I am.''

''I would imagine it's a comfort that he decided to stay on here living with you.''

Eugenie peeked out of one eye at Kelly. ''Dear, you misunderstand. He chose to let me stay. Everything became his once he turned twenty-one. Up until then, I was simply the executor.''

And he lived above the garage? Her interrogation gig took a surprise turn—not necessarily for the better.

She leaned back and half listened as Eugenie rolled out another story of Ethan the Neighborhood Menace. She didn't know what to do with all these new images of Ethan. Stories and vulnerabilities—and yes, imperfections—that made him all the more human. Not some bad-boy Adonis dazzling her before he blew out of town again.

This was a man.

And damned if he wasn't even more appealing in a way that made her envision rings and babies and all those things Ethan insisted weren't in his plans.

Yet, she couldn't stop herself from listening.

And dreaming.

Ethan roared into the garage, sliding his Jag in beside Cook's Beetle and the wall, his aunt's empty space gaping two cars down. Shutting off the engine, he worked the peppermint stick to the side of his mouth, flipping a second one between two fingers, leftovers from his and Kelly's day in North Carolina.

Frustration itched through him, thanks to too much unfinished business, first with Kelly, then Hatch's bizarre references to Aunt Eugenie.

At least Hatch had already reassured him Kelly's old professor was currently ensconced in an alcohol rehab, so he couldn't have been responsible. But who was?

Tension stretched within Ethan. Something had to give.

Just as he reached for his keys, the garage door hummed to life, cranking open again. His aunt's Mercedes pulled into the empty spot.

The passenger door swung open, two very feminine legs swinging out. Brown leather thigh boots wreaked hell on his libido.

Kelly had obviously found her own mark to place on Aunt Eugenie's fashion advice. She never wore heels, always opting for flats, but in a way that brought a new flash to her clothes. Boots skimmed up slim legs to a dress hem that hiked well above the knee as she scooched out of the car. Kelly stood, her wool coat swinging around her hips.

Why the hell did it take a grown woman so long to stand

and shake her dress back down to a decent length? Kelly
swept her hand down the loose-fitting slinky sweater dress.
Nothing fancy, but the brown dress had hints of gold shim-
mering in the fabric when she moved.

And she was moving too much.

Her hair glided with each turn of her head like some
shampoo commercial and it made him crazy. All of it. The
whole package. The whole woman. There wasn't anything
he hadn't already noticed before the accessories, but the
confidence in the tilt of her chin...

That was new.

Sexy as hell.

And he'd found her mighty hot before. Never would he
forget the scents and sounds of her pleasure in the mine. He
sat in his car and watched her and wanted her and couldn't
decide if his decision to stay put was born of selflessness
or cowardice.

He didn't need his window down to hear. And he listened.
Couldn't make himself stop eavesdropping just for the pleasure of hearing Kelly's voice.

Another damned blot on his already freaking opaque
character. Ethan clicked the peppermint stick to the other
side of his mouth.

His aunt stepped from the driver's side, no chauffeur for
her today. "Then there was the summer he learned to hot-
wire the neighborhood security systems so he could slip into
garages."

Gee, thanks, Aunt Eugenie. He slouched in his seat like
the guilty adolescent he'd been all those years ago.

Kelly shuffled shopping bags in her hands. "Oh, no,
please don't say he—"

"Of course not." Eugenie slammed the door. "He
couldn't drive yet. He was only twelve."

"So what was he doing?"

"Shoving bananas in tailpipes. The auto club made a fortune that day on all those stalled $100,000 vehicles."

Kelly's laughter bubbled free like French champagne. Sitting in his car, Ethan let it pour over him until it made him drunk with wanting her.

Her laughter dissipated, not that his desire for her faded in the least. His aunt stopped at the door. "Kelly, run on in without me. I left something in the car."

"Let me help."

Eugenie waved her away with a jeweled hand. "No need to wait for me. You go on inside."

"Okay, then. See you in a bit." The door clicked shut after her.

"Ethan," Eugenie called without the least question in her commanding tone.

Busted. He opened the door. "Yeah, Aunt Eugenie."

"You can come out of the car now."

Hatch should sign her on. Ethan stepped out. He never could run a damn thing past her. Thank God she hadn't been the rigid sort or he'd have been packed up and sent off to boarding school by seven.

He swung the car door closed. Now seemed as good a time as any to have that conversation with her and find out what Hatch had meant back at the mine.

Ethan called over the car, "The banana thing was funny, you have to admit."

"Of course it was. But I couldn't tell you that. I had to be a responsible adult." She strode across the garage in a swirl of orange silk and the finest faux fur money could buy.

He would have thought she'd stolen the floor-length monstrosity off a pimp if he hadn't signed the bill. Yet his eccentric aunt somehow made it look regal. "Thank you. I know you would rather have been shoving bananas in tail pipes, too, and instead you had to be that responsible adult for a kid who wasn't even your own."

Her smile creased lines on her face he knew he'd put there from worry.

She patted his cheek. "Oh, you're wrong there. You're very much my own."

An odd burn started in his brain. Hatch's words twisted through Ethan's mind. The strange emphasis on the word *aunt*. She couldn't mean her words literally.

Could she?

Not that it should be earth-shattering. She'd been his mother for almost as long as he could remember.

Regardless, his aunt harbored some kind of secret that he needed to know and now seemed the perfect time. Ethan forced his stance to stay loose, relaxed, in spite of the tightly coiled tension in his gut. "Am I your biological son?"

Eugenie's blue eyes, so like his, widened. She pressed a bejeweled hand to her heart while Ethan waited for her to catch her breath or gather her thoughts. His own heart thudded more than he would have expected. He told himself it didn't matter either way.

She gave him a tender smile along with a slight shake of her head. "No, you're very much your parents' offspring. Your mother had the labor from hell to get you here, difficult boy that you've always been."

"Okay." He processed the information and couldn't decide whether he'd wanted it to be true. Finally, he decided he was glad. Eugenie was already his mother in the ways that counted and he had to be relieved she hadn't felt the need to lie to him out of some sense of shame.

"What makes you ask now?"

She *was* lying about something, however, and he needed to know. "I'm going to ask you a question again. And this time I want the real answer. It doesn't matter to me what it is, as long as it's the truth."

Eugenie shifted her shopping bags in her hands, but stayed silent, her lack of a promise not escaping Ethan.

"What happened to my parents?" Still, she didn't speak, her face staying an oddly blank mask similar to the one he'd perfected over the years. He pushed on, determined she wouldn't stonewall him this time, "I'm days away from learning on my own, so if there's something you need to tell me, tell me now."

She stared back at him while the winter wind whistled through the eaves. She studied him with an intensity reminiscent of the time he'd asked to go white-water rafting. After consideration, she'd decided fourteen was old enough. He wondered what would concern her that much now.

Placing her bags on the hood of Cook's Beetle, Eugenie started toward Ethan. "We may not be biological mother and son, but we do share the same genetic tendencies. We're both unconventional. We love to travel." She traced a finger along the sludge-encrusted side of his Jag, leaving an indelible mark in his rudimentary field-craft tamper check. "What you don't know is that we share a common reason for why travel is so important."

Eugenie rubbed her index finger and thumb together until the dirt flaked free. "Nice trick with the car. But of course I used the same in the past. Ethan, I used to work for the same *employer* you do."

Shock rooted his feet to the cement. His aunt? Short and soft Aunt Eugenie, with her steel-gray bun and her hedonistic lifestyle?

His complete incredulity must have shown since she continued to explain, "You know the wealthy lifestyle offers the perfect cover for sliding in and out of countries. The circles our family ran in gave me entry to hearing more than you can imagine. Or maybe you can."

He could. And slowly the image of her doing the same shifted and settled with such clarity he couldn't imagine how he'd missed the possibility for so many years.

She glanced around the garage with a new edge to her eyes Ethan recognized well.

He nodded to her. "It's clean here. I sweep the garage and my rooms for bugs daily."

"Good boy," she said as if he'd brought home a clay paperweight from school. "I was recruited in my early twenties. I put in twelve good years before retirement. Not too shabby for a field operative."

A full-fledged operative. In the field. Not an entry-level

paper pusher. Those twinkling blue eyes of hers had seen the same harsh world he had. Those soft hands that had bandaged his banged-up knees had held a gun.

She'd given all that up, a job he couldn't imagine living without, to take care of him. The thought humbled him with the magnitude of the debt he owed her, beyond anything he'd imagined.

"My God, Aunt Eugenie. I'm sorry for what I cost you."

"Don't be so quick to jump to conclusions. I didn't choose to retire. Things went very wrong." She twisted her rings around her fingers, the diamonds refracting overhead lights in a disco display. "Not all branches of the CIA are squeaky clean. Thirty years ago, scientific research into genetics was just exploding onto the scene. There were so many new possibilities and the CIA needed to be on the cutting edge or the rest of the world would be there first. I had some friends in a Black Ops division called MEDUSA."

Ethan kept his face blank. ARIES fell under the MEDUSA header, the whole division and its section being given mythological names. "Friends?"

"We all started out as low-level operatives, but some were more ambitious than I was—Clyde Hanson, Samuel Hatch, Willard Croft, all went over to a secret section of MEDUSA called PROTEUS."

"Whoa. Hang on a second. You and Samuel Hatch knew each other?"

A smile flickered across her face. "Yes, Ethan. Samuel and I were…friends."

Ethan's world tilted at the implication, but then his aunt was only about five years older than his boss. Hatch's confidence about distractions from partners on the job suddenly took on a whole new complexion. "What does all this have to do with my parents?"

Eugenie smoothed back a lock of Ethan's hair as if he were ten again. "Well, there I was with my high ideals, thinking I was invincible, as all young people do. I asked the wrong questions about the genetic testing. I angered the wrong people in this country, as well as others. The next thing I knew, your parents were dead.''

A cold wad of certainty clenched in Ethan's gut. He knew too well where this was going, had heard of it happening to others, but never considered…

''The bullet in your father's head and one threatening phone call told me all I needed to know.'' Eugenie tipped her head back, staring unblinking up at the ceiling for a moment before leveling her gaze at Ethan and continuing, ''I was expected to shut up and get out, or my nephew would be next.''

The long-ago sound of that bullet popped in his memory. The swerve of the car. The lurch off the road, flipping, tumbling, his world rocking right along with it. Never quite righting itself again.

All the anger and frustration and even fear he'd felt then surged to the surface now. Renewed memories his child's mind had suppressed elbowed to be set free. He forced himself to function. ''Why didn't they just kill you?''

''Because unfortunately for my poor brother and his beautiful wife I documented what I know. It's tucked away as your life insurance. If anything happens to either of us, it goes to a friend of mine in the press.''

Ethan gripped her shoulders and tried to ignore the slight curve inward, from age or worries, he didn't know right now and couldn't afford the sympathetic distraction. ''Aunt Eugenie, you have to tell what you know. You can't keep secret something that might hurt others.''

''Says who?''

''Me.'' His grip tightened. He respected his aunt, but couldn't reconcile the shifting image of her. ''There's a code we have to live by. We may bend rules, but to protect people. Not to execute them. Whoever did this has to be stopped.''

Her jaw set with the same determination of years ago when she'd charged into his school to confront the headmaster for daring to use corporal punishment on her nephew. Ethan had hung up his tie for good that day.

Time to take another approach with her. No way would he win against that steely will if she was set on protecting him. "Okay, I understand why you felt the need to keep it secret then. You didn't know who to trust. You were alone and I was a still a child. But I'm an adult now. You don't need to protect me anymore. Whatever you know has to come out."

Her shoulders drooped another inch. She shook her head. "You don't know who you're dealing with. Even people on the inside can't be trusted."

She stepped away, swiped her bags off the hood and bolted into the house, pimp fur coat sailing behind her.

Ethan pressed his thumb between his eyes against the throbbing pressure. She couldn't mean Samuel Hatch? Ethan would trust the man with his life. Or more important, with Kelly's. But then he never would have suspected his aunt had been some Mata Hari in her day.

Or that his parents had been assassinated.

More memories long locked away blasted through his defenses in Technicolor. Of the day his parents died. The shouts. The smell of snow, gunpowder—and blood. The unleashed memories howled through his brain.

And in the middle of the hurricane, he saw one constant. One beacon of peace to reach for.

Kelly.

Kelly stretched her legs in front of her, reached, swayed, continued the constant toning motion. Tried to recapture the soothing effects of the greenhouse atmosphere. Tried inhaling the lush, transporting scents of gardenia and orchids.

With no success.

The evening of captivating stories about Ethan had taken their toll. Once clear of the garage and Eugenie Williams, Kelly had sprinted to her room for her workout clothes and a blanket. And, please Lord, some peace.

She tweaked the volume on her Walkman, but the increased sound of rushing waves did little to drown the distractions humming in her brain. Her hand gravitated to the slim chain around her neck that now held the aquamarine Ethan had bought at the mine. Sentimental. Silly. But a beautiful reminder of an incredible man. Forty-eight hours from now, she would be in the ballroom. Seventy-two hours and she would be through working with him.

Don't think about Ethan as a vulnerable, enchanting child.

Back to the ball. She gave up trying to escape into her exercise routine, instead closing her eyes and reviewing the upcoming mission. Their meetings with security liaisons, with the Marines and Secret Service. Updates with Carla Juarez and Robert Davidson, who would monitor surveillance from the ARIES war room. And of course Aunt Eugenie's requisite block of time to work her Cinderella miracle.

What would Ethan think of her?

Kelly hated the vain thought, even while a part of her thrilled at knocking the man off balance, making him regret what he'd missed. She skimmed her hands along her arms to dispel the chill of loss raising goose bumps along her skin.

Come hell or high water, she wouldn't ask him again. She might be on a quest to assert herself, but with that came a certain sense of her own worth. She deserved to be appreciated for herself. If Ethan wanted her, he would have to come begging.

What would it be like to have his hands on her and know he wouldn't stop? Or to have his eyes caress her from across the room, no-holds-barred, no reservations? Just total and complete promise?

Her skin heated as if his gaze already skimmed her every curve, the sensation so real she couldn't help but open her eyes to find—

Him. Ethan.

Standing just inside the closed doorway, he watched her,

his gaze so hot he must have negated any blast of air from outside that might have alerted her. She'd locked the greenhouse door and engaged the security system Ethan had installed. But of course he knew the code.

Even if he hadn't, he was that good at his job. She might be honing her skills, but his years of experience and natural talent gave him an edge. A dangerous and oh-so sexy edge. This Ethan she recognized well, even if she didn't know what had brought the shift back.

He jammed his hands in the pockets of his leather jacket and leaned against the door. "Tell me to go."

She might not be willing to ask him to stay, but she sure as hell wasn't going to tell him to leave.

Snowflakes glistened in his coal-black hair. "Like last time I came in here, tell me to get out. You had the right idea then."

She stayed silent.

"You know this is wrong."

Damn it, she was tired of his mixed signals and tempting half seductions. "Then go if that's what you want."

"I don't," he said, each word torn from him. "I don't want to go. But I don't always want what's right. I'm a selfish son-of-a-bitch, and one of us needs to do the right thing. Being honorable and cautious isn't my strong suit. You're the smart one. Help me out."

She was the smart one? Somehow she knew that wouldn't stop her from making a reckless decision tonight.

"Kelly, I want you so damned bad I'm shaking here. Please."

The final word rasped from him, and even though she knew he was begging her to make him go, she'd received her desired pleading. No, she wouldn't ask him to stay. But she knew what to say to guarantee he wouldn't leave.

Kelly draped her hands on her knees and met Ethan's gaze dead-on. "It's a dragon."

"What?"

"My tattoo." Her right hand trailed up her thigh until her fingers stroked a single finger in a swirl along her hip. "It's a dragon."

Chapter 12

Ethan couldn't suck in air fast enough.

He also couldn't make himself step away from the vision of Kelly lounging on a quilt, the aquamarine he'd given her swaying on a chain between breasts he ached to cup. Her hair flowed around her shoulders, temptation radiating from her warm brown eyes.

A dragon.

This woman of so many contradictions had chosen to brand herself with a dragon. Ethan surrendered to the inevitable, his defenses already in the negative numbers tonight.

"Tell me more," he demanded, shrugging out of his jacket.

Kelly arched her back in a languorous, feline stretch. "It's not very large, about two inches, and the tail curves around my hip." She scooped up her CD player and shoved to her feet, taking too damned long to dust off her bottom. "You said you had to know and now you do. Mystery solved. You're free to walk out that door."

Like hell.

If he were a better man, he would leave. But he wasn't and he couldn't, not tonight with the world shifting under his feet and this woman offering forgetfulness. He was through resisting her.

But first, he had to take care of one thing.

Ethan turned away. Kelly's light gasp of surprise behind him fueled him to move faster. He hooked his foot on a low shelf and swung himself up to the camera hidden in the corner among dangling ferns. Arm arcing back, he flung his jacket over the lens.

"How long has that been there?" Kelly called up to him.

He dropped to the ground. "Since the day after I found you in here."

She studied him through narrowed eyes, her body outlined in curve-hugging Lycra as she stood—too far away. "Have you been watching me?"

Maybe this would make her send him packing. "What do you think?"

"I think you have."

"You'd be right." He waited, certain now she would tell him to haul his sorry butt out of her greenhouse.

A slow smile curved her full lips, and she leaned one luscious hip against a table of potted flowers.

His mouth turned drier than the sack of soil beside him. "You're okay with that?"

"Of course. You were doing your job." Her eyes flicked up to his dangling jacket. "Can anyone hear?"

He shook his head. "There's no microphone. I couldn't have survived seeing *and* hearing you. Not and manage to maintain any objectivity while watching over you."

"So you were watching to keep me safe?"

"What do you think?" he repeated.

She tossed her head, hair rippling. Her lithe body exuded a newfound inner confidence in her own appeal. The whole package radiated such lush sexuality Ethan almost dropped to his knees.

Instead, he charged across the greenhouse. Five bold steps—he counted every one, begrudging each inch between them—and Ethan gathered her against him. He tasted her. No, absorbed the giving feel and flavor of her lips. Her arms flung around his neck without hesitation.

He gripped her hips, tucked her in a perfect fit between his thighs. "I gave you your chance to send me away."

She pressed closer. Hotter. "I know."

"If you ask me to stop, I will," he muttered against her lips.

"I won't ask."

Forcing himself to draw back, he stroked her hair away from her face. "Kelly, there can't be any question, not after what happened to you." He held himself apart from her, waiting. "I need to hear you ask me to stay."

"I don't want to talk about that now." She stretched up on her toes to nip his bottom lip, her soft hands gliding down his back. "Don't want to think about it."

"I know, honey, but I have to. For both of us."

She cupped his face in gentle but sure hands. "Do you have a condom tucked away anywhere?"

In his pocket, always had kept once close since the first time he'd kissed Kelly. He'd known this could happen. Would happen. "Yes."

"Then stay."

A rush of relief surged through him, quickly followed by a pulsing need to claim her. Finally. Fully. Damn the consequences. He had a truckload of regrets in his life, and he wouldn't add never knowing Kelly to the list.

He would be her first, if not her last. And he would damn well tap every ounce of restraint he possessed to make certain it was a "first" worth remembering.

Kelly watched every line of Ethan's body tense. She'd studied him long enough to know. He was coiled and ready to act. All that wonderful strength and determination would be directed at her.

He tapped the aquamarine between her breasts until it swayed gently. "Let's take this inside."

Forget delays of even a second. The cold blast of the snowy winds and outside world could too easily bring the chill of reality. She didn't want reality. She wanted her fantasy moment, her dream come to life with Ethan. "No. Here. Now. With the heat and the flowers."

A smile of wicked promise creased his face. "So you like the flowers?"

"I love flowers."

"Then you'll have flowers." Ethan's hand stroked down her arm and away.

He reached past her, returning with an orchid. With the barest whisper of a touch to her face, he trailed the bloom down her forehead, along her nose, over her lips.

"Hmmm." She inhaled, savored, smiled against the milky petals.

He tucked the orchid behind her ear. "A flower for you."

"Thank you."

"I'm not done."

She certainly hoped not.

The hard length of his body pressed her back against the edge of the wooden table. Slowly he plucked flower after flower and tossed them on the blanket.

Orchids, lilies, gardenias fluttered over her onto the puffy comforter, until finally he ended with crushed roses raining petals and perfume over her head, drifting and catching along every sensitized inch of her.

She clasped his wrist. "Ethan! Don't waste them all."

He pried his arm free and flung a fistful of daisies to their makeshift bed below. "They're mine to do with as I please, and seeing them against your bare skin would please me." His voice lowered, rumbling husky, dark, with even a hint of danger. "Very much."

Ethan draped his arm over her shoulder, drawing back until a yellow tulip grazed along her shoulder. She shivered in spite of the humid warmth of the greenhouse.

His eyes followed the tulip's trek down in a glide between her breasts. Her nipples tightened beneath her sports bra, already eager for his attention.

Ethan didn't disappoint her.

With the same finesse he managed in every aspect of life, he skimmed her top up and off without even dislodging the flower from her hair. The cold weight of the stone teased her skin. Every nerve tightened, from the brush of air or his eyes, she didn't know and couldn't scavenge the will to figure it out.

He retraced his path between her breasts, detouring lower to explore each curve, under, around. The petals kissed each pointed tip in turn, Ethan's hungry gaze devouring her. "Kelly," his hoarse voice echoed, "your breasts are so damned pretty."

Heat tingled all the way to her bare toes, but not from embarrassment. His compliment stirred a swirl of excitement. The sincerity of his words, the simple compliment, somehow seemed so much more believable to her than some lavish poetry about beauty she didn't possess and shouldn't be important.

She gripped his hands and flattened his palms to her breasts in a bolder move than she would have expected from herself on her first time. But she had to pack a lifetime of memories into the moment, in case there wasn't another with this man.

Kelly cut that thought free with the clean precision of a florist's scissors. "Finish."

A low groan rumbled up from Ethan's chest. His hands gentled against her, one sliding around to palm her back and draw her closer. His head dipped as she rose to meet him halfway. Chambray rasped a gentle abrasion against her skin.

Live for the here and now, she reminded herself. Take a page from Aunt Eugenie's book and savor the moment. Although Kelly didn't think Aunt Eugenie's plans would have necessarily included Kelly jumping her nephew in the greenhouse.

Yet was she really doing any jumping? No, she'd been too caught up in a sensual haze of allowing Ethan to take the lead. Making the most of this moment included doing everything she could imagine to bring Ethan as much pleasure as his hands on her body brought her. While she might be lacking in experience, she'd always had a fine imagination.

Kelly arched up into another kiss, gliding her hand down his chest to his jeans and palming the rigid length encased in faded denim. Even her fine imagination didn't do him justice. Her fingers explored his length, while her tongue explored the warm recesses of his mouth.

He tasted so good, like crisp, snowy air and maybe a hint of one of those peppermint sticks they'd shared. She'd dreamed of being with him, what it would be like having all that roguish experience devoted entirely to her.

Except he wasn't sending one of his wicked smiles her way now. Between deep heady kisses along her mouth, her throat, her breasts, he studied her with such somber, intense eyes. With a hint of reverence that humbled her even as he elevated her.

No, he wasn't the kick-ass bad boy from their office here. He was turning into someone she barely knew, but found no less intriguing.

Trapped between their bodies, her fingers worked the buttons on his shirt free, found the rigid planes of his chest, his stomach, finally the fly button on his jeans. He shrugged out of his shirt and kicked his jeans and boxers free with barely restrained impatience.

Reality was so much better than any of her fantasies.

Of course she never would have thought to place any of those fantasies in a greenhouse. All the same, she welcomed the haven of heat in the middle of winter.

Ethan lowered her to the blanket, flowers crushing beneath the press of their weight. A fragrant blend of perfumes clung to the humid air.

He hitched a finger in the waist of her leggings and waited until she smiled her consent. He peeled them down, one inch at a time, as if unwrapping the best Christmas present ever and enjoying every second of the process. Only once he'd tossed them aside did his gaze travel to her hip.

His low growl of approval sounded much like her dragon come to life.

"You like it?" she asked, as if she couldn't already tell from the leaping response under her hand.

A second growl offered a resounding affirmation just before his mouth lowered to kiss the tattooed patch of skin. The heat of his mouth seared her skin much as the needle had. His hand swept around, finding a purple tulip he'd rescued from somewhere. She didn't care where. Didn't care about anything but Ethan continuing.

While he rained hot kisses along her hip and her belly, he caressed the flower up the inside of her leg. Higher. Higher still.

Until.

She couldn't think at all.

The combination of the silken flower and his roughened fingers teased her into a world of sensation so intense the burn, the need, reached an almost painful clench of nerves.

And then he slid to his side, tore open the small packet and sheathed himself. Ethan kissed her once, twice. "Everything okay so far?"

She didn't want any reminders of the past. Being with Ethan had nothing to do with violence, but his concern touched her all the more. "Much better than okay."

Kelly reached for him and he rolled to his back, pulling her with him. "You're in control, Kel. Your pace. Whatever you want."

The position of command tightened her desire. Too intense. Her fingers dug into the steely wall of his chest. "I want to finish."

He guided her hips and she wasn't fool enough to reject the tutelage. He eased her down, slowly. The full, thick pressure giving her momentary pause, the stretch stinging until she tensed. She didn't want pain to play any part in their time—

Ethan's hands worked a gentle massage against her hips. "That's it, hon. Easy. You're almost there."

And she was. The stinging eased, her years of limber meditation paying off.

She looked down at Ethan. Tendons in his neck strained with his effort to hold back while he waited for her and she fell a little bit more in love with him. Maybe a by-product of the moment, but she couldn't pull up the will to stem her emotions for once.

So she smiled at him and moved against him, coaxing him to join her. No holding back. His answering smile painted itself on the back of her lids as her eyes slid closed and she savored. Man, did she ever savor every stroke. Her pleasure and his a focal point in a ritual far more mind-altering than what she'd stepped into the greenhouse seeking.

If only they could achieve the same synchronicity with their clothes on.

She squeezed her eyes shut against thoughts that would steal this moment from her. The glide of their bodies against each other, the touch of his skilled fingers, built the intensity, narrowed the focus. Tighter. Closer. Until...

The pinpoint exploded in a shower of sensation. Kelly arched against Ethan's bracing hand as wave after wave sparked through her. Each bolt of pleasure tearing a fresh cry from her. *"Mon amour. Mon jules."*

Words wrenched from her by the strength of her release. *My love. My lover.*

Again Ethan plunged upward, his deeper stroke and hoarse shout of completion triggering an afterglow through her shuddering body until she sagged against his chest.

Her words echoed back in the wind. In her heart.
Mon amour.

* * *

Ethan sprawled in a tangle of gray satin sheets, Kelly tucked against his side as he stared up through his skylight at snowflakes swirling above them in the starlit sky. He'd expected to regret being with her. But he didn't. He couldn't regret something so damned perfect, both times. Once in the greenhouse and again in his bed.

Which left him where?

About five minutes from hunting for a ring and begging her to take it.

Ethan crooked a finger in her necklace and twisted the chain around his finger. He'd known the minute he peeled those leggings down and off, the second he'd laid eyes on her dragon and slid his body into hers, that he'd taken away any choices. He'd crossed a line and there wasn't any going back.

Marrying Kelly. He let the image churn in his head but couldn't make the edges of the picture come cleanly together. Never could, a large part of why he'd never pursued her, because Kelly was undoubtedly the marrying kind. He couldn't picture what kind of future they would have and that bothered him—almost as much as the thought of letting her go.

Which was no longer an option. He knew damned well his aunt had spoiled him as a kid. Sharing had never been his strong suit, and he found now that there wasn't a chance in hell he could share this woman with any other man.

He was her first, and he damned well intended to be her last.

Which meant marrying her.

Ethan tugged her forward and kissed her with a familiarity that scared the hell out of him after only knowing her body twice. He untwined the chain and found the warm comfort of her hip beneath the sheet. "What would you have done if I hadn't had a condom with me in the greenhouse? Would you have sent me on my way?"

"No." She feathered her fingers over the bruise on his arm from the mine, then his injured shoulder blade, finally along the faint remains of the scratch from his near miss with a bullet in Gastonia. "I would have told you to follow me inside and we would have used the box in my room."

He pulled her hand away and kissed her palm as if that could erase her brush with the danger of his world. Hers, too.

He booted that thought out of his bed. Out of their bed. "Or we could have come straight to my place."

She swept her hair out of her face, revealing full, well-kissed lips. "Why don't you ever come into the house?"

"I do." He'd never be able to look at her hair swinging across her face again without thinking of sex. Incredible sex. The best sex of his life, with a virgin, no less. "What about when Jake and Matt came to dinner?"

She shook her head. "We ate by the pool. And I don't consider a glassed-in pool area a part of the house. Or the gym. I can't think of a single time you've stepped into the house since I arrived. Were you afraid I would jump you and drag you off to my boudoir?"

Her hand traveled southward.

He stopped her a second shy of her target and brought her hand up to his mouth. "Soon. Give me ten more minutes to recover."

And to get his head back together before this twenty-four-year-old, used-to-be-virgin flipped his world any more. He needed to find a fit for those edges. Soon. He couldn't do that with her hands on him and his body five seconds away from making a lie of his claim to need ten minutes. He rolled from the bed to his feet and pulled on his boxers. "Let's get something to eat."

Kelly dragged a sheet behind her and wrapped it around her naked body. "Why don't you come into the house?"

A pit bull in gray satin.

He ignored her question and charged down the stairs, the

computers from the loft above emitting a halo glow throughout the darkened apartment.

Her light tread followed. "Have you been staying away from the house because of me?"

"No." His feet padded across the chilly tile. "I don't spend much time there. It's not me. Too formal." Too many memories. "I feel like I need to put on a damned tie every time I walk through the door."

"Was that your parents' house?"

He nodded, already searching for a way to change the subject. "Aunt Eugenie and I had a talk."

Well, hell. That didn't do much for changing the subject. He yanked open the refrigerator, the light knifing through the dim room.

"About what?" Kelly dropped to a chair at the table.

He dug out a box of Chicago-style deep-dish pizza and dropped it on the table. He'd developed an addiction to the stuff in college and could use something to keep his hands busy until his mind engaged again. "About when my parents died."

"And?"

Telling her wouldn't jeopardize anything, and he didn't relish having his head ripped off again for keeping secrets. He'd explain what he could and try not to sweat the rest. "She used to do what we do." He reached into the freezer, where Kelly's ice cream had taken up residence in his kitchen the past two weeks. "Occupationally."

"No way!" Her grip loosened on the sheet.

His traitorous eyes homed in on the hint of dusky pink peeking from the sheet. "Uh-huh."

He turned to fish out a spoon before he caved to the temptation to crawl back in bed with her.

Not yet. Not until he reestablished some boundaries. While feasting on pizza instead of Kelly, he told her the rest of what his aunt had shared.

Kelly swirled her spoon in the carton of rocky road ice

cream. "So someone's still out there, responsible for issuing the order."

"If what she believes is true, then yes." He pitched the pizza crust back in the box. "And I believe her."

"Me, too." Her leg extended under the table, her foot caressing up and down his calf. "Questioning could rain down fire on your head."

"It could." He captured her foot and anchored it to his thigh. "I'll talk to Hatch in a couple of days."

"I'd like to help."

"Let me see what I'm dealing with first."

She toed his stomach.

"Ouch! That hurt, damn it."

"It was supposed to."

She dropped her foot to the ground, pinning him a look that rivaled her dragon's glare. "I know you tried to get Hatch to pull me off this case again."

Ethan closed the pizza box, stalling. Not that it helped him find a safer answer. "Did he talk to you?"

"No. It wasn't tough to figure out." She hitched her sheet higher with a dignity worthy of any Grecian goddess. "Why can't you see I don't need to be protected? You've had a chance to follow your dreams. I want to follow mine, too, and I think I've made a damned good start for twenty-four years old."

"Yes, you have—"

"Don't placate me," his pit bull in satin continued. "I may not be the most savvy agent in the DC area, but I'm holding my own. I'm advancing. I'm meeting the world on my terms and I won't let you take that away from me. My parents dictated what I did for years. I won't let anyone do the same again."

He didn't want to dictate anything. He just wanted to keep her safe. Ethan grabbed the pizza box from the table and pitched it in the trash. "There's a difference between controlling you and trying to keep you alive." He gripped the edge of the cool steel sink, his back to her, not that it erased the image of her burned in his brain. "I can't help how I feel. Mortality has taken a chunk out of my hide a few times too many for me to ignore it."

He threw his head back, staring up at the vaulted ceiling and drawing in steadying breaths.

Kelly slipped up behind him. Her arms circled his waist, her cheek falling to rest on his shoulder blade. He clasped her hands in one of his to stop her from saying something that would lead to a fight. God, he didn't want to fight with her right now.

As much as he hated dredging up the past, maybe it would make her understand so he could keep her safe. Ethan reached inside himself to find the words. For Kelly. "I have exactly three memories of my mother. I remember her tying my shoe in the front entry hall. Just a flash of time. Not much of a memory. Then there was another time we sat on a bench at the zoo. We watched the monkeys and pitched peanuts into the cage."

"Those are good memories to have." Her words whispered over his skin with warm comfort. "I'm sure she would be glad those things you did together stayed with you."

"I only mentioned two memories."

She rubbed her cheek against his back. "I know."

Ethan turned in her arms to face her. "How the hell do you get me to talk without asking?"

Shrugging, she waited in that Kelly fashion that always started him talking when a seasoned interrogator couldn't have pried a word from him. *Face reality, bud.* Somehow, she'd gotten to him, tempting him to share things with her he hadn't told anyone else.

He tucked her to his chest, his hands rubbing along her back, finding it easier to accept comfort somehow if he was the one touching. "I remember the day she died. I always told people it was a void, not unusual with accidents like that. Then I didn't have to talk about it. Made sense when

I was five. Became a habit later on. No one needed me to
fill in the blanks, since it was obvious what happened.''

Ethan buried his face in Kelly's soft hair, the scent of
roses and their lovemaking wafting up, his only grounding
in the present.

''My parents always bought the best of the best for safety
in cars. They insisted on a shoulder harness seat belt for me,
even back then. But the strap on this car came up high
against my neck. I remember my mother taking her scarf
and wrapping it around so the harness wouldn't chafe my
neck. My mother was asleep in the back. I was excited to
be up front with my father.''

Kelly stiffened in his arms, just before her hand snaked
up to his neck and soothed small circles against his skin.
He felt a tear leak from her eyes, down his chest.

He should stop. The burden was his to carry, and it was
damned selfish of him to have sought her out in the first
place. But he'd started and he knew his dragon lady would
make him finish.

Ethan lifted a strand of her hair and looped it around his
finger. ''Then there was this car beside us. I always liked
driving fast, so I wasn't afraid. I didn't really understand
until my father shouted to my mother to wake up.''

Staring at the dark strands, he lost himself in their luster
and softness. How long he spent wrapping the lock around
his finger, he didn't know, didn't care, just soaked up the
softness of Kelly to dull the edges of the past scraping at
his memory. ''Then they shot him.'' His finger crooked re-
flexively. ''The car slid off the road. Down the mountain.
Flipped, maybe four times, until it landed on the roof. My
mother didn't stand a chance.''

His finger numbed, and he realized he'd twisted the lock
of her hair too tightly. She'd never winced. Typical Kelly,
putting others first.

How much more would it cost her to be with him?

Untwining the hair, he eased her from his chest and shook
the circulation back into his finger. One hand still holding

Kelly, he stared over her head at his flickering computer screens above rather than face her tears yet. "My shoulder harness held, so I wasn't hurt. I hung from the ceiling for maybe…five minutes. Five hours. Forever. I don't know." His father hung beside him, open eyes staring unseeing. His mother lay below. Already dead. "I remember the smell of her perfume on that scarf with the seat belt tight against my neck."

He swallowed against the phantom constriction. "Still can't stand a damn necktie to this day."

Her cool fingers continued to stroke his neck, soothing the fever in his skin, almost reaching through to the memories, too. "What happened next? How did you get out?"

Ethan dug through the years. He hadn't thought much about afterward. Of course he'd only been five at the time. "There was snow outside the window, on the ground. I stared out the window at that while I waited."

He paused, an image inching its way to the surface in hazy detail.

"What?"

Holy hell. "Kelly, there were boots outside that window." He looked down into her eyes, red and puffy from crying tears over him. Something he'd vowed he would never cause.

"The rescue workers? Or someone come to help?"

He shook his head. "Any of those would have called in to me. No one spoke." The long-ago crunching of steps through the snow faded. "The boots turned and walked away."

"Ethan, you weren't the only one to survive the accident that—"

A beeping pierced the air, drifting down repeatedly from the computer loft.

Ethan jolted. Dread pierced him.

His computer. The security system. Someone had broken onto the grounds.

Shoving away from the counter, Ethan tore himself from the lure of Kelly's arms and tear-stained eyes. Hadn't he learned his lesson after Gastonia? No emotions on the job. A mistake he damned well couldn't afford to make again.

Chapter 13

Kelly sprinted up the stairs behind Ethan, the computerized alarm cutting through the air. She tripped on the tail of the sheet, stumbled, caught the banister and righted herself.

"Damn. Damn. Damn!" She yanked the satin sheet from around her foot and resumed her charge. Past his bedroom to the next level in the open computer loft. Already, Ethan sat at his desk, clicking through keys. Images on the surveillance screens shifted, flickered, focused.

Outside her bedroom door? Her door clicked closed.

But she locked it. Always.

"Hell." With a vicious shove, Ethan rolled his chair back and shot to his feet.

"Ethan!" Kelly shouted at his bare back, flinging her tangled sheet aside before chasing him. Modesty would have to take a back seat to speed and keeping Ethan from rushing headfirst into heaven-only-knew what. "Find out who it is first."

Ethan bolted toward his bedroom. "Didn't put a camera in your room out of some damned stupid sense of honor," his voice jabbed at the air, lowering as he darted into his room, "emotional crap that gets people killed."

Kelly trailed him just as Ethan jammed his legs into a pair of sweats. She yanked on her tights, grabbed one of Ethan's T-shirts from the floor.

He pulled his 9mm off the dresser. "Stay here."

"Like hell I will." She dug in the bag she'd taken with her to her workout, beneath her CD player, her hand closing around the grip of her SIG-Sauer. Her constant companion since Ethan had startled her that first time in the greenhouse.

She sped down the stairs on bare feet, through the great room, just catching the door before it swung closed after Ethan. Damn, he was fast.

She should have been on guard.

But she'd been too caught up in Ethan. Herself. How they felt together.

She tore through the garage, into the hall leading to the back stairs into the main house. He'd been so right about staying apart to keep objectivity. Now she had all those images of him as a little boy, not just the playful images, but also ones of him hanging by his seat belt for hours, staring down at his dead mother.

Had his tears fallen onto her body?

Kelly gasped past a hitch in her side that had nothing to do with running through the endless corridors or the minor aches to her newly loved body. Dimmed lights cast shadows along her path, offering cover for someone to lurk. Her hand clenched around her weapon.

Lush Persian rugs padded her steps. Framed landscapes and portraits marched along the walls, so far her only companions.

She rounded the corner. Ethan stood with his back flattened to the wall beside her door. A crystal sconce slashed yellow light across the hard planes of his face. He lifted a finger to his mouth.

As if she needed reminding.

She plastered her back to the wall on the other side of

the door, the flocked wallpaper tickling her arms. Ethan gripped the knob, turned, slowly, until the door creaked open.

Silence.

Ethan swung around into the doorway, gun drawn. Kelly's heart thudded while she waited as backup, staring at his bare chest, such a broad and vulnerable target.

Silently, he gestured all-clear. She followed him into her room, the soothing blues and pewter grays offering no comfort now.

Light sliced across the carpet in a slim line from the door to her private bathroom cracked open a couple of inches. The beam flickered across the plush carpet as someone moved inside the bathroom. A slight figure in a lime-green sweat suit hovered over the tub.

Adrenaline singed Kelly, along with a hefty kick of anger. How dare anyone break into her room? Invade her privacy?

Ethan crossed the room with pantherlike grace and silence. Before Kelly could more than blink, he kicked open the door.

The figure whipped around.

Kelly stopped. "Brittany?"

Brittany screamed.

Her hands shot behind her back. A bottle thumped to the floor. Kelly's shampoo bottle spun like a kissing game gone mad, liquid splattering the walls.

Dripping.

Eating the paint from powder-blue walls.

Kelly shivered. Suddenly the cellophane treatment didn't seem so torturous after all.

Ethan advanced, gun by his side. "What the hell's going on here?"

Brittany's belligerent gaze flicked from half-dressed Ethan to Kelly in Ethan's shirt. The teen's eyes filled and her chin quivered. "I thought you were doing your Pilates stuff."

"She was," Ethan answered, defying Brittany to argue. "And what were you doing?"

"I was helping you realize how wrong she is for you," the teen whined. Brittany collapsed to sit on the edge of the garden tub, blinking back tears. "It wouldn't have actually hurt her."

Ethan's set jaw broadcast that he wasn't as forgiving. "Like the weights? Or the Jacuzzi temperature?"

Brittany stared at the floor and flipped the corner of a bathmat with her toe.

While they were on a confessional roll, Kelly went for the whole shebang. "Did you really think you could get away with following him without our noticing?"

Brittany shrugged. "I only wanted to see where you lived when he went to pick you up that day, and maybe check out what you did sometimes. I couldn't believe it when Miss Williams announced he was bringing a woman here. So yeah, I followed you and messed with the hot tub. Big deal."

Sympathy tweaked Kelly. Fried hair seemed a pretty juvenile prank from a kid with an adolescent crush, and she knew too well how crush-able Ethan Williams could be.

The teen gripped the edges of the marble tub. "I wasn't really gonna hurt you or anything. I just wanted him to see what a klutz you are."

Kelly's kinder feelings disappeared faster than the paint under Brittany's toxic shampoo mix.

"I mean, like, really." Brittany rolled her eyes. "What does he see in you?"

The girl just didn't know when to quit.

Echoing from the hall, shouts and footsteps saved Kelly from answering. Not that she knew the answer.

The bathroom door swung wide, Eugenie silhouetted in surprisingly sedate blue silk pajamas, the butler and cook standing behind her. "Oh, my." Eugenie's eyes assessed Ethan and Kelly side by side, then Brittany, finally landing on the peeling paint. Her face hardened. "Oh, my."

"Exactly," Ethan snapped. "Kelly, you were the one she was after so you're the one to decide. What do you want to happen to her?"

Brittany whimpered.

Kelly mentally flipped through options. Could all of those incidents really be that simple? Or was Brittany linked to someone else? If so, she likely occupied the low rung on the ladder. In which case the best thing would be to let her go and have her followed.

As much as Kelly relished the idea of seeing the spiteful twit carted downtown and deloused, she knew what to do. "Let her go."

And get to the nearest secure phone ASAP.

Ethan nodded.

He'd been testing her, and she'd passed. A rush of pleasure surged through her greater than when she'd aced her graduate proficiencies.

Brittany stormed past without a single thanks—the ungrateful brat.

Ethan nodded to the butler standing in the door. "See that she leaves the property."

"Yes, sir," the butler said before leaving.

Kelly sagged against the sink, her SIG-Sauer heavy in her hand as she stood alone with Ethan and his aunt.

Alone and definitely under-dressed.

Eugenie nudged the bottle with her fuzzy slipper. "Cook will send someone up to clear this away. We'll obviously want to replace all your beauty products immediately."

"Thank you." That wouldn't take long. Even with Eugenie's makeover, Kelly still shied from too many products. Simple meant fewer goofs for Kelly the Klutz.

"Well, goodnight, then," Eugenie called as if ending a formal dinner party. "I'll leave you two to find your own way back to bed."

Eugenie paused, turned and reached past Ethan's head. Her hand came back with a rose petal. "Ethan Williams, I haven't had to get after you for picking my flowers since you were ten.''

She patted his cheek and spun away with a low laugh.

Ethan, however, looked far from amused. Where had her tender lover gone? Kelly touched his chest. Ethan flinched.

She jerked her hand back. Confusion, hurt and more than a little anger wrestled for control within her.

''Come on.'' He gripped her arm and tugged her toward the door, his touch far from loverlike.

''Ethan.'' She dug her feet into the carpet. ''Ethan!''

He gave her a slight tug, his face as immovable a mask as one of Eugenie's mud treatments. ''No time to waste. I have a call to make.''

At least he wasn't leaving her in her bedroom. She doubled her steps to keep up as he hauled out of the house.

Her ire eased along with her confusion. Of course he wanted out of the house. He'd all but admitted to staying away because of the painful memories. The fact that he wouldn't sell it but avoided entering said much about how his parents' death still affected him.

Ethan charged through the garage and back up the stairs to his apartment. He slammed the door closed behind them. The cavernous room echoed with silence and memories of what they'd shared in the room just a few minutes earlier.

''Go to bed, Kelly. I'll take care of making sure Brittany leaves.'' Ethan climbed the stairs.

Man, she was getting tired of chasing his hunky back. ''I'll wait up until you're done.''

He dropped into his computer chair and spun to face the screen. ''I need to call ARIES.''

''Okay.'' She perched a hip on the desk beside him. ''I'll wait.''

His gaze fell to her legs, held, then scorched up to her unrestrained breasts. Her body heated at the memory of his touch, of his mouth on her skin. Her breasts tightened beneath the cotton in an invitation he couldn't miss.

Ethan shifted, looked away and hammered keys. "I'll be sleeping on the couch."

Her body still humming from the passion in just one look, she couldn't believe what she was hearing. "You're kidding, right?"

He clicked until the surveillance screens shifted to views of Brittany's car. "I can keep watch better that way."

Like he would actually sleep at all. She expected he would park himself in front of the screens all night. "Then we'll both sleep on the sofa."

"No."

What the hell was going on? She might be inexperienced, but she couldn't have completely misread him.

Old insecurities threatened. He'd had her and was through. Or worse yet, he'd found her lacking. The sleep excuse was just that, an excuse to get rid of her.

Her chest constricted. Even the thought hurt, so much more now that she knew exactly what she would be losing if he walked away. Damn him. She deserved better than this. "So is this the big brush-off, then? Sex was great, now we're done?"

"No."

"Can you give me a polysyllabic answer?" She thumped his shoulder. "And could you quit being so cold and look at me?"

His jaw worked. Slowly, he spun his chair to face her. His shoulders lowered, his face lined with exhaustion for the first time since she'd met him.

His hand fell to rest on her knee, his other hand clenched in his lap. "Tonight was…incredible, Kelly."

The ache inside her eased.

His hand fell away. "But it's time to get back to the real world. Go to bed. In less than forty-eight hours we'll be standing down a room full of jewel thieves. I need a partner who isn't asleep on her feet and can watch my back."

Turning away and shutting her out, Ethan reached for the secured phone and pulled the key from a hidden drawer.

Twisting the key that guaranteed protected communications, he punched in the number. While waiting, he rubbed a hand along his neck, just as he'd done when telling about his parents' murder.

Self doubts faded, replaced by a new understanding. The day he'd lost his parents had left its mark in more ways than one. He didn't like ties…fabric or emotional. Losing Celia had only cemented his defensive need for distance.

All his revelations of the past hours poured over her, the reliving of his parents' deaths brought to the surface by the revelations about his aunt. While he barked out an update into the phone, the harsh lines on his face mirrored those she'd seen when he'd stepped into the greenhouse.

His hardened agent exterior covered pain.

He'd come to her earlier because he was hurting. He hadn't sent her from his apartment, but his emotional walls were in place, high and impenetrable.

And in that moment, a deeper ache spread, because now Kelly knew. Her quest to learn more about Ethan and banish her crush had worked. Her infatuation was truly a thing of the past.

She loved Ethan Williams, a man who wanted her body, even her friendship, but would never risk accepting her heart.

Ethan sprawled in the steel-backed chair in the spacious ARIES tech lab while Kelly, Juarez and Davidson discussed listening devices. With her legs crossed, Kelly swung her foot in a lazy dance back and forth, the delicate arch of her calf all but hypnotizing him.

Another thirty-six hours and he could put this case behind him. Ethan tapped a folded memo along the table, flipping it over and over in his hand.

He didn't know what the hell to do about Kelly after that. Sure, he'd thought about marriage, but now he wondered if Kelly might be better off without him. He'd lived day-to-day for so long, planning for the future could scare the sludge off his Jag. If he screwed up as he'd done last night, Kelly paid the price.

The hell of it was he could *not* touch her again until he had his head on straight and a plan of action in place. Sleeping on the sofa sucked when the woman he wanted waited warm and willing up a flight of stairs. She deserved better than some half-baked plan for a day-to-day future.

The future. Sweat beaded Ethan's brow.

Director Hatch leaned against the wall, arms crossed over his chest as he watched without a word.

Did the man ever sleep? Ethan wrestled with images of a younger Hatch and Aunt Eugenie tearing up the world in their field-agent days, a reminder that this lifestyle didn't last.

How would he and Kelly end up? Going separate ways? Both of them living out their lives alone? Ethan returned his attention to the discussion at hand.

Carla Juarez grasped tweezers and pinched the miniscule listening device, rolling her wheelchair toward Ethan. The size of a grain of rice, the device would lie out of sight in his ear canal. He never questioned how it stuck there. Wasn't sure he really wanted to know. Juarez had proposed they give Kelly a dry run using the device to become accustomed to multi-tasking with several voices transmitting through the earpiece. Ethan had welcomed the chance to leave the apartment and put some people between himself and Kelly.

Except it wasn't helping.

Hatch pulled a roll of antacids out of his pocket and thumbed one free. "We finally caught up with your tour guide from the mine. He says someone paid him a thousand dollars to send you down the wrong shaft and rig the generator. Said the guy gave the excuse of being a jealous boyfriend. We've got a sketch artist working on it."

Ethan had been hoping for more. "And Brittany Hill?"

"No suspicious movement." Hatch popped the antacid in

his mouth and clicked it to the side. "We're keeping a tail on her."

Juarez leaned closer, the tweezers tickling Ethan's ear. "The power of young love."

"Very funny, Juarez." Ethan scratched a hand over his burning gut.

"Quit fidgeting!" Carla Juarez chastised him. "Do you want me to rupture your eardrum?"

"Lovely image. Thanks."

"No problem, hotshot."

Ethan flipped the folded notepaper between his fingers again like a quarter in a sleight-of-hand trick. The message from Samantha had arrived just as he'd warmed up the Jag while waiting for Kelly. He still didn't know how he planned to handle Samantha's request that they meet, whether to include Kelly or not.

She would be mad, but he couldn't afford to let that influence him.

"All done." Juarez wheeled her chair around. "Okay, Kelly. Your turn."

Kelly hooked her feet together and tucked them under her seat—ankle boots her footwear choice of the day designed to make his life a living hell.

Juarez winked. "You look great, kiddo."

Kelly smiled. "Thanks, Carla."

"I'll say." Davidson emitted a low whistle from beside the map of the ballroom on the wall. "You do clean up well, Taylor. Pencil me in on your dance card. I'll rest up this bum leg of mine just for you."

Kelly swacked his arm. "You'd better not set one foot out of headquarters and leave me high and dry with no backup."

"No fair. Rich boy over there gets all the fun." Davidson pitched a marker at Ethan.

Ethan shot him a glare in the timeless communication of one male to another that said without question, *mine.*

Davidson cocked a brow before stepping back with a slight nod of acknowledgment.

Juarez rolled away from Kelly. "Okay. All set." She passed Ethan and Kelly each a tiny clip-on microphone. "Tech support is working a set into your clothing buttons now. With a heist in the works, we decided planting the mikes in jewelry might not be such a wise idea."

Kelly turned her back and whispered, "Ethan? Are you there?"

Her voice echoed in his head—sheer pleasure and torture in one silken-toned package. He shifted in his seat. "Yeah, Kel, I'm here."

Her laugh tripped free as she spun to face him. "Oh, man. This is so cool."

Cool?

It seemed mighty damned hot in the room to Ethan.

Juarez passed Ethan and Kelly each a small plastic case. "Your contact lenses. They're tinted to just the right level to counteract the effects of the Laser Dazzler if it needs to be activated."

Kelly cradled hers as if they were the crown jewels. "You came through."

Intellectually, he understood the need to keep the volume low so as not to burst the eardrum, but God help him, her husky tones spiraled through his mind like tendrils of smoke.

Juarez grinned. "Didn't want you to have to resort to one of those other options suggested by the Marines over in the Urban Warfare Battle Lab."

Davidson chuckled. Good. No temptation in hearing that voice.

"Ah, come on." Davidson rubbed a hand along his thigh absently. "It would have been fun watching the Gastonian ambassador try to wade through the sticky foam. Or the microwave gun singe the polyester right off the girlfriend of the Holzberg secretary of state."

"All in the name of compassionate combat," Juarez

chimed, her wheelchair offering a glaring reminder of the price of war. She rolled toward the door. "Come on, Kelly. Let's take a spin around the office and gab with people, while the guys talk in here. You can get used to processing all the different channels of information coming your way at once."

Kelly held open the door. "It's so wild hearing you in double, literally and through Ethan's mike."

"You'll also have the command post voices back here to contend with, but you'll adjust before you know it," Juarez said, her voice dimming as she wheeled into the hall. The door swished closed behind them.

Too bad the image of Kelly's animated face remained in Ethan's mind as real as her voice in his ear.

Hatch shoved away from the wall. "Davidson, run through the security checklist again. Taylor can listen in. Won't hurt to hear it repeated."

"Sure." Davidson grabbed another marker from the metal tray. A map of the ballroom with the plastic overlay for notes sprawled across the wall.

Ethan tipped back in his chair. Markers squeaked as Davidson drew a series of Xs resembling a basketball play grid. Their background chatter would offer enough for Kelly to process as she walked the halls back to her desk.

Soaking up compliments from too-damned-pushy men.

She wouldn't be lacking for date offers after this op ended. Offers from a pack of fools who hadn't been able to appreciate her diamond-in-the-rough beauty before.

She deserved better.

Better than him, too, for that matter.

Her voice caressed his ear. His eyes slid closed. Excitement pulsed through her words, as it had the gems at the mine, later when they'd shared a simple snowball.

A kiss.

Going sentimental over a snowball?

Lack of sleep must be screwing with his self-control, but

he would sleep when they caught the scum responsible for Alex Morrow's disappearance.

When he had Kelly safely behind her desk again.

For how long, a voice taunted? How long before she landed her next field assignment and ended up with bullets tearing through her mojo and into her back like Juarez?

Kelly laughed over something. What? Damned if he hadn't been following the conversation. Her silky tones rolled around in his head, a part of him he couldn't escape when his emotions were too damned close to the surface.

The sound of her blended with memories of her sighs of pleasure in the mine and later in the greenhouse. He could almost feel her under him. Need pulsed through him, thick, hot and without warning. Just like Kelly in his life.

His breath huffed in and out, every drag of air heavier than the next. He wanted her. Any way he could have her and damn the consequences. He wanted her now. Just give him ten minutes alone with her in a closet where he could hike that—

A cleared throat broke into Ethan's concentration. He bolted upright, his eyes snapping open. Davidson stared at him with an ill-disguised smirk. His soon-to-be-pounded buddy snagged a red marker and scribbled on the board. *Do you need a cigarette?*

Ethan growled low, "Bite me, bud."

A gasp sounded in his head. Kelly. "What?"

"Nothing," Ethan mumbled. "Just Davidson making a fool out of himself."

Hatch crossed to his case sitting on the table. He snapped it open and pulled out a file. "Nice work, people. I'll leave you to do your job."

Walking toward the door, he placed the file on the table beside Ethan, dropping a roll of antacids on top without hesitating. The door clicked shut behind the director.

Davidson capped the marker. "What's that?"

Ethan scooped the antacids off and flipped open the first

page of the file. His parents' names leapt out, along with his aunt's.

Adrenaline seared him. He had it. The file on his parents' murder. No doubt Hatch had computerized copies, but Ethan had what he needed.

Yet the thrill faded as quickly as it had surged. All he could think of was Kelly.

Mine. Again the single word pulsed through him. Became a part of him.

He was a selfish bastard who couldn't let her go. But he also couldn't spend his life eating rolls of antacid and wondering if she'd made it through the day alive. Even if he cut himself out of her life, she would always be there in his head, as she was now, earpiece or not. Kelly had become a part of him no amount of distance could slice free.

Which left him with only one option.

Ethan crumpled the note from Samantha in his hand. He would decide after the meeting if Kelly needed to know the results of what he learned.

For now, he would get through this assignment. Do whatever it took to keep Kelly alive.

Then come hell or high water, when the clock struck twelve on Kelly's Cinderella mission, Hatch would have two resignations on his desk.

Chapter 14

Kelly raced up the stairs to Ethan's apartment, too jazzed to wait until supper to meet him as they'd arranged. Every step pumped her excitement from work up another notch. She planned to entice Ethan out of whatever had brought on his bad mood and celebrate.

God, she loved her job. The whole day at ARIES trying out equipment had been a blast. She'd worked the ops-support end for two years, all but salivating when others donned the high-tech tools of their trade. ARIES had the best of the best, thanks to their unlimited black ops budget. Nowhere in the world were operatives better outfitted.

And now she was one.

What would Hatch have for her next?

Restless energy charged through her. She wanted the next days to whiz past.

Then what? Would Ethan's walls come down or double in height?

Her feet faltered on the landing.

She wouldn't let him.

Kelly punched in the code to Ethan's alarm and let herself inside. "Ethan?"

He'd said he needed time to shower and change. Well, she planned to surprise him in the shower and change his attitude.

The silent apartment greeted her. Strolling through the kitchen, she trailed her fingers along the rim of his coffee cup where his mouth had rested. A poor substitute for the man's kiss, especially when she would likely spend another lonely night in his bed while he sacked on the couch if she didn't make some headway.

"Ethan?"

No answer, not even the sound of a shower.

A tingle started up her spine, a newly developed sixth sense she'd developed over the past two weeks.

He'd left her alone. He rarely did that anymore, always insisting they stick together.

Overprotective lout.

So what was he doing now?

Kelly bolted away from the table and up the stairs to the computer loft. Time to use some of those skills he'd taught her. Dropping into his chair, she clicked through the grounds surveillance commands until she found him.

And Delmonico's ambassador pro-tem, Samantha Barnes. His former girlfriend. Sitting on a lounger together by the indoor pool, Ethan beside the cool beauty, his head ducked close to hers.

Those old insecurities kicked in with a vengeance. Samantha Barnes was everything Kelly had once dreamed of being. The stunning redhead was brilliant, confident and an acting ambassador of an important American ally in an unstable region.

No. Kelly halted the green-eyed monster in its tracks.

Ethan may have cut a wide swath through the female population, but always one at a time for as long as she'd known him. She trusted his innate sense of honor enough to know he would completely set her free first. And he hadn't done that. Yet.

So what was he doing?

She clicked through computer keys to try and up the volume, but Ethan had chosen to talk by the swishing hot tub.

No doubt deliberately.

If she had higher tech skills in this arena, she could probably weed through the interference. But she didn't. Why was he meeting with Samantha so late when she should be resting up for the major embassy function in the works?

The embassy. Samantha's job as ambassador pro-tem to Delmonico.

Kelly straightened. While Samantha didn't know about Ethan's ARIES status, she did know he had intelligence connections.

The meeting was business.

Relief threatened to swamp her. Too much. More emotion than she wanted right now when she didn't know how Ethan felt.

Kelly stared at the computer screen, taking in the two heads bowed close together, deep in conversation. She might not be jealous. But she *was* mad as hell. Anger felt good. Tangible and a lot less painful than what she'd experienced when he announced he'd be sleeping on the sofa.

How dare he pull a stunt like this? Kelly considered racing down there and simply entering the meeting as if she'd been called to participate. Except he might leave before she arrived.

Her eyes slid to the telephone. Ethan's first lesson in field craft drifted through her mind.

Sometimes the simplest answers worked the best.

He always carried a cell phone in his pocket.

Kelly reached for the receiver, never taking her eyes off the computer screen. If she and Ethan stood even an infinitesimal chance of working out, he needed to come to grips with accepting her as a fellow operative and equal.

Starting now.

* * *

Ethan took the computer disk from Samantha and wished he could come up with some words of comfort to offer a friend with too much pain in her eyes.

Others might be fooled by her calm exterior, but he'd lived in that same hell for too many years and for the first time wanted to find a way out of it other than getting himself killed on the job.

The cell phone in Ethan's shirt pocket hummed, vibrating against him. Samantha jumped back, elegance in place again, if a bit brittle.

Ethan slapped a hand over the pocket. "I'd better take this." He pulled the phone out and glanced at the LCD screen to find his apartment number. Kelly. Panic punched him. He shouldn't have left her alone. He flipped the phone open. "Kelly? Everything okay?"

"Just peachy, partner."

Her over-bright tone set off alarms in his head. "Did you need something?"

"Yeah," the cheer in her voice faded, "I need my partner to be straight with me and not hold out on meetings with sources."

Ethan's eyes shot straight up to the security camera in the corner wet bar. Busted.

"That's right, ace. *I'm* watching *you* this time." Kelly's voice shimmered through the phone waves with an extra electric kick of anger.

Samantha patted his arm. "I should go."

"No," Ethan said. "Hold on—"

"It's okay." Samantha stood. "You have what you need. Work's the best thing for me and I have a pile of it waiting back in my hotel room."

"Kelly, be with you in a second." He flipped the phone closed on the distraction he did not need right now. He would deal with Kelly's jealousy in a minute. "You'll be at the summit ball tomorrow?"

"Of course."

He couldn't come right out and tell Samantha about the potential threat at the gala, and damned if the need to do so didn't tear him up. Alerting the public would send the perps deeper into hiding and only make it tougher to catch them, leaving others open to the threat without the blanket of protection Ethan and Kelly had orchestrated.

Ethan settled for a simple, "Watch your back."

"Of course." She jabbed a finger at his chest. "And you remember to treasure what you have." Whipping her coat off a chair, she stopped him with a raised hand. "I'll see myself out."

Spine straight, she glided toward the door.

See herself out? Training wasn't easily ignored. He stood at the door and watched until she pulled safely away from the house.

Prideful woman. He recognized the resistance to accepting help well. Now Samantha would just have to find the right person to help her through it. As he had. A person he damned well *did* intend to treasure and protect.

As soon as they got past a serious head-butting in their future.

Ethan pivoted on his heel and shot through the hall to the back entrance in the garage. Taking the steps three at a time, he framed his words to reassure Kelly. Christ, he would never, never cheat on her. Couldn't fathom ever wanting another woman. Damned well looked forward to exploring a thousand ways to make Kelly sigh with pleasure.

However, while he wasn't used to accounting for his actions—to anyone—he recognized she carried a lifetime of insecurities, thanks to her parents.

He paused outside the door to give himself a second to gather his thoughts. Then remembered she was likely watching him anyway.

She made a hell of a student. He punched in the code and swung the door open. "Kelly?"

The low squeak of his office chair spinning above offered the only answer. Kelly lounged at his wall of computers in the loft, her arms draped over the rests with negligent ease. Her legs stretched for endless miles in front of her.

The fire in her eyes sparked a shower of ire upon his head.

"Kelly, it's not what you think." Was that cliché the best he could come up with? This woman stole his ability to think, reason and apparently his ability to talk rationally, as well.

"Then what was it, Ethan?" She stood, her voice picking up speed and anger with every word. "Explain to this junior operative what I misunderstood about my partner meeting with an embassy source without telling me."

Busted. Truly busted.

Well, hell. He'd underestimated her. She wasn't jealous at all. Not even a slice insecure.

She was professionally pissed.

Kelly started down the stairs, slowly, every word punctuated with a step. "Tell me why half the team keeps from the other half what's going on."

Somehow he suspected his "keeping her safe" answer wouldn't gain him any ground.

She cruised toward him. "Make me understand why it's smart ops to hamstring your partner by insisting she sit in a freaking apartment all the time rather than utilize the skills you taught her."

He opted for a shot at a bluff. "Samantha lost her husband, Kelly. She's going through a rough time. She needed someone to talk to."

Her arms folded over her chest. "Good try, Williams. I'm not buying it."

Kelly waited, her face smooth and expressionless.

When had he lost control? The first time Kelly spoke to him. "Damn it, Kelly, I taught you that poker face, so you can just cut it out." Still she didn't budge. "Fine. Yeah, I was meeting with her to discuss business. She had some intel to pass along about an intercepted message. She wanted it off the record and untraceable back to her."

"And you didn't see fit to tell me?" Her voice rose with the color in her cheeks. "I could have had something to offer, and instead I'm sitting up here with nothing but a stack of crossword puzzles."

Screw this. She wanted to know, he'd tell her. "Well, at least you're safe!"

"I don't want safe!" She thumped his chest with both palms. "I want to do my job the same as you do." Her breast heaved under her dress, before she spun away. "God, there's no reasoning with you."

"Don't walk out on me." He grabbed her arm.

She jerked free. "You can watch over me with your cameras. Then you won't have to worry about any messy arguments or emotions. You can keep your distance and brood, rather than face what we did together. What we felt. Hell, you can't even commit to a real partnership. It's no surprise any hint of a real relationship would send the big bad agent running for the hills."

Her words raked across emotions already too damned raw, fired the gut-burning desire he'd held in check all day. For months. For years, around this woman.

He studied the set line of her jaw. The rigid brace of her shoulders. She burned for this job just as he had for so many years, even before he'd lost Celia.

Kelly wasn't going to give up. She lived for this job. And damn it, so did he.

His mental image of those resignations went up in flames. He could almost see the edges blackening, curling, turning to powder. With them went his hopes of scratching out some kind of future with Kelly that wouldn't send him to the nuthouse worrying about her.

"Fine. You want real? Here's reality. Nobody's running now." His hand shot behind her head, tangled in her hair and tugged her head back.

Before she could do more than gasp—perfect since parted lips suited him damned fine—his mouth crashed down on hers.

Ethan drew in the taste of Kelly. The scent of her. The feel of her soft body under his hands. Every bit of her saturated his senses with as much potency as her voice.

He cupped her bottom, lifted, rocked their hips against each other.

She whimpered under his mouth.

Control. He had to find it. He eased back, hands shaking. "I'm being too rough."

"No," she insisted, drawing his bottom lip between her teeth, "you're not."

He rested his forehead against hers. "Do you want—"

"Yes!" She jerked his shirtfront. "I want. Do I ever *want.* I want you. I've always wanted you and don't know how to stop."

And neither did he.

He slanted his mouth over hers. Without breaking their kiss, he backed them toward the stairs. Bodies locked, they kissed and stumbled up the steps, flattening against the wall to tunnel hands under clothing. Finally, they made it to the landing. He reached for the door, but before he could twist the knob, Kelly hooked a leg behind his and rocked their balance. Or maybe that was the effect of her kiss.

They fell to the floor, Ethan twisting at the last second to cushion her from the floor.

"Now," she whispered against his lips, kicking off her shoes. "Here."

She didn't have to tell him twice. His hand burrowed under her dress to whip her stockings and panties down and off. He pitched the pink wisp fluttering over the banister.

In a tangle of arms and legs and need he rolled her under him. She worked the fly button free on his jeans with a newfound expertise. No fumbling, she found him. He gave a brief thought to undressing, but Kelly's insistent touch, her kisses, nips, sighs urging him on, told him she wanted this as much as he did. Slow would come later.

He tore his wallet from his back pocket and found protection.

Damn it, never would he lose sight of protecting Kelly.

And then he was in her. Only fair since she'd been inside him all day. All month. For as long as he could remember and right now he couldn't seem to remember anything but her.

And the feel of her gripping him with moist heat.

Under him, in him, a part of him.

He moved within her, holding back until his every muscle strained, screaming for release. The longer he held back, the longer he kept her, the longer he didn't have to contemplate what could happen in the next twenty-four hours.

That he couldn't let happen.

He couldn't lose her.

He couldn't lose—

Her cry of release ripped through him, her beautiful body arching up and into him once, and again. His own shout mingled with hers until he sagged on top of her, absorbing her aftershocks.

Keeping her with him a few seconds longer.

Chapter 15

Kelly trembled with the residual waves of pleasure rippling through her.

She'd wanted him. Wanted this. But hadn't fully understood the storm churning through Ethan. The intensity of whatever tore at him radiated in waves. She'd grappled her way over his wall and now didn't know what to do with what she'd found. There weren't books for her to study on this one, and her lack of experience in relationships left her with precious little to draw upon.

She kissed his neck and waited for him to talk, a better option than to risk saying the wrong thing. Ethan rolled off her and sat with his back against the wall, dragging in air.

He traced a finger along her neckline, dipping in to pull the chain around her neck, down to the stone dangling from it, the aquamarine from their mine trip. "You're right. I should have told you about the meeting with Samantha."

Shock kept her from talking more than indecision—and hope.

Maybe…

"It's been a hell of a day." He untwined the chain and stood.

Ethan straightened his clothes, then extended a hand to her. She rose to stand beside him, ready to curl up in his bed and savor whatever time they had left together, to grab some intimacy with this elusive man.

Instead, he turned the corner and climbed the last few steps to his computer wall. He reached past her to his side of the computer console. "Hatch gave me the file on my parents' murder."

Kelly rubbed the tensed muscles in his arm, trying to understand where he was going with this. "That's good. What does it say?"

"I haven't read it yet." He held it as if testing its weight. "But I can't stop thinking about it. And yeah, I misstepped earlier. Thinking about them…hell, yeah, I want to keep you locked up tight here."

He held up a hand. "I know. You don't want protection." Ethan dropped the file on the desk beside her. "Here."

Kelly picked it up. "You want me to look?"

"Go ahead," he shot over his shoulder as he loped down the stairs to the kitchen.

Already she could see him pulling away, but this time he'd left a piece of himself behind. While Ethan pulled water bottles from the refrigerator, Kelly flipped through pages, icy horror chilling away the remains of passion. Was he trying to tell her something by showing her the brutality of how his parents had died?

A line item snagged her attention. "Ethan," she called, her eyes still scanning the pages, soaking up the words with dawning horror, "where was your au pair—Iona—from? The woman who supposedly passed along your locale to the attackers?"

He returned to the loft, placing a bottle beside her. "From what little I could find out the past couple of weeks, Iona's passport listed her as a Swiss National."

Kelly tapped the paper. "That's not where she was born."

He tugged the yellowed paper sealed in a plastic sleeve. "Bastia. But that doesn't—"

"—exist anymore." Cold certainty hardened within her. "It was absorbed into the shifting borders of—"

"Rebelia. Damn it. Here." He pitched the computer disk Samantha had passed along onto the computer console. "See what you can make of that. Samantha lucked into this message intercepted by Delmonico's intelligence. She says even if you break the encryption, it came from Rebelia, which means I'm screwed as far as interpreting it anyway."

She jammed the disk into her computer, activating the software to decode the encrypted message while Ethan waited beside her, edgy restlessness pulsing from him.

Words shifting before her, she typed out the translation and found…

"Oh my God," she gasped, leaning back from the computer. "Read."

Ethan canted forward, his eyes scanning, widening with dark realization. "If this is right, someone in Rebelia is targeting jewels all around the world. Specific jewels. This isn't some random heist. They're out for the Gastonian ambassador's blue sapphire."

Kelly leaned back in the chair. "Aside from the value of it, the diplomatic repercussions alone could start an all-out war between the countries."

All roads led back to Rebelia. Eugenie's diggings into CIA workings back then and operative Alex Morrow's disappearance now.

Could a small country like Rebelia actually have had an intricate spy network in place for over thirty years?

Of course it could. The magnitude of what they were facing rolled over her. And apparently rolled over Ethan, as well. He grabbed for the phone. "Screw this. I'm calling Hatch and telling him to cancel the whole damned summit ball."

She clutched his wrist. "What about Alex Morrow? And whatever else is planned with the rest of the next heist and the one after that."

He jerked his arm away and shot out of the chair. "Fine. Then your unreasonable boyfriend is asking you to sit this one out at headquarters so I can think."

She stood, toe-to-toe, determined to have her answers this time. "And what about the next op?"

His silence and stony face answered her too well. He really expected her to give it up for him.

"You want me to quit?"

Still he didn't disagree. Instead, he moved closer, hips molded to hers as he stroked his hands down her back, lower. "You want to travel, I'll take you anywhere you want to go." His hands journeyed sensuous paths over her body with a lover's knowledge of where to touch. "I have enough money for ten lifetimes and we'll spend it all in one. You'll be so busy, you won't have time to miss ARIES, or anything else."

"Don't," she pulled herself away, anger and passion making painful companions in her belly. "Don't try to manipulate me."

His throat worked, none of the Ethan lightheartedness in sight. "I love you, damn it. I never wanted to love anyone this way again. Hell, I never *have* loved anyone this way. That has to count for something."

Everything within Kelly went silent and still. Ethan loved her?

And she couldn't do a thing about it.

Blue eyes she'd dreamed of for so long stared back down at her. Part of her yearned to take anything he offered. Another, stronger part of her knew better.

"There was a time I would have given anything to hear those words from you. But Ethan, you've taught me I'm worthy of more." She let herself touch him, her palm to his chest, a bittersweet pleasure. "I've spent years trying to be something I'm not to make people love me, which is silly because then they don't love the real me, anyway.''

Kelly held her eyes wide and unblinking. She wouldn't cry. If he saw her weakening, he would push and she didn't trust herself to hold strong.

She stroked her hand over the steady beat of his heart. ''I can't promise you I won't die. But if you take away my right to stand up for myself, then I'm not truly living.''

His face hardened at her rejection. He stepped back, putting distance between them with his cold eyes as much as his retreating body. ''That's a great speech, Kelly. Of course you always did have a way with words. Well, I'm not so good with twisting around languages, but I can tell you this straight up. I'm not some damned fairy-tale prince, but I would have given you everything I had.''

As she watched him walk back up the stairs, she wondered if maybe her summa cum laude brain had misled her this time.

Wearing his tuxedo and counting down the minutes until Kelly descended the spiral staircase, Ethan stood in the cathedral-ceilinged entry hall of his aunt's house.

His house.

His parents' home.

He slid his finger along the neck of his tux shirt. Damn tie pinched.

Eugenie stood beside him, swathed in a purple ball gown and eager to unveil her creation. So many times she had stood at the foot of those same stairs while he slid down the steps on a sled. Or had that been his mother? He hated being inside with ghostly memories attempting to push through, but Kelly deserved to have her escort waiting for her.

He took comfort from the solid weight of the 9mm secured in his shoulder harness. Some comfort. Not enough.

Hell, none of it felt like enough—the army of a hundred security personnel outside the historic hotel where the summit ball would be held. The thirty armed guards inside posing as guests and waiters. Not to mention the room full of heavily armored forces waiting as a contingency backup.

He and Kelly had spent the entire day increasing security. They'd met with Hatch about the potential threat from Rebelian nationals and tried to pinpoint their link to Alex Morrow's disappearance. But the ambassador to Gastonia wouldn't cancel his appearance. There was nothing left to do but forge ahead with additional security in place. CIA, FBI, Marines, even local law enforcement were all woven together in a joint operation, yet none of them had seen his or Kelly's faces to link them as the masterminds.

In his ear, the low voices of Juarez, Davidson and occasionally even Samuel Hatch himself already hummed with feedback from the command post in ARIES headquarters. Just as when multiple frequencies piped through his headset when he flew his plane, Ethan sorted through the voices. Kelly's receiver would be turned on in minutes.

Not that he needed the sound of her voice to keep her in his head.

Eugenie tapped his arm. "Ethan. She's here."

Ethan looked up. Kelly stood above him.

She stole his breath, and he'd been prepared for her to look beautiful. Yet even he hadn't expected this.

He had to applaud his aunt for her choices. She'd restrained her own extravagant tastes in favor of elegant simplicity that didn't distract from Kelly. Heavy white fabric—brocade maybe—draped her in a straight sheath. Off the shoulders, her dress accented the graceful arch of Kelly's neck, exposing a creamy expanse of skin waiting for the jewels inside the case in his hand.

No elaborate twists or curls for her hair, Kelly's ebony hair was swept back into a low braided bun, a stark style that only the most classic of bone structures could carry off. Only *Kelly* could carry off. He'd always been able to see the beauty beneath her baggy clothes and curtain of hair. Now the rest of the world would see, too.

Her foot peeked free from the hem as she descended the stairs, one satin ballet slipper descending to the next step. No ridiculous heels to hamper her if they needed to act later.

If.

He shut down even thoughts of the possibility.

Kelly stopped in front of him, her eyes full of doubts and desire. He could play on both of those so easily to win her. Her inexperience with relationships would give him leverage.

But he couldn't do it.

Honor sure bit sometimes.

Resigned, but determined to give her his protection if nothing else, he draped the ruby necklace along her pale skin—jewels to entice a crook her way. Ethan reminded himself of her training, and the fact that he would be there with her. He wouldn't take his eyes off her until they had the thieves in hand.

No great hardship, looking at Kelly all night.

He closed the clasp on the ruby necklace, allowing his hands a brief detour along her silken shoulders. No doubt her SIG-Sauer waited strapped to the inside of her silken thigh.

He dragged his mind away from thoughts of her soft, white thighs. Dangerous territory tonight.

Ethan snapped an orchid from the vase of flowers. With the familiarity of a lover—his by rights, damn it, if only for one more night—he secured the flower into her gathered hair. He pressed his lips to hers and whispered, "Be careful."

He heard himself echo the very words she'd spoken to him before he'd left for Gastonia, the words that had alerted him to her feelings. And he realized for the first time what watching him leave for that assignment had cost her.

"Ethan, you've taught me well. Now it's time to trust me." With a single brush of her mouth against his, she stepped back and waited for him to offer his arm.

He would have offered this woman more, but Kelly had

made herself damned clear. He'd given her everything he had. But as he'd known from the start, what he had left within him couldn't be enough. Not anymore.

He just prayed like hell his mojo that had carried him through ten years and more operations than he cared to remember would hold for one more night.

Kelly sipped her glass of club soda, the crowds and conversations swelling around her in multiple languages while she conversed with Ethan's friends. No champagne for her. She had to stay clear and sift through the interpretations.

She absently pressed her palm to her chest, where her aquamarine rested inside her strapless bra. Her good-luck charm was far more precious than the rubies around her neck because it had come from Ethan the man—not the multimillionaire.

The scent of the orchid in her hair wafted forward, a constant reminder of Ethan and his touch on her shoulders. The touch of his eyes even now. Always on her.

Kelly forced a smile and nodded while Jake Ingram's fiancée Tara rambled on about her latest purchases for the wedding. Easy enough to stay silent and listen.

Strains from the string quartet drifted through as unobtrusively as the security personnel. Men in tuxedoes stood by the doors, looking more like bouncers than dignitaries. Others talked covertly into their sleeves. Their lack of humor marked them more than their size or actions.

Nerves strung within her as tight as the violin bow.

Cases of jewels marched down the middle of the room. Inside rested necklaces, rings, solitary stones—some historical, others new and ostentatious. Rubies, emeralds, diamonds, sapphires perched in artistic displays, cradled or suspended, all arranged with tiny halogen lights refracting sparkles beyond comprehension.

Masses filed by. Men in tuxedos or military uniforms of various nationalities. Women in designer gowns and the traditional costumes of their homeland. Not that anyone allowed their awe for the jewels to show. Everyone from Mrs. Mega-Bucks Blasé to Ambassador Nonchalant cruised past the velvet ropes around the exhibits with low hums of "lovely, lovely" as if viewing an attractive floral arrangement.

And they all accepted a Nebraska farm girl's right to be there.

Incredible.

She'd pulled it off, with Eugenie's help—and most of all because of Ethan's confidence in her as a woman. If he could only trust her as a partner, as well.

Unable to stop herself, Kelly searched for him. Finally, she spotted him across the sea of bodies, standing with Samantha Barnes and White House advisor Matt Tynan. With them stood Eugenie and the Gastonian ambassador. Ethan hadn't left the man's side all evening, just as Kelly hadn't left the jewels.

Ethan's face creased with his laugh, a deep rumble that echoed in Kelly's ear, along with background noise from ARIES headquarters.

Only she would recognize the underlying edge or how Ethan longed to ditch the formal garb. His tuxedo fit his body with a negligent élan. So often she'd seen him in a suit at ARIES and thought the same thing, never realizing the true Ethan preferred ragged jeans to designer clothes.

He knew how to adjust to fit into the world around him when necessary, while no one ever realized he held a piece of himself apart. Never noticed he didn't allow himself to belong.

Kelly accepted another round of congratulations from Ethan's social set, along with eat-dirt-and-die glares from more than one woman. No doubt Ethan would have plenty of consolation after their post-mission breakup.

Would he share with one of them why he hated ties?

Kelly willed away distracting thoughts and flipped her wrist to view her diamond-studded timepiece. Only fifteen minutes left in the cocktail hour and then the guests would all shift to dinner. The jewels would be stored away. The transfer to and from the armored cars could be controlled. No worries there.

Could the whole thing have been a hoax to divert their attention? Or had word of the additional security leaked, scaring away the thieves? In which case, they might not have a security heads-up next time. Alex Morrow might not have a second chance.

Ethan's voice stayed with her as her constant companion, an ever-present reminder that even if she succeeded in the evening's mission, she had still failed him. Failed *them.*

Where was the compromise?

The string quartet on the corner dais faded to a stop.

Adrenaline simmered, heated, tingled through her.

"Attention, ladies and gentleman," the speakers blared with the announcer's voice as the lights dimmed. "If you'll direct your attention to the displays so generously loaned, we'll begin our laser show and highlights of tonight's features."

Across the room, Ethan nodded to his friends and stepped back, his gaze raking the crowd. "Show time," he mumbled.

"Got it."

"What?" Tara asked.

Kelly pulled a smile. "Got to step back so I can see better."

Tara looped her arm through Jake's. "Of course."

The laser show spotlighted jewels, strobing through the room, flickering, distorting images away from the cases into choppy, fragmented disco movements. Kelly blinked. Looked again. Her SIG-Sauer lay like a cold block of ice against her thigh. If only she could have worn a shoulder harness like Ethan.

"Kelly, check your six o'clock," Ethan called the warning to look behind her. "Why does that person look familiar in a wrong way?"

She glanced over her shoulder at the mass of bodies.

Slowly, her eyes focused on…the hairstylist from Peter's salon? Then his cashier. Two, five, then ten of the salon's employees moving. Reaching into their jackets for…

"Gun," Kelly ducked to speak into her mike.

"Security, guard your eyes," Ethan barked. "Dazzler, go."

With barely a flicker, the lights adjusted, shifting to the military-developed Laser Dazzler. A hum of noise started from the crowd two seconds before disorientation set in.

Pandemonium reigned.

Guests stumbled in uncoordinated confusion. Couples clutched each other. Jake Ingram braced an arm around his fiancée's waist. A waiter tripped over a potted tree, champagne glasses sliding, shattering on the floor.

Twenty men with guns surged forward, aiming wildly. Guards swarmed the ballroom, wearing protective eyewear.

Screams echoed up to the crystal chandeliers. Keeping her post by the jewels, Kelly karate-chopped the guns from two men's hands. The damn dress limited her from kicking.

One gunman somehow staggered past the fountain toward the Gastonian ambassador. "Ethan! Coming your way."

Bodies swayed, dropped to the floor. If a shot went wild… Ethan plowed through, launched himself on top of the ambassador.

"Ethan?" Kelly forced her voice to stay calm, her focus on the mission, essential for keeping Ethan and the others safe.

"Secured and clear." His steady bass rumbled reassurance through the airwaves. "Check right."

"Roger." Kelly turned in time to trip the salon's valet and call another warning to Ethan. "Two possibilities coming your way!"

Ethan pivoted, bodyblocking one figure while shouting to his aunt.

Eugenie swayed, averted her head and righted. She hefted a near-empty pewter punch bowl from the table and clocked the gunman on the head. The man collapsed back into a jewel case, glass shattering.

Alarms blared as the punch bowl thumped to rest on white velvet.

And it was over.

That fast.

After two weeks of intense planning and praying. A multiservice security force of unlimited funds brought the op to a successful conclusion in less than three minutes.

But worth every penny for the lives saved. God, how much worse this could have been without prior warning to plan.

Feds swarmed the room, making arrests and taking statements. Kelly's ear buzzed with cheers from Juarez and Davidson. The general consensus circulating through the crowd seemed to attribute the disorientation to prior planning by the jewel thieves. Fine by Kelly as it kept their role downplayed, the goal of all ARIES operatives to maintain cover. An APB had been put out for Peter Miller.

Peter the masseur.

An American spy? Or Rebelian national? His flat accent that sounded like *studied* newscaster tones thrummed through her memory. At least they'd found out before anyone died.

Kelly slumped against a wall, the draft from the hall cooling sweat she hadn't even realized had beaded her skin. Her heart thudded in her ears. She'd done it. They'd done it. Ethan had to see how well they'd worked together.

If only they could find the same balance in a relationship.

Kelly's hand gravitated to her breastbone where the aquamarine lay nestled and hidden inside her dress. What had happened to taking charge of her future? So she and Ethan had argued. One fight. A really big one with no apparent compromise in sight. But she'd been willing to battle for her job. Why had she fallen short of giving the same effort to a relationship with Ethan?

Because the failure would hurt more.

A pitiful excuse for not going after what she wanted. A woman with a dragon on her hip and love in her heart didn't back down so easily anymore.

Kelly spun away from the wall.

Smack into a chest.

A masculine chest and the man of the hour everyone was seeking. Too late, she realized her shock and fear must have shown—and alerted him. An arm hooked around her waist.

"What are y—"

A hand slapped over her mouth. Strong and masculine. Peter Miller yanked her into the corridor.

"Kelly?" Ethan looked left to where FBI agents cuffed and hauled away suspects. Right to where a society matron draped in diamonds sobbed on her companion's shoulder. Who the hell could see anything in the mass of people? "Kelly? Talk to me. What's happening?"

He surged into the crowd, searching. Wingtip shoes crunched shards of glass along the hardwood floors.

"Walk," a masculine voice growled through the earpiece.

Ethan's steps faltered. "Kelly?"

Her breath huffed heavier, faster into the mike. Ethan's joined pace. Only now did he realize how their breathing had become one over the past two hours since they'd left the house. "Kelly? What the hell's going on? Where are you?"

Kelly gasped. "It would be easier to walk if you'd take your hand off my eyes and the gun out of my side."

A gun on Kelly. Ethan's gut twisted, burned. Only minutes ago he'd been reeling with relief over keeping Kelly alive. Even if she did walk away from him, at least he didn't have her blood on his soul. Now his worst nightmare exploded in front of him and all he could think about was the time he'd wasted arguing with her.

"Davidson, do you copy that? Kelly's been taken." Ethan flung through the door into the hall while ARIES affirmed his transmission. "Keep talking, Kelly."

"Ow!" she squawked. "It would sure be nice if you didn't bump me into walls. This hall has too many corners."

Fear grabbed Ethan in a stranglehold as he listened to her voice. "The hall. Got it, Kelly. Davidson, give the order. Have security fan out. I'm looking, Kelly. Hang tough. We're looking."

Kelly panted, the sound of running feet pounding through the mike. "You won't get away with this, Peter. Why are we going upstairs instead of leaving?"

Peter. She'd found Peter Miller. "Good, Kelly. Keep it coming." Ethan forced his voice to stay even, hell-bent determined to keep her calm, reassured even as his feet double-timed toward the service elevator. "Davidson, did you get that? Peter Miller is here and he has Kelly."

"Roger that," Davidson barked from headquarters. "We're trying to track you, Kelly. Keep talking."

A door squeaked and clicked.

"Peter, stop. You don't want to do this." Kelly's voice rose for the first time.

The hair on the back of Ethan's neck prickled.

"Get in the room and shut up."

What the hell was the man thinking? Peter Miller was in a load of trouble in a place crawling with agents of every kind. The guy shouldn't have a second to spare…

Unless he'd lost hope and planned a standoff—with a hostage.

In a room. A hotel room. Alone with Kelly.

No. No. And hell no! Fury fired through Ethan while fear iced his spine. He didn't want to hear what he was almost certain would come next.

"Take off your dress."

Ethan's world exploded into a red haze. Not Kelly. Not that.

"No!"

Chapter 16

"No!" Ethan's shout reverberated in Kelly's brain.

She slapped a hand to ear. Her eyes teared up from Ethan's shout. Not just from the physical torture to her eardrum, but from the anguish in his voice.

Thank God her captor hadn't heard.

"Take it off," the wiry masseur ordered again from his position in front of the door to the cleaning service supply room. He bore little resemblance to the gentle, new-age masseur who'd taken time to mix ylang ylang bath oils for her.

Kelly stumbled away from him, reaching behind her for anything—a mop, a jug of cleaner. Some weapon.

She wouldn't allow this to turn into the nightmare of her experience with the college professor. Kelly scrambled to think of something to say that would reassure Ethan while still figuring out a way to get out of this hell.

Why would Peter waste time on this?

Unless he had nothing left to lose.

She wouldn't, absolutely wouldn't let this happen to her.

And she wouldn't be separated from the tiny microphone inside her dress button. Peter hadn't said anything to lead her to believe her cover had been blown. She needed to hold on to that.

"Whatever part you had in what went down tonight, you don't want to make it worse." Her grappling hand closed around an iron. "Ethan will be looking for me any minute. Give—"

Peter backhanded her.

Kelly reeled, slammed against a shelf. Towels and brooms rained around her, the iron thudding to the ground. Pain exploded through her head for a second time, but she held back her own scream for Ethan's sake even though the smack must have transmitted.

Ethan's growl rumbled in her ear. "He's a dead man."

His cold vow chilled her soul.

She wanted to let Ethan know she would make Peter pay big-time. Once she found her opening. Let Peter think she was weak now. She'd kick his ass soon enough, regardless of how strong the wiry man was from years of giving massages.

Thank you, Ethan, for giving her the tools to do it.

She'd learned. She would make it.

She hoped.

Peter snagged a housekeeping uniform off a hook. "Here. Take this."

Kelly sagged with relief. He just wanted her to change. She needed to let Ethan know before he lost it and barged through in some reckless dash. "Oh, you want me to—"

"Shut up." He leveled the gun at her temple.

Fair enough.

Kelly inched her zipper down. Revulsion swelled into nausea. Twice Peter had touched her while giving her a massage, looked at her, and she'd never known.

Swallowing down bile, she distanced herself. Besides, she wore a bra and slip beneath her gown. She was still covered, her 9mm out of sight.

She wasn't the helpless student from all those years ago. She was a government agent, with training. She could keep herself focused, protect her gun in the white garter-belt holster until she could button that housekeeping smock.

"Kelly!" Ethan barked through her earpiece. "Damn it, Kelly, find a way to talk to me. Now. Give us your twenty."

The gun never wavered. She couldn't risk talking yet and feared he wouldn't be able to hear her anyway, not with the growing space between her and her button microphone.

Kelly wrestled into the khaki jumper, fumbled as slowly as she dared with the buttons. Done. She straightened in time to see Peter pitch her gown into a cart of dirty sheets. He yanked her toward the door.

"Kelly!" Ethan demanded. "Kelly, damn it, say something."

The edge to his voice worried her more than the gun, and she was seconds away from leaving her mike. She gathered her thoughts and gave one last shot at communicating with Ethan. "Peter, why am I changing—"

He dragged her into the hall and kicked the door closed.

"Kelly?" Ethan's call echoed. "Talk. Let me know you're all right."

He couldn't hear her.

Peter wrenched her arm. "I hate the delay, but it was necessary. I had to make sure my hostage wasn't wearing a wire and or one of those listening devices. But then I guess it was ridiculous of me to think *you* might be some kind of undercover cop."

"Yeah, silly." He'd pay for that one later, Kelly assured herself.

He jammed the gun in her side. "Not a sound."

Kelly slowed as much as she dared along the hall, Ethan's voice her constant companion.

"Kelly, I'm with you," Ethan rumbled through, steady, strong. "No matter what's happening right now. I'm with you. Know that. Listen to me. Do what you have to do to stay alive. I'm gonna pray you're kicking the crap out of him right now.''

She heard his heartbeat thudding harder, faster.

"But if you're not—" his voice turned hoarse, pain radiating from his quiet words, "that's all right. You do what you have to do. Just zone out. Go to that far-away place in your head when you're meditating. Anything you have to do to stay alive.''

Tears burned her eyes as his words seared into her mind. Yes, she heard him. Every ounce of his love and hurt transmitted and stabbed right through her.

Finally she understood what he meant, how love could be wonderful, but it could be hell—their pain as tightly entwined as their joy. She'd thrown his love and his need for her back in his face. Which didn't say much about the love she thought to have for him.

A love she hadn't even told him about, and now she might never have the chance.

"We're looking for you, Kelly. By God, we're going to find you. So just hang on. Hang on, Kelly. I love you. I hope to God you can hear me. I love you.''

Again, she heard him, as did everyone in ARIES. This time, she believed him and grieved she hadn't listened before. If—when—she got out of this, she would remind him he'd made his vow to a host of listening ears. *No holding back, Williams.*

And she would give him hers, as well. To a room full of people. From atop her damned cubicle if she had the chance. She wouldn't give up, couldn't give up, because of Ethan. She couldn't do that to Ethan.

He needed her.

Peter rounded the corner, stopping in front of the stairwell. Would he go down or up?

"Okay, Kelly-girl.'' He swung open the stairway door. "Time to hang out on the roof and wait for my ride, while everyone downstairs cleans up the mess I left behind, patting themselves on the back for what a good job they did.''

He scooped his hand into his pocket and withdrew...

A rock. A fist-sized sapphire. On the inside of his wrist, usually covered by sweatbands, scrolled a tiny tattoo with Rebelian lettering woven into a snake. "I've got what my leader asked of me, anyway, and a valuable hostage. I'll bet Williams pays big-time to get you back from Rebelia."

All roads led to Rebelia.

"How did you get the sapphire?" Her mind flashed through the evening. All the jewels had been secure...

Except for the case crashed open by the Gastonian ambassador's body.

"So nice of Miss Eugenie to drop that punch bowl into the case and cover the missing jewel, not that she intended to help. But I'll take it any way I can."

At least he still didn't know her part or Ethan's or that they knew she was missing. It bought her an edge.

If she could just lead Ethan to the roof. Even if these scum received ransom ten times over, they would never release her. She'd studied their like in ARIES profiles too often. Once she climbed into that helicopter, she'd be as good as dead, taken from the country and tortured—if they weren't shot down first.

She pressed a hand to her thudding heart. The gemstone necklace tucked in her bra cut into her skin.

The necklace.

Kelly eyed the doorknob.

Slowly, she inched a finger into her bra to hook onto the chain, easing it up and into her palm. Hand clenched, she dropped her fist by her side.

Willing any remnants of Kelly the Klutz aside, she glided her hand along the door and slid her chain over the knob.

Okay, Williams. Time to live up to that hotshot agent rep.

Because she needed him every bit as much as he needed her.

Ethan tore down the halls. Fourteen more floors to go. The elevators were out. Only eight minutes had passed since communications with Kelly had gone down.

Eight endless minutes. He fought roiling nausea in his gut.

He couldn't think about what might be happening to her. He had to focus on finding her. Someone would find her soon.

The hotel was just so damned big.

Through his earpiece, a barrage of voices filled the waves. None of them Kelly's. At the ARIES command post, Hatch had assumed control, clipping out commands in rapid succession for additional backup.

Ethan listened, all the while chanting through a litany of heaven-only-knew-what to Kelly in the hopes that she could still hear him. Damn it, he customarily made security checks on people in his aunt's life and Miller's record had been clean. The fact reeked of a scope of influence Ethan didn't even want to consider. Not now.

He rounded a corner, ready to search the next floor.

A flash of light sparked.

His feet slowed. Ethan squinted, looked closer as he closed in on a glistening pendulum swinging on a door at the end of the hall. A chain with Kelly's semi-precious stone dangled from the stairwell to the roof.

Kelly wasn't in one of those rooms. Relief almost drove him to his knees.

A temporary reprieve.

If they'd headed to the roof, Peter intended to leave. A hell of a lot worse waited for Kelly if they got away.

"They're heading for the roof. Send backup." He looped the chain off the knob and clutched it in his fist. "Aquamarine, Kelly. Message received and I'm on my way up. Not much longer."

Ethan charged up the stairs. A helicopter hovering out of radar range could swoop down in seconds and be gone just as fast. He wasn't too late. He wouldn't let it be too late.

He stopped at the door. Don't go blasting in. Think. Pull

that mojo out of exile and put it to work. Go on the assumption Peter didn't know they were looking. Give nothing away. He spoke softly into his mike, "Kelly, I'm coming onto the roof."

Ethan tucked his gun in his pocket, donned his idle-rich facade and pulled open the door, his most important undercover op yet, with Kelly's life the stakes. "Kel, hon, you up here? Don't be mad, babe. I just want to talk to you."

He stalked across the roof, all of historic Alexandria sprawled below. Frigid wind tore gusts of steam from vents, blasting snow in a near-blinding swirl. Good. That would make landing a helicopter damned near impossible.

If they hadn't left already. "Kelly?"

"Over here, Ethan my boy." Peter Miller stepped out of the shadows, Kelly tucked against him, gun in her side. Two henchmen, more spa workers, loomed behind him.

Ethan allowed himself three precious seconds to absorb the vision of Kelly alive, and apparently unharmed, other than the hint of a bruise on her face.

Peter Miller would pay for that. Slowly. Painfully.

But first he had to take care of three sets of enemy hands holding guns. Two-against-three odds. Not what he'd hoped for but losing wasn't an option.

"What the hell's going on, Peter?" Ethan bluffed.

The feds couldn't be more than a couple of flights below. Stall. Pray the helicopter couldn't land and that there wouldn't be a hail of gunfire.

"You should have stayed downstairs, Williams. Now we're going to have to take you, too." Peter nodded to one of his henchmen who swung around and aimed a Glock at Ethan. "Of course you shouldn't have started asking all those questions about your parents. I had it good here and you screwed it up. Now I have to leave."

Ethan kept his stance loose, deceptive, trying not to think of the gun pointed at Kelly. She stood limply against Peter, no doubt luring him into assuming weakness. The wind blasted snow around her feet. Her teeth clattered but her eyes sent a clear message of honed training.

Ethan eased forward. "Messed up a good thing?"

Crooks always loved to brag, ego ruling them. He could use that to distract Peter, and get as much of the confession as possible into the mike. Ethan eased closer. "What do a few questions have to do with a jewel heist?"

Peter asked. "You're thinking small. I've been collecting secrets for years and giving them to my country. I wish I'd killed that bitch Eugenie and taken my chances with her ridiculous press-release threats."

"But you didn't."

"No. My mistake then, but not now. Too bad you didn't die in the mine. That would have paid her back. Her snooping cost my homeland a big piece of what the CIA had going on back then." His boots moved backward as he dragged Kelly with him. The odd shuffle, the snow, the boots all merged with the image of another pair of boots in Ethan's memory.

The day his parents died.

"Or maybe I should kill you after all. I walked away from you alive once before thirty years ago. I won't make that mistake again. So what if the old bat talks? Who'll care about one of your long-gone turncoat agents selling my country a few laboratory secrets thirty years ago anyway?"

The irony of it nipped Ethan with more power than the tearing wind. There had been a Judas in their social ranks all along—Peter Miller. The guy had been using his position catering to the DC politically powerful to pilfer secrets, and had no doubt used his position to watch over Eugenie, as well. The stakes were too high for Peter to negotiate. Any hostage was as good as dead. "Let Kelly go. I'm a more valuable hostage anyway."

"How short-sighted of you. It's not just about money. It never has been. It's all about country." The barest hint of an accent slid past his flat broadcaster's voice. "My sister

Iona was prepared to die serving our homeland, and so am I.''

Peter and Iona, linked, thirty years ago and now, danger so close. Every muscle in Ethan contracted with the magnitude of what could have happened. He'd been so focused on Kelly and future threats, all the while this slime had put his hands on Kelly and Eugenie countless times. Hell yes, Ethan could understand well a fury that would rage for years—for a lifetime.

Helicopter blades slapped the air in the distance. Closer. Time to trust his partner.

''You're not leaving with Kelly.''

Peter shifted his gun from Kelly to Ethan. ''How do you plan to stop me, pampered rich boy?''

''I won't need to.'' Ethan smiled at Kelly and winked. ''My partner will.''

Kelly jammed her elbow back. Stomped Peter's instep. And whipped out her weapon.

Ethan rushed the nearest henchman while Kelly swung her gun and fired at the other, twice, in a clean double-tap. Blood pumped from the man's shoulder. He stumbled back off the roof.

The helicopter eased out of the haze, hovering inches from the roof and swaying in the wind.

Peter shoved a hand into his pocket. Ethan stiffened, ready for anything. Another weapon. A grenade. Anything...

Except a rock?

Roof lights gleamed off a fist-sized sapphire. Peter backed away, turning, running and pitching the sapphire ahead into the helicopter cockpit.

Ethan sprinted after him, even knowing he wouldn't make it in time. At least it would give him a closer shot. Peter's back made a perfect target, a deserving target after what the man had done to Ethan's family. To Kelly.

''Ethan! Think. Don't let the past screw with your mind.''

Kelly shouted with the uncanny ability to read his intent. "Damn it! He can't talk if you kill him."

His logical Kelly.

Peter's back might offer the perfect target, but Kelly's voice offered the perfect promise for tomorrow. A promise he couldn't throw away. Years of survivor's guilt peeled away in soul-releasing loads. Time to step out of the past and into a life with Kelly.

Ethan adjusted his aim. Squeezed the trigger. Pumped two quick bullets into Peter's kneecap. Blood spurted.

Three steps shy of the helicopter, Peter stumbled, fell. Screaming in agony, he rolled on the ground. Immobilized.

Just as Ethan started to launch forward, feds poured through the door, swarming the roof and surrounding Peter and the other downed henchman.

Leaving Ethan free to focus on Kelly.

Three strides and he locked her to him, against him, a part of him.

Alive.

Warm and alive. He backed her away from the scene. Their time had faded. ARIES operatives didn't take credit. Hatch would clear away any hint of their participation, already the director's voice echoed in Ethan's ear with orders to that effect.

Ethan wrapped Kelly closer to his chest, breathing in her scent and molding her body to his.

"Kelly," he whispered against her hair.

Just Kelly. A single word said it all.

The helicopter rose out of sight. One jewel, one man flying an escape. But millions of dollars worth of gems and a ballroom full of people saved. And foremost, the location of Alex Morrow had been narrowed considerably from anywhere in the world to the small region of Rebelia. Not bad odds for one op.

He and Kelly made a damned fine team.

His hand clenched around Kelly's semi-precious rock that had purchased her priceless life. Now, he just had to convince her to take a chance on him. No doubt, a riskier proposition than dodging bullets on a snowy rooftop.

It was well past midnight. His Cinderella stood on a windswept building rather than in a ballroom. Her coach was nothing more than a dirty Jaguar. Her gown exchanged for a maid's smock, she was covered in sludge and blood, hair falling in her face.

And never had his Kelly been more beautiful.

Ethan's hand clenched around the chain and the aquamarine. He might not have a princess-cut diamond on hand, but he had something far more precious and lasting.

He had a future. If he could just convince Kelly to share it with him.

The night inching toward the next morning, Kelly counted as church bells chimed the hour. Three, maybe four times. Stepping out of the hotel lobby into the crisp air, Kelly didn't know for certain. Didn't care.

Ethan's jacket around her shoulders, they made their way through the snowy back lot for his car. Valet service was a bust tonight in the mass exodus of guests, not that any agent worth his salt would ever use a valet service and risk car tampering. Thirty-degree weather tempered the adrenaline heating her.

The cold reminded her they were alive.

Snow whispered down on the stragglers leaving, a handful of police checking out, a couple that looked suspiciously like Aunt Eugenie and Director Hatch.

Kelly stayed silent. Let them steal any moment together that they could.

Life should be savored.

Peace echoed in the parking lot and in her ear, the listening devices deactivated. Mission complete. They'd linked the thieves to Rebelia, where, it was hoped, Alex Morrow would be found. Better yet, they'd disbanded an entire network of Rebelian spies in the DC area.

After the shoot-out on the roof, Ethan and Kelly had assumed their roles as concerned guests accidentally caught in the crossfire. Kelly preferred it that way, always having liked the secret satisfaction of one-upping the unsuspecting with her deceptively unassuming exterior.

They'd retrieved her dress, crumpled mess that it was. But it was warmer than the overall and she hadn't wanted any reminders of Peter's eyes on her. So she'd put the gown back on and snuggled into the warmth of Ethan's tuxedo jacket draped around her shoulders. They strolled to his car, side-by-side; they hadn't touched since that moment on the roof.

Until now.

Hands on her hips, he hiked her up onto the hood of his Jag. At least she didn't have to worry about the dirt ruining her dress.

His fingers dug a gentle massage into her hips. "Congratulations, Agent Dragon Lady."

"Thank you." She waited for him to make a move, anything, but for once he seemed unsure of what to say. She slipped his tie free and pitched it over his shoulder. "Where do we go from here?"

Ethan took her hands in his. "During that time when I thought…" he paused, head tipped back toward the stars. His throat moved with a swallow.

All his words earlier rolled back over her. "Ethan, I'm sorry. I tried to tell you, but—"

"I know." He looked back down at her and smiled. "That's not my point. I realized none of this other mess matters. However I can have you, that's how I want you. I won't waste another minute that I can spend with you."

His words soothed over years of rejection. He wanted her. Brainy Kelly, who preferred messy hair and clunky shoes. She owed him the same acceptance.

After hearing the anguish in his voice earlier, absorbing his pain into her, she understood well what the offer cost him. She loved him all the more for making it. "I realized something in there, too. I heard you, Ethan. Every word you said. I heard it all. Even more than that, I heard what it did to you, and you're right. I love you too much to ask you to go through that again. If it's a matter of having you or the job, there's no question. You win. Hands-down.''

His hands glided up to cup her face. "There was a time I'd have taken you up on that." He shook his head, snow drifting to her lap. "But I'd have been wrong. Seeing you tonight, Kelly— God, you were magnificent. You were made for this. I can't take it away from you."

He clasped her wrist in his hand and kissed her palm. "Besides, after tonight, I'm finding I'm not quite ready to be put out to pasture yet. The way I see it, we make a pretty good team. I'll rest easier if I'm the one watching your back, and if you're the one watching mine. How about we give this a joint effort?"

"See the world and let the government pick up the tab?"

"Make love in a dozen different war zones in a dozen different languages."

She draped her arms over his shoulders. "Oh, you're making me hot."

"Told you I wasn't ready to be put out to pasture just yet."

She toyed with the hair on the back of his neck and looked forward to the day he could let it grow again. "Wanna come prove your youthful virility?"

"I think this old warhorse can manage." He brought her face to his and kissed her with an intensity that proved he could manage that and a lot more.

Kelly shivered against him, sagged into the warmth of his chest and looked forward to a lifetime of toe-curling kisses more exciting than any op.

One last question niggled at her logical brain. "What about children?"

His hesitation clenched her stomach. She'd just assumed he meant marriage.

He dropped a kiss to her head. "I want them before I'm

ready for the nursing home, so that gives me a little while longer to wait until we retire from active operations.''

Kelly exhaled. He did mean marriage and family. How could she have doubted him? Sure he wanted compromise, but that was okay.

She truly believed she could balance it all, but had learned to embrace his fears, as well as his dreams, just as he'd taken on her own. Life wasn't about fairy-tale fantasies but real-life balance and compromise. ''I think maybe five or six years in the field will prepare me for the hazards of motherhood.''

A smile worked its way up his face and into her heart. He threw back his head and laughed. She started to scoot off the hood. ''Let's go home.''

He stopped her. ''Wait. I'm not done yet.''

Ethan plopped her back on the hood and dropped to one knee in the snow-covered parking lot.

Her heart thudded.

His hand came out of his pocket. His fist opened. Nestled in his palm rested her semi-precious stone that meant more to her than any princess-cut diamond because Ethan had given it to her.

''Kelly, will you marry me? Be my partner, my lover, my love. Take on the world with me…take on me. Forever.''

He stared up at her. Waiting. Moonlight illuminated the unease shifting in his eyes. Not that edgy need to run she'd seen so often in him, but something different. A genuine fear of losing her. Kelly stared down into those worried eyes, searching and saw…

Ethan.

Not the millionaire playboy, but the whole picture. All the layers to Ethan Williams—the charming bad boy, the seasoned agent, the youthful avenger who jimmied electric gates, the tender lover who made her a bed of flowers. And yes, the stubborn, overprotective lout, as well.

He'd been right when he'd told her he wasn't some fairy-tale prince. He was something better. A real man with flaws.

And she loved him, flaws and all. The real Ethan. Just as Ethan loved her and had wanted her long before her Cinderella night.

The real Kelly. A stronger Kelly than she'd been two weeks ago. A woman past girlhood crushes and ready to embrace the love of the incredible man at her feet.

A deeper realization and peace settled over her as she accepted her own self worth. How odd that only through accepting herself could she appreciate what was really beautiful about Ethan. And oh, he was such a beautiful man through and through.

"Yes, Ethan, I love you and I'll marry you. *Oui. Si. Ja.* And again yes, in any language, my answer's the same. Yes."

She launched off the hood and into his arms. He rocked back, braced a hand on the asphalt and steadied.

Not that she intended to let him stay that way. She looked forward to rocking his world for the rest of their lives.

Kelly sagged against him, lured him with a kiss and lost her own focus for a heart-thumping minute. Then sent them both sprawling to the snow-cushioned parking lot. "You bet I'm happy to take you on, Williams. Starting right now."

She lowered her face to his and began her own determined assault on his senses.

Ethan palmed her hips, his best bad-boy smile in place for her and her alone. "Well, my dragon-lady partner, this is one time I'm more than happy to let you have the upper hand."

Epilogue

D<small>r.</small> Alex Morrow was alive.

Samuel Hatch sensed it deep in his sixty-year-old, in-
stinct-seasoned gut. And luckily, he didn't have to rely on
his gut alone.

Hatch adjusted the sunlamp on the thriving sprout of his
potted strawberry plant. No need for antacid today.

Thanks to Ethan Williams and Kelly Taylor's top-notch
ops work, an entire ring of Rebelian spies and jewels thieves
were in custody, half of whom were more than happy to
talk in exchange for lighter sentences. Alex Morrow's cap-
tivity in Rebelia—if not the exact location—had been confirmed. And most important, their leader intended to keep
Alex alive.

Peter Miller was proving difficult, but they wouldn't be
cutting deals with that bastard anyway. His litany of crimes
was long—the jewel heist and Taylor's abduction merely
starting the list. He would pay in full for his assassination
of Ethan's parents.

Lifting the yellow watering can Rita had favored, Hatch

liberally sprinkled a shower over the soil. He'd read on the Internet that water plumped the fruit. He could swear he saw the first hint of a bud even now.

Soon to be ruby-red.

Rebelia's leader Bruno DeBruzkya had ordered his legions around the world to gather jewels. Worldwide efforts to freeze assets of countries sponsoring terrorism had left DeBruzkya seeking alternative methods to finance his network. Whatever the sick bastard had planned for Alex, DeBruzkya had to be stopped.

Replacing the watering can, Hatch stared at his map of the world with agent locales marked, the pin identifying Robert Davidson slowly gaining prominence in his mind. Given Davidson's familiarity with the region and its people from his assignment there two years ago, he would make the logical choice for the next stage. Davidson would ascertain Alex's exact location.

No question about it.

Hatch's instincts had carried him through situations that would have downed most operatives, and his instincts had seen him through again. He'd been a hundred percent on the mark in pairing Ethan Williams and Kelly Taylor for this mission.

Professionally and personally.

From one of the monitor screens lining the wall, a cheer drifted, swelled. He'd left the security camera on the ops-support office in anticipation of Ethan and Kelly's triumphant visit.

The victors had arrived.

In a job with never-ending stresses, Hatch had learned fast to savor the celebrations when they came. Crises would invade soon enough.

He strode past the wall of monitors and the lengthy conference table, out into the ops-support room of cubicles where Kelly Taylor had once worked. Keeping a low profile, he watched from the periphery of the crowd. Beside her old desk stood Ethan Williams and Kelly, unabashedly holding hands.

Cheers built as heads popped up above the divider walls—prairie-dog style. Carla Juarez wheeled backwards.

Climbing up onto Kelly's chair, Ethan never relinquished his hold on her hand, as if he might be wary of fate stealing her away. Hatch leaned against the wall, watching from the outskirts. *Wise boy, Williams. Cherish her while you have her and make every day count.*

Ethan whistled between two fingers until the room quieted. "Everyone, listen up. I have a question that needs addressing." He turned on the chair to encompass the whole room. "Is there anyone here who doesn't know how crazy in love I am with this woman?"

Laughter rippled past the cubicle walls in an infrequent but welcome bout of brightness.

Gazing down at Kelly, Ethan continued, "Because if there's any doubt, I want to make sure it's cleared up right now."

Hatch enjoyed a rare smile. Eugenie owed him a big thanks for delivering this one. He looked forward to the day his old friend whipped out photos of her grandchildren.

Watching young love in action, he couldn't help but remember how he and Eugenie had given it quite a run in their day. Of course they'd always known they weren't cut out for a life together. Not the way he and Rita had later been meant for each other.

The way Ethan and Kelly fit.

Eugenie liked her freedom and he needed peace in his personal life to balance out the turmoil of his work. But those days with Eugenie Williams did make for some damned fine memories.

Juarez pitched a pencil at Ethan. "Yeah, Williams, I think we all got an earful of you and your undying affection during last night's mission."

"That you did." Ethan's eyes clouded with memories,

before clearing again with a mischievous twinkle. "But then, what's not to love about Kelly? She's smart, funny, gorgeous, packs heat with a purpose. Knows what a moron I can be, but is willing to take me on anyway."

Ethan jumped down from the chair amid office chuckles and nudged Kelly into the aisle. His eyes perused her body with the same slow glide she'd given him two weeks ago that had prompted more than a little water-cooler gossip. "And she has absolutely the best...*assets* I've ever been lucky enough to behold."

Kelly flushed all the way to the roots of her shining hair, a damned pretty blush that brought more than a whisper of regret to the eyes of other men in the room. The fools had missed what had been a cubicle away all along. But not Ethan, smart agent. After all the boy had lost, he deserved the best and now he certainly had it.

On top of everything, Ethan had a solid start in achieving justice for his parents. Hatch knew he wouldn't be able to stop Eugenie from going to the press about what happened thirty years ago, but that might well be a good thing. Certainly his nose was clean, and the agency could always use the occasional cleansing of scum.

Ethan hooked a hand over Kelly's shoulder and drew her close. "Which brings me to the important part of this little speech." All traces of humor disappeared from his face. "I'm retiring."

Gasps echoed from the twenty ops-support personnel. Hatch barely held his own back. He'd never seen this coming, but couldn't begrudge Ethan his exit, if that's what he wanted. ARIES would lose much when he and Kelly stepped out the door for the last time.

That devilish grin slid right back across Ethan's face as he lifted Kelly's hand to kiss. "Retiring from bachelorhood, that is."

He landed a kiss beside a five-carat princess-cut diamond Hatch had once seen gracing Ethan's mother's hand.

Juarez eased forward and tugged Kelly's fingers for a closer look. "Wow, what a rock! Give us the skinny on how he proposed."

Kelly toyed with a chain around her neck, thumb rubbing over the aquamarine like a talisman. "Let's just say he was perfectly romantic."

Juarez released Kelly's hand. "When is the wedding of the century going to be?"

"Next week." Ethan tucked Kelly to his side. "I don't plan to give this woman a chance to change her mind."

Kelly Taylor, soon-to-be-Williams, linked her fingers with her fiancé's. "We're flying out in the morning for a small ceremony. Ethan's aunt and my parents will be joining us."

"Sorry the rest of us will miss it," Juarez said. "Can we at least know where? Come on, Williams. Details!"

"I guess there's no need to keep it a secret since you could find out if you decided to make use of your gadgets." Ethan scratched his shoulder over his tracking device.

Kelly cupped a glass paperweight from her desk and tipped it until the tourist attraction shone in the fluorescent glare. "We're going to be married in Paris at the base of the Eiffel Tower."

Ethan scooped the paperweight from her hand and flashed his vintage bad-boy grin. "I wanted to hear Kelly say her vows in French."

Juarez snorted. "But your accent sucks, Williams."

"No problem. I have the best tutor around." Ethan turned to Kelly, his bad-boy grin fading to one of tender affection. *"Oui, mon amour?"*

Her smile mirrored his. *"Oui, mon jules."*

Hatch shoved away from the wall and backed toward his office, continuing to watch until the last minute. A damned fine day for ARIES all the way around—a successful conclusion of one mission and hope for the next. No question about it, his instincts told him Williams and Taylor were one hell of a team to have in the ranks.

* * * * *

Be sure to pick up the next exciting story in the
FAMILY SECRETS *series,*
THE PHOENIX ENCOUNTER
by Linda Castillo,
and learn about agent Robert Davidson's
dangerous ARIES mission!

Coming in March 2003

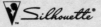

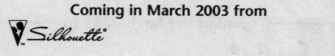

If you enjoyed what you just read,
then we've got an offer you can't resist!

Take 2 bestselling
love stories FREE!

Plus get a FREE surprise gift!

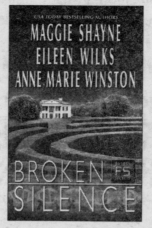